Jeremy,
Thanks for your encouragement

BLIND SPOT

Marilyn [illegible]

Disclaimer
All characters in this book are fictitious, and any resemblance to actual persons, living or dead, is purely coincidental.

Cover Design: Marilyn Kleiber

Library and Archives Canada Cataloguing in Publication

Temmer, Marilyn, 1941-, author
Blind spot / Marilyn Temmer. -- First edition.

Also in print and electronic formats.
ISBN 978-1-927890-10-3 (paperback).--ISBN 978-1-927890-11-0 (pdf)

I. Title.

PS8639.E55B54 2015 C813'.6 C2015-907216-6
C2015-907217-4

Printed in Canada

Published by Sun Dragon Press Inc., Canada
www.sundragonpress.com
First Edition, 2015

BLIND SPOT

BY

MARILYN TEMMER

Sun Dragon
Press Inc.

DEDICATION:

This book is dedicated to the members of my writing group: Maggie, Ursula, Wendy and Joan. Their support and encouragement have made this book possible

ACKNOWLEDGEMENT:

With many thanks to Ron Head, sculptor and fireman, for his patience and assistance. Any errors are mine alone.

Blind Spot

CHAPTER 1

1885 LONDON, ENGLAND – MID APRIL

Amanda Wentworth hurried up the stairs to her front door. The basket over her arm bumped against her hip. London's atmosphere promised another pea soup fog, the worst possible weather for those with consumption.

"I'm home," she called softly. If her father slept, she didn't want to disturb him. Their upcoming move to Canada formed a major part of the plan to restore his health.

An ominous stillness greeted her query. "Hello," she called again, "Mother? Faith?" Where were the familiar and terrifying wheezes of her father's desperate gasps for air? From coughing and shortness of breath to spitting blood and then to complete bedrest, Amos Wentworth's three-year fight to regain his health seemed doomed. Once again Amanda regretted the time taken to make arrangements to move to Canada and fresh, clean air.

Suddenly, she knew. She dropped the basket, flung her cloak at a hook, gathered her skirts, and sprinted for the stairs. As she neared the top, she could hear the murmur of her sister trying to comfort their mother.

Amanda stood in the doorway, her own tears threatening to overflow. Elizabeth knelt by the bed, cradling her husband's head against her cheek. One of Faith's arms curled lightly around her mother's shoulders, offering silent support in a time of grief and pain. Her free hand held a handkerchief, its sodden state of little benefit in stemming her tears.

Amanda knew. Even without the evidence of such a scene of overwhelming sorrow, she knew that her father was dead. Their ship sailed in less than a week.

✿✿✿

Six days later the three women boarded the ship. Amanda directed the appropriate disposal of their luggage. Faith made her mother comfortable in their cabin.

What else could we do? The question repeated over and over in Amanda's brain, even while she made arrangements for the funeral and took care of other last minute details for their trip. She had still to shed her tears. Only by doing one chore and then another had she been able to cope. Now she would have three weeks in which to mourn. And think.

She felt her sister's arm steal around her waist. "I just wanted to say goodbye to England before I waved hello to Canada."

Amanda returned the embrace, but Faith forestalled her anxious query. "I wanted to say goodbye, too. Mother is finally asleep." Amanda tried to smile, but knew that her expression more closely resembled a grimace. Faith removed her arm and held onto her hat with both hands. "Stop worrying so. Our only chance to support ourselves is to fulfil the contract Papa signed. You know the equipment's well on its way, and the signatures of both parties are on the contract. You did exactly the right thing. Mother thinks so, too."

"Are you sure? It seems I have made plans without consulting either of you."

"What else could you do?" Unconsciously she echoed Amanda's thought. "Someone had to take care of the funeral and get us on board. You know that mother all but collapsed. I hope this sea voyage might help her recover her health."

"I hope so, too, Faith." Silence encompassed them as they watched the shore recede, then disappear.

✿✿✿

"Mr. Waters, is Mr. Montgomery in the dispensary? I need more of my little green pills."

"I'm sorry, Mrs. Thronley. He will be back in about an hour. He is making a special delivery for the Jansen's young lad. They're afraid his cold will worsen into pneumonia."

"Such a fine young man. We were lucky when he bought this place from Mr. Maddley. *He* certainly couldn't be running here and there." She crossed her hands at her waist and drew in her chin. Her companion, Miss Calliope Carstairs, nodded agreement.

"Why, Mr. Maddley was so crippled with the rheumatism he could hardly walk, even with those two canes of his." Mrs. Appleby nodded.

"Yes, and his memory wasn't as good as it might be, either. Much better to have such a fine, modern-thinking young man who respects tradition to take care of us. We'll be back later this afternoon, Mr. Waters."

Henry Waters watched the two elderly ladies leave, their steps tottering, but determined.

✿✿✿

ONE MONTH LATER - CANADA

"Almost there, Mother."

"Thank you, dear." Her voice was wispy with fatigue and grief. The train from Toronto to Marcher Mills swayed and lurched, calling for the last reserves from the three women.

Amanda reflected that her mother's strength and endurance in the face of physical and emotional upheaval was remarkable. Her father's death had devastated all three women.

While maintaining a façade of optimism, Amanda kept her fear of their rejection to herself. She was prepared to fight as long and hard as necessary to establish their practice in this new and overwhelming land. In the aftermath and shock of the loss of the head of the family, she comforted her mother and sister.

"Remember, the contract with Wentworth Optometry Services has been signed and witnessed. It is not a contract with Amos Wentworth. Mr. Montgomery will not be able to go back on his word." When her mother and sister argued that women did not run businesses, Amanda retorted.

"If Mr. Sebastian Montgomery tries to wiggle out of this contract, I will shout his despicable actions from the highest rooftop. Think of what people will say. They will be horrified that he would treat a widow and her daughters so shabbily."

She resolved to make a living for her family in this new country. So much land. It was astounding to realize that her homeland could fit into just this province of Ontario many times over. The distances were vast. Even the people they had already encountered varied enormously—in appearance, manners, and accents—and nothing was as it had been.

Faith continued to be a rock of emotional support and strength. In the frantic days before sailing, Amanda had often railed against the irony of her father's death. Now the fresh air he so desperately needed filled their lungs, while he rested in England's soil.

She became aware of her surroundings and told herself that her body was swaying in response to the rocking of the railway carriage, and not from exhaustion. The prospect of organising her mother, sister and a small mountain of luggage was daunting. Only the thought of a strong cup of tea and a chance to stop moving kept her going. The sun promised a further hour or two of light. *At least we won't arrive in the dark.*

Recent experience of Canadian train engineers, keen adherents to the screeching brake and billowing steam school of locomotion, had taught her to remain seated until the train came to a complete stop.

A brisk exchange of letters with Henry Waters, business manager for Montgomery Enterprises, promised that the Wentworth family would arrive in Marcher Mills today. The trunks containing the equipment for the manufacture and dispensing of eyeglasses had preceded them and should, even now, be *in situ*.

Sebastian Montgomery, elder son of the Montgomery family, felt the addition of Wentworth Optometry Services served a dual purpose: it provided a necessary service to the community and added prestige to his pharmacy. It also fitted in nicely with his plan to provide the most up-to-date and modern services for his community. He prided himself on a modern approach to his business. The pharmacy, as well as the Montgomery manufacturing plant and home all boasted a telephone.

✿✿✿

Dear Mother and Father,

Thank goodness you arrived in England safe and sound. I know there have been tremendous advances in rail and marine travel, but Atlantic storms wait for no man. I will now admit I had some concern in that area.

Apparently my beautiful new niece, little Miss Beatrice Matilda Chalmers, has worked her magic on her Canadian grandparents – with probably the English parents and grandparents giving them a good run for their money. Edward regrets he is unable to write just now, but asks that I pass on his congratulations and best wishes. As you have probably guessed, he has left all his classwork to the last possible minute, and is now frantic to graduate with grades high enough to suit his family. I wish him luck.

Henry Waters is amazing. It is due entirely to his unrelenting efforts and astounding ability to organize and delegate that I am able to spend so much time in the pharmacy. For instance, this afternoon I received a telegram and have to be out of town tomorrow – the very day that Mr. Amos Wentworth and his family are due to arrive. What a comfort to know that Henry will meet the family, get them settled, and give Mr. Wentworth an opportunity to see his new premises. I am very much looking forward to having him occupy that empty room adjoining my shop. He assures me that his daughters are very skilled in all aspects of the business, and are eager and willing to help.

I must say goodbye, now. The carriage is at the door. Mrs. Smithers has packed an overnight bag for me.

With deepest affection and respect,

Sebastian

✿✿✿

Amanda was long accustomed to conducting business on behalf of her father. Initially she had dutifully signed all letters as A. Wentworth, at first in good faith; later in tremulous hope. She blessed the fact that she and her father's Christian names both began with the letter A. She planned to use these circumstances, backed by a signed copy of the agreement, to bludgeon her way into the only means available to support her family.

A skilled optician, she was particularly gifted in diagnosing the exact requirements of her father's patients. Her competency in grinding lenses was unquestioned and equalled by her sister. Her mother, reeling with grief, had left everything in Amanda's capable hands. Her sister's pointed questions about their legal and financial situation had resulted in a full explanation, as Faith's cooperation and skills were an integral part of Amanda's plan. A soft query interrupted her reverie.

"Would you like me to take care of our things and help mother while you organise the baggage?" Her sister smiled to indicate her eagerness to help.

Amanda sighed with relief and reflected that Faith had proven her mettle on the journey. "That would be wonderful, and I accept absolutely! Let's hope that Mr. Montgomery will be at the station to greet us as he promised." Clutching the baggage tokens in one hand, she prepared to descend to the platform. She prayed that all the boxes and trunks had arrived; her constant fear had been that some would be lost, and valuable items disappear forever. She braced to see once more the trunks still bearing her father's name.

✿✿✿

Gladys Whiffletree surveyed her parlor with pleasure and a deep sense of satisfaction. Harold had been gone for ten years, but this house showed that he had been a successful man, well able to leave his widow in comfortable circumstances. The parlor stove provided warmth for body and soul. Her gaze lingered on special objects in this favorite room.

The pump organ, resplendent with its velvet-covered pedals and shiny woodwork, offered the perfect spot to display her many family photos. Her two sons and their wives, replete with attendant children, flanked the large photograph of her husband. Other precious pictures of various sizes, dimensions and frames, nestled in front, beside, or peeked from behind the larger ones. The table beside her bed was the resting place for her wedding picture. She always said goodnight to her sweetheart with a smile and a kiss. Sometimes, when she compared the image of herself in the picture and then in the mirror, she wondered at her generous acquisition of lines, wrinkles, and pounds.

Objets d'art, gifts from a doting husband, decorated various pieces of furniture throughout the house, but the parlor remained her favourite. The small, round table and its four chairs invited company. Her cup, filled with freshly-perked coffee, waited on the kitchen table, right beside a plate of cookies still warm from the oven. Just one more thing to do before she took a well-earned rest. That task was to check if the yard boy had done the lawn and flowerbeds as directed.

Jimmy Sewell could be a good worker, but the quality of his

efforts varied. She referred to it as his hit and miss approach. Unfortunately, he was frequently more miss than hit with edging and weeding the front beds. She opened the front door and gasped, placing her hand on her heart. The man standing in the doorway started to tip forward as he released his grip on the doorknocker.

"Mrs. Whiffletree, I'm sorry to have startled you."

Catching her breath, she smiled and reassured him. "I guess neither of us was expecting the other. And enough of this Mr. and Mrs. nonsense, Henry. We've known each too many years. My husband always admired your business practices. He often mentioned that Mr. Montgomery senior knew what he was doing when he hired you thirty years ago."

Henry grinned. "Thank you."

"Now just you come right in. There's coffee hot in the pot and cookies just out of the oven." Henry, eager to taste Gladys' cookies and warm himself with a cup of coffee, stepped across the threshold, removing his hat as he did so.

"If you're going to spoil me with cookies and coffee, don't let me hold you back." He grinned. "I can certainly manage to hang up my coat and hat."

She smiled and bustled away. "Sit in the parlor, Henry," she called over her shoulder. "I'll be right there."

Fifteen minutes later, social pleasantries observed, Henry got to the reason for his call.

"As you know, Sebastian has hired an optometrist. He's arranged for the house the Chatham's used to have to be available for them when they arrive next week."

"The entire town and surrounding territory know about that new service. Those advertisements he's running in the *Marcher Mills Clarion* even included the name of the gentleman. Does Mr. Amos Wentworth have a family? Will they be coming with him?"

She felt she knew what Henry's request would be, and she'd

be delighted to oblige. Indeed, she was hard pressed to wait for the request before she agreed. Not only would the Montgomerys be grateful for her help, but the inside track on information that everyone was anxious to hear would be hers, and hers, alone.

"Mr. Wentworth has a wife and two daughters. The daughters will help him in the store, especially the older one. Her name is Amanda; the younger one is Faith."

Well, well. Two pieces of fresh information already, and they'd hardly started. Speculation about the new service and its provider had occupied the gossips for some time. She would just tell this tidbit to one or two notorious gossips, making sure to let them know it was confidential. The news would spread with its usual dizzying speed.

"So, Henry, what would you like me to do—although I have a pretty good idea of what you're going to say?"

"You probably do. If you could find it in your heart to order some basic supplies for them at the mercantile, I'll arrange to have them delivered. Also, Sebastian asked if we could count on you to help smooth their way for those first few days. An ocean voyage and long train journey are exhausting."

"Of course. I'd be delighted. Such kindnesses are so typical of Sebastian. I'm going to Zeke Marshall's store tomorrow for myself. Don't worry about arranging for their delivery. I'll do that when I order my own things, and tell Zeke to charge them to the Montgomery account. I'll just need the key."

"Wonderful. Thanks so much. I was sure we could count on you!" He reached into his waistcoat pocket and extracted the key.

Gladys refrained from commenting on the large sigh of relief accompanied the placing of the key in her hand. *Not as sure as all that, were you, Henry Waters?* She was preparing to elicit more details, but Henry pleaded a full day's activities yet in store. Still, she had a great deal to mull over. A dull, overcast, and chilly early spring day had brightened unexpectedly. As she escorted her guest to the door, she remembered to check the lawn and flowerbeds.

The recent death of the town's handyman caused considerable scrambling for those residents who used his services on a regular basis.

Her initial glee when she obtained Jimmy's services faded quickly, and she was coming to regret her decision. Pushing Jimmy into doing an adequate, let alone outstanding, job on his assigned tasks almost equalled the effort of doing them herself. One quick look from the verandah confirmed her suspicions. The edges of the beds looked as if a myopic rabbit had grazed on them, and the weeds rivalled the flowers in height and frequently surpassed them in vigor.

She grimaced. Mr. Hit-and-Miss had missed again.

✿✿✿

Why aren't you here, Sebastian? An emergency meeting in Toronto just isn't good enough. You were supposed to meet and welcome the Wentworth family to Marcher Mills. I'm not very good handling this sort of thing, as you well know.

Henry vaulted from his carriage and cursed roundly, albeit under his breath. A series of mishaps had all-but-guaranteed he would be late in meeting the train. He admitted that Sebastian was the only person to handle the emergency meeting, but he really was *not* very comfortable with people in social or semi-social situations. His speciality was organization and paperwork. Problems on production lines, glitches in deliveries, even handling employee situations fell well within his area of expertise.

The screech of brakes had reached him while still a block from his goal. He took the steps to the station house two at a time, thanking his stars that organising a family of four and then collecting the luggage took time. He adjusted his speed to a more respectable walk as he rounded the stationhouse, casting his gaze about for Jed Baker, stationmaster, ticket seller, and organiser of all things in his little kingdom. As he searched he noticed that Bert Stiles and Al Anderson had placed themselves in a position to monitor the activity on the platform. He wondered what the two troublemakers were up to. Whatever it was, someone was sure to suffer.

Just then he saw Jed supervising the loading of two large crates and several trunks from the baggage car onto his wheeled trolley. Henry could practically smell the paint from ten feet away. That trolley was Jed's pride and joy, and the town joke was that he could never use it, as it always seemed to be wet with paint.

Coming toward the station house were two figures: one draped in widow's weeds, complete with veil; the other also in mourning, but without a veil. He scanned the platform again. Where was Mr. Wentworth? And wasn't there another daughter? He turned his gaze once again to the trolley, now rumbling toward him in a stately manner. A slim female, also in mourning, accompanied Jed. No other strangers were in sight.

He noticed that Bert and Al had altered their path to intersect that of the trolley. They were commonly referred to as B and A, or BA, for bugger all — an epithet delivered with considerable venom. Bert frequently had Al in tow. Al could be very useful when performing simple tasks. His understanding was not great, but when the actions were simple and instructions repeated several times, he had his uses.

Bert's vision of himself as a sharp businessman did not agree with the perception of others. The community at large considered him perilously close to a scoundrel. He had a reputation for shady dealings, but so far he conducted his Marcher Mills activities strictly within the rules of good business practices. Yet the reputation persisted.

The other figure hurrying towards the trolley was Zeke Marshall. As the sole proprietor of the town's general store, he met most of the trains. It was no surprise to see him counting boxes and barrels and checking them against a waybill.

Just then the young woman accompanying the widow addressed him.

"Are you Mr. Henry Waters?" The voice was soft; the diction, precise.

Whipping his hat from his head and bowing slightly, he responded. "Yes, I am. Welcome to Marcher Mills."

"Thank you. I am Miss Faith Wentworth. We are very happy to be here, Mr. Waters. My mother is urgently in need of a cup of tea and a chance to rest." Henry bowed again, this time to Mrs. Wentworth. Faith turned in response to light, firm steps crossing the wooden platform, and smiled. "And this is my sister, Miss Amanda Wentworth. Amanda, Mr. Waters is here to meet us, just as he promised."

Henry turned to greet Amanda. She must have been the lady almost hidden by the trolley and its contents. He took her proffered hand.

"Good day, Mr. Waters. We are so relieved to be here. As you can see, we have our personal luggage, but did the equipment reach the pharmacy safely? There should have been a large trunk and three wooden crates."

Henry responded to her greeting and verified that the goods had arrived. He noted signs of exhaustion and grief in all three ladies. Miss Faith was holding up bravely in support of her mother, who looked very close to collapse, leaning into her daughter's young strength. Miss Wentworth was accustomed to being in charge. In spite of pale cheeks and heavy lids, resolution surrounded her. This was a woman who met life head on.

"Mr. Baker is very efficient. The trunk and crates are safely in place at the pharmacy. I've made arrangements for your personal things to be sent directly to your house—to which I am delighted to take you." He smiled, relieved to know he could depend on Jed.

"Also", he continued, "your neighbor, Mrs. Gladys Whiffletree, has fires lit and the kettle on the hob. Her motto has always been that a 'good cup of tea' can solve any problem."

Elizabeth Wentworth thanked him for his thoughtfulness. "A good cup of tea and a journey's end will be bliss, indeed." Her daughters smiled in agreement.

He could see that grief had drained Mrs. Wentworth's small reserves of strength, and she was holding on by sheer willpower and a determination to be there for her girls.

Henry was somewhat surprised to find himself swept along, herded, as it were, by a small-but-determined sheepdog, as insistent as it was efficient. He looked around again and remarked, "I don't see Mr. Wentworth. Is he coming on a later train?" He had hesitated to ask, especially in view of the sea of black surrounding him. Mrs. Wentworth turned her head away, the hand holding a black-edged handkerchief disappearing under her veil.

"My father died shortly before we left, Mr. Waters. My sister and I ran all aspects of the business for the last year." Amanda delivered the double shock in a voice that shook slightly, in spite of her efforts to hold it steady.

"My sincere condolences, Mrs. Wentworth, Miss Wentworth, and Miss Faith, on your tragic loss." He assisted the ladies into the carriage and turned the horse towards 42 Portland Place and the promised cups of tea.

His mind was reeling. Thoughts of Sebastian's reaction to this disaster, especially in view of the appointments already made for his brand-new service, gave him pause. They jostled with those of the enormous effort, physical and emotional, of three women making their way alone. Desperate to offer more than empty words, he was inspired to remember the local churches.

"We have an Anglican church in Marcher Mills. I will ask the vicar to call in a day or two. Is there anything else I can do for you?" The offer was gratefully and graciously accepted.

All was quiet in the carriage as Henry turned the rig and merged into the traffic on the main street. "Miss Wentworth, you say that you and your sister virtually ran your father's business for the last few months?"

"Yes, indeed, Mr. Waters. My sister and I are experienced and competent, well qualified in diagnoses, as well as the design and manufacture of frames and lenses, and will manage very well."

Henry gulped. Sebastian's views on women were rigid and traditional. They graced one's table, appeared to advantage on one's arm, and knew how to run a home and to entertain. Their place was solidly and irrefutably within the confines of home, church, and children.

"Do you perceive a problem, Mr. Waters? You have mentioned in several of your letters that Mr. Montgomery's plans for the pharmacy include offering the very best and most up-to-date services. We therefore concluded that his openness of mind extended to spheres outside the narrow boundaries of commerce." She noted that his Adam's apple bobbed up and down several times and resigned herself to hearing, yet again, a reiteration of the male conviction that "a woman's place was in the home". Her hands, hidden by the folds of her skirt, fisted.

"Well, yes, I…that is, I…well…." He cleared his throat, gathered his thoughts, and began again.

"Mr. Montgomery's determination to offer the best and most up-to-date services in his pharmacy is certainly true. His views on women, however, tend to the traditional." Henry kept his eyes glued to the road. He appeared absorbed in his efforts to guide the team around the worst ruts.

"I feared that such might be the case. It so often is."

Henry saw Amanda's shoulders slump. She obviously realised that her posture was reflecting her weariness and despair and promptly straightened her back.

"As it is already four o'clock, would you please be so kind to tell Mr. Montgomery that I will keep the appointment tomorrow morning, as arranged? You will appreciate, I am sure, that after such an extended journey, it is vitally necessary for my sister and me to settle our mother in our new home." She braced herself for the answer.

"Yes, yes, Miss Wentworth. There is no trouble about that whatsoever. Mr. Montgomery will be quite amenable to your meeting." *And may I be forgiven for that lie.* "He has several appointments lined up for you. Would you like him to call on you? I know he would be glad to do so."

"No, thank you, Mr. Waters. I will visit him in his establishment. You may tell him I will arrive at eight o'clock tomorrow morning."

"Thank you, Miss Wentworth, I shall do so. And here we are at your new home, as promised." He was grateful for the opportunity to change the subject.

The four occupants of the carriage viewed the new abode with quite different thoughts.

Elizabeth considered with great pleasure the prospect of *not* having to cope with a moving surface, and of being sure her foot would hit the floor exactly as it should. A house was so *still.*

Faith could hardly wait to settle her mother and sister so she could explore new vistas. Her secret investigations about the freedom of young ladies in the colonies had garnered the assurance that it was quite proper for her to walk out alone. Only in the daytime, of course, and only to such places as the high street for shopping or to church, for devotions. Faith, however, was adept at finding the most circuitous routes and had promised herself some delightful—if deliciously scary— times.

Amanda gazed at the house with satisfaction. It would do well as a base from which to defend her right to provide optometry services in her new community. The neighborhood was solidly middle class. The properties on this street exhibited societal values held in esteem: gardens neat, walks well swept, and brass door knobs and trappings shining brightly. No censure could be forthcoming from even the most censorious when confronted with such irreproachable respectability.

Henry experienced mixed feelings. On the one hand, he could, and would, thankfully deposit his charges to the tender mercies of Gladys Whiffletree. On the other hand, there was no denying the fact that the duty of informing his employer of the drastic change of circumstances would be uncomfortable, to say the least.

✿✿✿

"That should do it for the Wentworth family, Zeke. I'll be home in an hour to receive my own order, so I can open their house for you." Gladys took her time adjusting her shawl. Nerine Appleby had just told Charity Marshall, Zeke's wife, how many yards of flannelette she needed. Her daughter's baby was due soon, and she had promised two dozen nappies as a welcoming present.

Nerine was active in the Methodist circles in town. The Anglicans and Methodists prided themselves on exhibiting Christian tolerance and brotherhood to their sadly misguided fellow worshippers. And to each other.

They had an uneasy and loose alliance that included Presbyterians and Wesleyans, were wary of the Baptists, and considered the Roman Catholics next door to heathens. But, regardless of the path by which community members approached their religious observances, or even if they ignored them altogether, *everyone* was interested in the new optometrist and his family.

"Gladys, did I hear you say the Wentworth family would be here on this afternoon's train?" The query, delivered in an offhand manner, did not disguise her anticipation of the response.

"Hello, Charity." Gladys feigned surprise. "I didn't realise you were finished with Mrs. Appleby. Yes, they will. Of course, the Montgomery family will give them a warm welcome. Sebastian asked me to get the house ready for them, and see that they have a few supplies to start with."

"Will he be meeting them?"

"No. I understand that he had to make an urgent trip to Toronto, so Henry Waters will meet the four o'clock train in his stead. He will deliver them and their luggage to the house."

Two more women drifted closer. Decisions about children's shoes could wait. This was important.

Gladys relished the increase in her audience. "You can imagine their exhaustion after travelling constantly for almost a month." She rested her shopping basket on the counter, and prepared to enjoy herself.

"I don't for one moment believe that an ocean voyage is relaxing. Pitching and tossing, having to hang on for dear life any time you dare to creep out to get some fresh air, cramped cabins—and water from barrels that have been sitting in the sun for the entire crossing? No, thank you." She picked up the basket and turned toward the door.

"But Gladys, people pay huge amounts of money to take sea voyages. The upper classes have yachts."

Carefully returning her burden to the counter, Gladys fought to keep a straight face on the most unusual pronunciation of the word *yachts*. It rhymed with matches. She prepared to defend her position.

"I still say they'll be ready to collapse, especially the parents. Of course, young people bounce back faster." Her hand changed its grip on the basket's handle. She had brought it to carry the yarn she had just purchased. With luck, she could get her stitches cast on and a couple of rows completed before the delivery of the heavier goods.

"But they'll be seeing so many new things on the train. I remember when we came over, even though I was only five years old. It seemed that it was one long circus."

"Somehow, Alice Smith, I think you've forgotten the vast stretches of unending forests. England has towns and villages every few miles; Canada's towns and villages occur every few hundred miles!" Having given herself an excellent exit line, Gladys bowed, smiled graciously, and gave a superb imitation of a ship in full sail. The basket hung at her side, like a small and officious tug guiding its vessel in the designated direction.

CHAPTER 2

Henry plied the knocker with more vigor than was his habit. Mentally he was composing, he hoped, a compelling argument that would persuade Sebastian to give the ladies a trial run.

"Yes, Mr. Waters? Can I help you?" Clara Smithers was an exemplary housekeeper. She was calm competence personified.

"Yes, Clara. The matter is most urgent."

"I'm sorry to hear that, sir. As you know, Mr. Sebastian has been called out of town. He told me not to bother with supper and not to wait up for him. He wasn't sure if he would be returning tonight or early tomorrow morning. Something about supplies for one of the factories, I think." She remained placid in the face of Henry's obvious agitation.

"Are you sure? Perhaps I could go to him."

"Well, I suppose you could, sir, but as I said, I really don't know exactly where he is. I do know he mentioned going to Toronto, and having more than one meeting." Her demeanor remained unruffled.

Henry was frantic. His prey had escaped. "Then I'll have to write him a note. Please be sure he gets it the minute he arrives. It's really very urgent."

"Of course, sir. I'll just get you something to write with." She left the room with her usual stately gait. Henry longed to help her increase the tempo of her steps.

Whatever Sebastian's reaction at the prospect of having either a female optometrist or no optometrist, combined with the rash of appointments already made in good faith, the fact remained that he really had very little choice. Henry began to organise his thoughts while he waited for the paper, pen and ink to be delivered. A furious pounding on the door accompanied loud shouts of "Fire! Fire!"

He leapt from the chair and dashed outdoors. The caller was already running to the next house to give the alarm. A recent spate of fires in outbuildings and garden sheds had plagued the community. He headed for the fire station.

Smoke filled the late afternoon air, and an ominous red glow appeared over the south side of town. It silhouetted fellow members of the volunteer fire brigade as they rushed to the station. Derry and Dasher would be harnessed to the pumper wagon, ready to pull the water truck as soon as enough members had assembled.

✿✿✿

That Bert was really something! He was up to every nasty trick in the book. Al loved the fact that people had to be nice to him, even when you could see that they hated doing it. That was the kind of power he wanted, too.

"Hello, Mr. Stiles." Or, "of course, Mr. Stiles". Al wheezed with laughter.

Bert had ears like a cat. It really beat all how he could manage to walk past someone, seeming to pay no attention whatsoever, and hear everything. For instance, now he knew that the man who was to have been the optometrist was dead, and that his daughter would take over—or thought she would take over.

Al, product of a fundamentalist Christian sect, was disgusted—*women didn't know their place, no more.* "But don't you worry none, God, because I will teach that uppity woman to know her place. And any more who think they are equal to men." He muttered, then spat for emphasis.

Because they knew that she would be going to the pharmacy, but not at what time, he and Bert agreed that Al would be in the alley from seven in the morning. Any woman who thought she could be as good as a man would be more than likely to arrive early and hope to catch somebody doing something wrong.

CHAPTER 3

Amanda Margaret Wentworth, you just march right down that street. No more excuses. Mother will benefit from having to supervise Faith with the unpacking. Now move!

Pushing up the spectacles sliding down her nose due to nervous perspiration, she straightened her shoulders, checked that her hair remained in its plain chignon, and convinced herself that the hatpin still anchored her favorite headgear in a suitable manner. The reticule dangling on her left wrist swung gently against her body as she walked along the boardwalk.

Mentally she read the names on the storefronts as she resolutely marched toward her destination. Marshall's Emporium, Zeke Marshall, Prop. Henry Soames, Lawyer. First Chartered Bank of Marcher Mills, owned by the Rice family. The Rices, like the Montgomerys, were a force to be reckoned with, claimed their new neighbor.

The next building was empty, but beside it was a delightful little store: Betty Keppel, Seamstress. Betty's penchant for keeping up with the latest fashions from Toronto assured her of a brisk business. Today her window featured a hat guaranteed to make any woman's feet itch to slip through the door and try it on.

One-two-three-four-five-six. She realised that she was focussing not only on the number of steps left before her ordeal, but on the sound of her footfalls on the boardwalk. Tap, tap. Every tap seemed louder than the one before. Clearer. More important. Demanding her attention.

A steady clip-clop heralded a wagon coming up on her left,

the harnesses jingling a tune in counterpoint to the sound of their hooves. Men shouted and laughed as they harassed the smith with good-natured banter.

Just a few more steps—past the alley—and her goal was at hand. Her stomach roiled at the thought of the confrontation ahead. She would need all her skill as a shrewd negotiator to reconcile Sebastian Montgomery to the truth of her claims of expertise and a realisation of the degree of her determination.

✿✿✿

Al waited for the brazen hussy to pass. He had peeked out a minute ago and seen her gazing in the shop windows. Carefully following Bert's instructions was finally workin' real good.

Setting fires in sheds and outbuildings in this town was like taking candy from a baby–easier, in fact. He giggled silently as he remembered the furor of last night's little blaze. The machine shed, the new one Marv Sanderson had just built, had burned hot, hot, hot. He had helped until he was sure people had seen him in the bucket brigade, then disappeared for a good night's sleep.

Bert was pissed off just because he had fired the wrong building, but it was too late now to change anything. And firing a bigger building made the blaze bigger. And better. Much, much better. Fire was so beautiful.

Wrenching his mind back to the present, he monitored the sounds of the approaching footsteps. He knew just where she was, just as he knew his duty to Bert and to God. Women like her were an abom…abomshun…well, God knew, and that's what counted. He'd show her about thwarting God's will—and about vain adornment, too.

✿✿✿

Thirteen-fourteen-fifteen-almost there. She veered toward the opening between the buildings in order to avoid a suspicious lump on the boardwalk. A hand grabbed her arm, jerking her into the shadows. She blinked in an attempt to adjust her eyes to the darkness.

Before she could see her assailant, a musty odor of unwashed body and sour whiskey threatened to make her vomit. Short, powerful breaths stirred the veil on her hat and caused a few errant curls to tickle her ear.

"Bitch. You're just a harlot, wearin' those tools of the devil!"

Her spectacles were snatched from her face with a curse. The world now appeared as a series of blurred outlines.

"Jezebel. Whore. Wimmen ain't meant to try to change God's will. You be satisfied with what you got."

A blow to the side of her head sent her reeling. She windmilled her arms in a frantic attempt to avoid a fall and felt one hand slap the side of a building. Panting, she adjusted her hat which had tilted over one eye and was threatening to fall off. She was grateful for the rough, splintery support as she tried to focus.

Her attacker had disappeared, but the smell of whisky seemed stronger as she staggered back to the boardwalk. Waves of nausea threatened to overwhelm her. Only an iron will kept her upright. The combination of blurred vision and the after effects of the blow caused her to sag against the front of the pharmacy. An ignominious descent toward the boardwalk was punctuated by the loud bang of a door thrust open hard enough to collide with the wall. Consciousness was fading quickly, but she still heard the condemnation in the word "whiskey" as a pair of strong arms caught her just before she was engulfed in darkness.

"Henry, hold the door for me." Sebastian, grateful to see his friend and business manager hurrying toward him, lifted his burden with ease. "Disgusting—not even noon and she reeks of whiskey. Falling down drunk on the main street. Let's get her inside and out of sight before Mr. Wentworth arrives."

Henry, all too aware of the firestorm about to break over his head, braced himself even as he held the door wide. He knew the alcohol-scented bundle in his employer's arms was the expected, in his case, dreaded, A. Wentworth.

As a result of the stubborn fire last night, he had barely had time to rush home to bathe and change before arriving at the pharmacy. The bath had been a necessity. Even after scrubbing himself from head to toe, he was convinced that he still bore the odors of the burning building on his person. His desperate attempt to contact Sebastian before the fateful meeting had been useless. She was here!

He knew Sebastian's strong views on the delicate little creatures. How he thought these same fragile beings managed homes, children and childbirth was a mystery.

Too many of those knights-in-shining-armor tales when he was growing up, no doubt. Too bad I haven't had an opportunity to tell him that the A was for Amanda; not Amos. Now we're in for it.

Henry watched Sebastian angle his body in order to accommodate the full skirts of the lady's dress as he carried her into the back room of the pharmacy and propped her firmly and none-too-gently on a chair. His grip shifted to her shoulders to prevent an inevitable slide to the floor.

"Water, for God's sake, man—water! Don't just stand there, she's still out cold." No amount of vigorous flapping of a handy towel produced the slightest response.

When Henry supplied the requested glass of water, he was horrified to watch Sebastian pour a goodly amount into his palm and fling it on Amanda's face.

The method, though crude, was effective. Her eyes flew open and she gazed with bewilderment and trepidation at the tall, scowling figure looming over her.

"What on earth do you think you're doing?" she sputtered, wiping her face with her hands. Her grey eyes sparkled with indignation. "And where am I?" Her back straightened.

"Are you working with that degenerate who attacked me?" The lady's voice rose in register and increased in volume with each query. The last, delivered in something perilously close to a roar, caused its owner to flinch as she gingerly touched her head. The graceful motion halted abruptly. Her hand returned to her face, groping as if to find something. She lowered it again and frowned at the blood on her glove.

"What happened to me? And where are my spectacles?" She started to open her reticule, then stopped. "No, no, I remember what happened." Inhaling mightily, she continued with commendable determination.

"Give me that glass. And the towel." Without waiting for a response, she grabbed both objects from his unresisting hands, dampened the towel, and applied it with exquisite care to her poor head.

Henry, unseen by either of the combatants, backed slowly toward the door. Discretion, not foolhardiness, was called for. Any hope of finding a reasonable solution was fast disappearing.

He resolutely refused to think of Sebastian's reaction when he learned the truth. A strategic withdrawal was definitely in order. His excuse would be that someone had to mind the store. And if that didn't work, then he could claim to be looking for the lady's missing spectacles.

Herbs, patent medicines, tinctures and whiskey—the scents combined to cause Amanda's head to swim. But judging by the steely stare of dark green eyes and flushed complexion of her tormentor, this was not the time to let her mind wander. The pain subsided to a strong, but bearable, throbbing, and she became more and more aware of her physical surroundings. She realised that she had reached her destination, albeit in an extremely unorthodox manner.

The man she had first supposed to be working in conjunction with her attacker must run the pharmacy for Mr. Montgomery. No doubt he was convinced that his height and gender, not to mention his place in the community, allowed him to behave rudely. She straightened her hat with due regard to her wound, adjusted her skirts, and rose.

Or tried. Half-way up she found herself firmly seated once more. The brute had grabbed her shoulders in an abrupt manner and forced her to sit. He opened his mouth to speak when the murmur of voices from the front of the store caught his attention.

"Stay here and don't move. I have a great deal to say to you, madam." With that, he removed his hands from her shoulders, turned on his heel and strode from view.

I hope he adjusts his expression before serving his customer. That face would scare anyone! She continued her musings, dabbing absently at her wound. *I wonder if Mr. Montgomery knows of his attitude. It's a good thing this is the only pharmacy in town, or all his business would flock to his competition.*

She looked for Mr. Waters, who had vanished. Her attention then turned to the room which would be part of her daily life.

Order and method ruled. Containers aligned with painstaking precision, sported labels written in the finest copperplate. *Probably glared every utensil and vessel into submission.* The normal odors associated with a pharmacy faded into the background, except for that strong smell of whiskey. *A secret drinker—I might have known.*

Rising from her chair quickly caused a slight dizziness, but grasping the counter for a moment and standing quite still provided respite. She peeked out the doorway to see her opponent bowing and scraping to a well-dressed customer.

I'll just see if I can find that whiskey—and dump it down the drain. The idea that he would dispense mixtures and tonics that could be fatal if not made correctly and with precise directions given for their use, is appalling. But the smell of whiskey is all through the room—he must drink quite a bit.

She moved slowly, ensuring that there was always something near for support. She searched with diligence and perseverance. Then, with mounting horror, she realised that the smell not only permeated the room but also her skirt. The garment was quite damp. No wonder the odor had failed to dissipate. In disbelief she bent to verify her discovery and almost toppled over. Quickly grabbing the counter once more, she looked around for the towel. She soaked it under the pump and sponged the offending spot with considerable concentration.

CHAPTER 4

Always a stickler for punctuality, today Sebastian gave thanks that Mr. Amos Wentworth had not appeared as arranged. Standing in the doorway and watching his unwanted guest, he resigned himself to the fact that at the very the least he must see to her wound and make sure she got home safely. Henry could provide that last service, since Mr. Wentworth's arrival was no doubt imminent.

Her performance was excellent. He could almost believe she was unaware of being observed.

Ensuring a prop was always to hand, she carefully moved dispensers and bottles. She pulled them out, peered behind, and returned them to their original position. An air of furtive determination accompanied her actions. He realized that the inspection would not have been apparent if he had not seen its progress.

She must have seen him from the corner of her eye, for the start she gave when she discovered the whiskey-soaked patch on her skirt, followed by her ostensibly careful sponging of the offending spot were both very well done.

Even her expression of horror, disbelief, and repugnance was superb. Large grey eyes and saucy brown curls notwithstanding, the lady was both resourceful and talented.

Still she continued with the pretence that she was alone. The vigorous application of dampened towel to skirt continued until her nose was no longer wrinkled in distaste. She gave a final rinse to the cloth, wrung it out with vigor, and draped it over the side of the sink.

He looked around for Henry and spied him chatting with Mrs. Vanderburgh, an inveterate gossip. His annoyance changed to gratitude when he realised that his friend was keeping the busybody away from his inebriated and unwanted guest. Turning his attention back to the lady, he noted that she had continued to remove and replace each container with the same uncanny precision; a skill she had no doubt acquired in her illicit consumption of alcohol. Or drugs. The thought of drugs had occurred only when he noticed her relentless and furtive search; before then he had assumed alcohol because of its strong odor about her person.

Just then Amanda raised her head and pretended to see him for the first time. "You," she said, in tones of disgust. "Does Mr. Montgomery know of your need for the consumption of alcohol? Does he know you all but wring your hands in false humility as you no doubt encourage customers to purchase things they neither want nor need? Does he know that you use your looks, height, and false air of respectability in such shameful ways?"

Back straight and the light of battle shooting sparks from her eyes, she continued. "I'm sure he will be very interested when I inform him of your shabby habits. You should be ashamed, sir! Your family sacrificed for your education in order to hold the post of pharmacist, and this is how you pay them back."

As she drew breath to continue, Sebastian jumped in. "Well, madam, you're a fine one to talk, and such big words, too. Just how do you explain being falling-down drunk at eight in the morning? Your actions refute your façade of respectability. I'm sure your mourning clothes give you tremendous leeway in your actions."

The lady opened her mouth to retaliate, the light of battle in her eyes. Sebastian gave her no chance to jump in.

"No, no, no excuses. I'll have Henry make arrangements to see you safely home. Just give me your address. I have an appointment and no wish for my guest to meet you." He sneered.

"Indeed, in spite of your best efforts with towel and water, and your gifted performance for my benefit, you still reek of the demon rum—or whiskey, as the case may be."

Amanda's eyes narrowed in preparation for a blistering attack which would leave this degenerate whimpering for relief. Just then Henry stepped into the room and cleared his throat. The combatants, eager to continue their joust, turned. Two faces exhibiting identical expressions of annoyance greeted his interruption.

"Sebastian Montgomery meet Miss Amanda Wentworth—A. Wentworth—your new optometrist." It would be difficult to say which of the duelling duo was more taken aback.

"You... you... you're Mr. Sebastian Montgomery? You?" Her jaw closed with a snap. Head up, back straight, she made her best curtsy in spite of a fiery blush, then extended her right hand in a regal manner. "How do you do?"

Sebastian was furious. Why hadn't Henry told him of this? "Miss Amanda Wentworth? What happened to A. Wentworth? All the correspondence was signed A. Wentworth." Years of habit had Sebastian making his bow and shaking her hand, albeit with more force than was customary.

"Is this some kind of joke? If so, it's in extremely bad taste and not at all amusing." He was furious. A man who set considerable store by his personal dignity, he felt very much at a disadvantage. His brain worked overtime trying to assimilate several facts simultaneously. Fact: the lady reeked of whiskey. Fact: she did not seem the least bit drunk. Fact: the letters bore the signature, A. Wentworth. With this last fact came the realisation that something was very wrong. Fact: he had assumed drunkenness. Fact: he had not even mentioned her injury. Fact: neither had she played for sympathy. Fact: she was a snoop. Fact: she *still* reeked of strong spirits.

Amanda, too, was finding it difficult to put all the facts together. Nothing could have been more unfortunate than being attacked—bathed in a cloud of alcoholic fumes—and unable to see clearly, swooning into the arms of the man she had still to reconcile to the matter of having a woman share his business premises. Whilst she was able to prove her skill as a diagnostician, creator, and dispenser of eyeglasses, there was an enormous societal bias against females working outside the home.

Women's roles were those of helpmates; providers of a sanctuary of peace and tranquility for the mighty male. Of course, this did not apply to those menials who cooked, cleaned, and had other less-savory occupations. Deemed "the lower orders," their lot in life was to serve their betters. Her chin rose a fraction and she assumed a brisk, businesslike manner.

"I am, indeed… :

"Please accept my apologies… ."

Both started to speak at the same time. Sebastian, finally remembering his manners, gestured for the lady to continue.

"Thank you." Amanda could be gracious in victory. "I wrote the letters, initially on my father's behalf, and then on my own. I have…had…taken care of his correspondence for years." Her breath caught as she fought a sudden overwhelming grief. After regaining control, she continued.

"My father died very suddenly a few days before our ship sailed. Apparently he had a heart attack. That, in addition to the consumption, was too much for him to manage." Her complexion was chalk white, her back straight, and her gaze unflinching.

"That's all very well, Miss Wentworth, and I certainly wish to discuss this with you at length, but first please accept my apologies for ignoring your injury. Sorry. I meant to express my condolences on the sad passing of your father." He felt at a standstill. How crass to ignore her obvious grief and refer only to business matters. Any derogatory thoughts she might have about uncivilized colonials had just been confirmed. Sebastian's complexion was somewhat flushed.

"At least let me see how severe it is and give you something for the pain." Even as he spoke, he took her elbow preparatory to guiding her back to the chair. Amanda, realising the strength of this bargaining chip, acquiesced.

"Thank you, sir." She settled her skirts and removed her hat. Sebastian set a tray on the chair by her side. It contained a bowl of water, alcohol, some bandages, and iodine. She determined that the iodine would stay in the bottle.

"How is it you were injured?" He decided to leave the matter of the whiskey until later. If he were extremely lucky, the lady would volunteer an explanation. He was very much aware that she occupied—for the present—that part of the battlefield that offered all the advantages.

"As you know, our appointment was for eight o'clock. Just as I passed the alleyway next to your premises, someone grabbed my arm and pulled me between the buildings. He snatched off my spectacles, then struck me on the side of my head.

"My God, madam, I am so sorry to hear that. How many times did the blackguard strike you?"

"Once was more than enough," she said wryly. "Because I am almost blind without my eyeglasses, there was no hope of identifying my assailant—unless one can do so by the foul odors of his breath and clothing. Bathing was not his priority, I assure you. Now that I consider the matter, he must have poured whiskey on me. Also, I seem to recall something about 'Jezebel' and 'vain adornment', but that makes no sense. I'm wearing mourning, as you can see, and no jewellery whatsoever."

Sebastian and Henry were shocked. They could hardly credit that after being attacked the lady was able to converse in such a calm matter. It was their experience that women were more likely to have hysterics.

Trying to smooth the waters, Henry interjected. "But Miss

Wentworth, you must let me drive you home. I know that Sebastian would be more than willing to meet with you in a day or two, when you have recovered from this dreadful incident. I'll fetch a carriage immediately."

"Stay, Mr. Waters." She held up her hand, palm toward him. "Your offer and consideration are very much appreciated, but Mr. Montgomery and I have a great deal to discuss."

"So we do, but not today." His voice was courteous; his manner implacable. "Henry, you fetch the carriage and I'll finish treating Miss Wentworth's wound." He nodded to Henry who immediately left on his errand. "Will you receive me tomorrow, madam? I should like to call on you and your family."

Amanda was just about to agree when she realised that by so doing she would lose the moral high ground. Mr. Montgomery was feeling guilty, and this was the perfect time to press home her advantage.

CHAPTER 5

"Well, did you follow our plan, Al?" Bert Stiles waited with some trepidation. Al had been well drilled on his actions, but on occasion had tried to make things "better", which usually ended in botched results. A perfect example was his torching of the wrong building last night.

Bert had waited a long time to set certain things in place. Sebastian's defence of a younger boy whom Bert was tormenting might as well be yesterday. He could still taste the bile that rose to his throat every time he remembered. As he fled the scene, eyes blackening and nose bleeding, he vowed vengeance. Finally, finally, the opportunity was here. He would make sure to destroy all that Sebastian and his uppity family held dear.

The attack on Amanda Wentworth would create a diversion which would aid in the execution of the next step of his scheme.

"Yessir, I certainly did. Called the bitch a few names, too, and dumped half a bottle of good whiskey all over her skirt. It sure hurt to do that, though—what a waste!" Al had, indeed, felt it a waste of good whiskey, especially when poured over a worthless woman. But Bert paid him well for his efforts.

Bert had also promised him a series of jobs which would provide enough money to escape Marcher Mills, and had sort of—almost—indicated that he would accompany him. Al took this as a pledge of partnership.

"Not at all, Al. You got half a bottle of whiskey for free, Miss Wentworth got no more than she deserved, and things are in good train for the next step. Meet me tomorrow at our usual place at eight o'clock. It's time to start the next phase."

Al wouldn't understand the term "phase", but knew that more money would be forthcoming. It was enough.

✿✿✿

"Mr. Montgomery, you appear to be a man of honour and of considerable stature in the community. Any worries I may have had about your unwillingness to honour the contract with A. Wentworth and Wentworth Optometry Services are now at rest.

"Thank you so much for letting me have the equipment delivered directly to my new premises. My sister and I will be here tomorrow morning at seven o'clock in order to begin putting things in order." She ignored his attempted interjections. This was a fight not only for her, but for her mother and sister: they had no other source of income.

"Mr. Waters has indicated that you have been kind enough to set up appointments for us. Never fear that we will be ready to honour your commitments on our behalf and to serve our customers."

Sebastian inhaled, determined to indicate the absolute impossibility of having women dispensing these services. "Miss Wen…"

Amanda, played her trump card. "Now, sir, I must confess that you were absolutely correct. The effects of my recent misadventure are making themselves known. Would you please let Mr. Waters know that I am ready to accept his kind offer of transportation?" She rose and extended her hand. Sebastian, awash in her waves of seemingly logical discourse, made one last attempt to save himself.

"But Miss Wentworth, you cannot have considered…"

"Again you are right, Mr. Montgomery—I have not considered how much of your time I am taking explaining that which you have already grasped. Perhaps you would be so kind as to help me to the carriage. I suddenly feel a little dizzy." She rose to her feet, swayed in a manner nicely calculated to hover between an obvious play for sympathy and imminent collapse.

Sebastian, routed, offered his arm. He was concerned for her wellbeing, annoyed that she had used her feminine wiles—so like a woman—and verbal acuity to win this skirmish. His determination to stop her idiotic plan increased. As he assisted Amanda into the carriage, inspiration struck.

"Henry, you hold the fort here. The very least I can do is to see Miss Wentworth home and explain to her family just what happened this morning."

Amanda, rightly judging this a ploy to get her mother's agreement to the unsuitability and socially-precarious ramifications of her darling daughters setting up in business for all and sundry to gawk at, demurred.

"Not for the world, Mr. Montgomery, would I put you to such an inconvenience. You are the only person who may dispense certain drugs and nostrums."

Sebastian, realising that his companion was on to his plan, riposted, "The very least I can do is see you home to the arms of your family. What kind of a welcome to your new community is shown by shoving you in a carriage to make your own way?" He realised that he was speaking through his teeth and strove to unclench his jaw.

"Pooh. No such thing. Remember that you had assigned this time-consuming and unimportant task to Mr. Waters. A wise decision, as it met nicely your obligations for hospitality and care for a mishap which occurred beside your premises and those that require your presence in the pharmacy. You may rest assured that my mother will wish to visit you shortly to express her appreciation of your tender care." Amanda's glare matched the temper seeping into her voice. She appeared to stumble and transferred her grip to Henry's arm.

Sebastian, rightly guessing that the lady would have a glib response to any remarks on his part, ignored her last statement, and advised the driver to proceed to Portland Place. By dint of forcing her to accept his help into the carriage, he was able to shoulder Henry out of the way and take his place beside her. The silence which followed his command swelled to envelop the vehicle's occupants.

CHAPTER 6

Henry approached the back door of the pharmacy with some trepidation. He had had no opportunity to speak with Sebastian since he had left to escort Amanda home. The arrival of one of the factory managers with an urgent problem precluded any but the most cursory of greetings when Sebastian returned to the store. Henry and the manager left immediately to resolve the matter. This morning his anxiety matched that of yesterday, in spite of the fact that A. Wentworth's identity had been revealed.

After locking the door behind him, he placed his hat on the third peg from the left as usual, and then froze in place. Feminine voices created a soft counterpoint to the scrape of furniture being rearranged. The peace that prevailed gave notice that Sebastian had yet to arrive. As he approached the doorway to the portion of the building designated as The Optometry, a skirt hem flicked past.

"There, I think that's exactly what we need, Faith. Mr. Montgomery cannot possibly object to our borrowing the plants from his front window. They form the perfect screen between the waiting room chairs and our examination and work area." Just then she noticed that her sister's attention was directed toward the doorway.

"Good morning, Mr. Waters," they chorused. Faith continued. "What do you think of our little kingdom? We feel we've achieved just the right balance between professionalism and a soothing atmosphere."

"Yes, and we're particularly glad that you're here, as there doesn't appear to be a stool or even a box we could stand on.

Would you please be so kind to help us hang the pictures? They'll add the final touch." Amanda trusted her anxiety was not apparent. She firmly believed that the best defence is offence, and if they were ready to greet their first appointment, due at nine o'clock, their position would be strengthened by the *fait accompli*.

Henry, caught between wishing the ladies well and the sure fact of Sebastian's wrath, did his best. "Very fetching, indeed, ladies. I would be confident of your expertise were I to take advantage of your services."

The jangling of the bell saved him from trying to find additional polite phrases which met the exacting requirements of containing equal amounts of truth and tact. Unfortunately, that same bell also heralded the arrival of Sebastian, no doubt with fire in his eyes.

"I'll say goodbye for now. That's Sebastian, and we have a great deal to discuss." Rapidly disappearing into the back room, he braced for the worst. He hovered just out of sight, ears cocked for the battle about to commence.

✿✿✿

"Good morning, Mr. Montgomery." Amanda's voice barely trembled. She noticed that his hat remained on his head, a sure barometer of his agitation. "Please let us thank you for having the crates opened. Your thoughtfulness has allowed us to be ready for our very first appointment. You may also be assured that the Montgomery tradition of outstanding service will be upheld."

She struggled with her breathing. The increasingly red hue of Sebastian's complexion did not bode well. He removed his hat with great deliberation.

Amanda continued. "Your kindness in taking me home yesterday made all the difference. Thanks to your care and consideration we were able to reassure our mother that the incident was trifling and there was no need to worry." She hurried on, determined not to give him time to respond. His hat, now clenched in both hands, appeared in danger of a sad and painful demise. His breathing became heavier and louder.

"The plants from your front window form a splendid divider between our waiting area and the working space. Since we're partners, we felt sure you would be glad to donate them to our common cause." She snatched a quick breath, concerned that his face and neck were both scarlet. Perspiration stood out on his forehead. He bared his teeth.

"Notice how they give a feeling of calm. Some people find it stressful having their eyes examined. They always seem to think we'll tell them they're going blind." *Stop, stop, you're babbling.*

Sebastian gave up trying to be polite. "Madam, whatever gave you the idea that I would in any way endorse your setting up shop in this area?" His attempt at control was shown by his increasingly agitated manipulation of his headgear. No hatter could possibly restore it to its former glory.

"Really, Mr. Montgomery, where else on these premises did you wish us to do so?" The light of battle in her eyes was reinforced by the placement of her hands on her hips.

"Our crates of equipment were in this room—opened for easy access. The exact number and size of tables and chairs requested were also in place. Your advertisement in the *Marcher Mills Clarion*, which Mrs. Whiffletree so kindly showed us, states that the optometry services start today."

Sebastian's shirt buttons strained against the expansion of his chest. His face had gone from red to an intriguing shade of purple.

Amanda's heart was in her mouth. So much depended on winning this battle. Refusing to give in to her panic, she raised her chin another notch.

"Mr. Waters repeatedly stressed your high standards of service, the emphasis you place on truth, and your admirable reputation of meeting your commitments. He assured us…."

Sebastian found his voice. "At no time… ." His adversary ignored him and charged ahead.

"… that you had several appointments booked. He also promised you were a man of vision, one who was determined to bring the best services possible to his community. He… ."

"But… ."

"… assured us that the equipment had been delivered, and was even kind enough, as I mentioned before, to have the crates opened."

✿✿✿

Sebastian took another mighty breath, only to be outmanoeuvred once again. His frustration increased with the need to find words which would convey his outrage, but still be at least marginally acceptable in polite company. Impervious, the petite steamroller pressed on.

"If your obvious irritation is about the plants, they may certainly be returned. However, since the optometry service is connected so closely with the pharmacy, and since the idea was yours, we presumed that your interests dovetailed with ours."

"Presume is right, madam." Finally he was able to get a word in. He was appalled to hear the volume of his voice. Someone might even think he was shouting. Men of breeding and education—gentlemen—had no need to shout. They employed reason. Logic. Control. He continued in more modulated tones. "You presumed to lie to me about your identity. You presumed that I would be compliant with your wishes. You presumed that since a few—*very* few—appointments had been booked, I would have no recourse but to let you continue. You presumed that I would ignore fraud and misrepresentation and false pretences, and that your life would continue in merry fashion. And you presumed to TAKE MY PLANTS!" Aware that his voice had once again reached stentorian levels, and that a customer might appear at any minute, he struggled to regain his control.

Desperate to forestall his next diatribe, which would no doubt be a declaration for the Wentworths to leave and never darken his door again, Amanda played her trump card. A single tear welled up and began its journey down her cheek. She pretended to fumble for her handkerchief.

Sebastian was both incensed and appalled. Anger at her use of the ultimate feminine weapon jostled with his realisation that he would never have railed like that against a man who set himself up in opposition to his plans.

"Here, take this," he rumbled, handing her a fine linen handkerchief. A short wrestling match with his conscience permitted the next words to leave his lips. "I never meant to upset you to this degree, Miss Wentworth. Please accept my apologies."

Amanda abandoned strategy in favor of outrage. "*To this degree*, Mr. Montgomery? Am I to take it that upsetting business partners only to a particular degree—on a scale wholly of your devising, I may add—is acceptable?" By this time the opposing parties were practically nose to nose.

Faith and Henry had prudently withdrawn from the line of fire. With one accord, they now deemed it advisable to interject a note of sanity. Faith beat Henry to the draw by a scant second.

"Amanda, I'm sure you didn't mean what you just said. Consider Mr. Montgomery's thoughtfulness in driving you home and his kind inquiries about our mother."

"Sebastian, you know you have trouble accepting change. Instead of ringing a peal over Miss Wentworth, why don't you give her, and Miss Faith, a chance to prove their skills?" Henry's usual good sense, combined with the time granted by this interjection, had given Sebastian an opportunity to reassess his position. He could continue to his own disadvantage, or put the onus on

Miss Wentworth and her sister. A thoughtful response to a knotty problem precluded any accusations of undue pressure.

"Very well, Miss Wentworth and Miss Faith, you have two weeks to prove that you can, indeed, provide the services contracted for. However, let us be clear. We are *not* partners, nor will we ever be so. You are to fill the requirements as outlined in the agreement. Failure to do so will result in your immediate eviction from these premises."

He glared. The tears had ceased.

She took a deep breath, regrouped, smiled, and responded."Thank you, Mr. Montgomery. We accept your terms. I perceive a lady approaching who is no doubt our first appointment. The bell on your shop door has just rung twice. I suggest that we both get to work." She turned on her heel and seated herself at the table hidden by the plants. Faith moved forward to extend a gracious welcome to their very first client.

Henry tugged on Sebastian's sleeve and gently removed the beleaguered hat from its owner's grasp. "I'll put the kettle on while you take care of Mr. and Mrs. Appleby. I'm sure a cup of chamomile tea will help settle your nerves." He beat a strategic retreat. Sebastian detested chamomile tea and Henry knew it. And Henry had best keep to himself any comments about the entertainment to be derived from seeing his friend bested by a hundred pounds of female determination.

"Henry, how does she do it?" Sebastian was obviously still exercised by his rout. "I'm a reasonable man. I am. You know that when we have problems at the plants or offices, or with tenants, I provide a voice of reason. I do not shout. My teeth don't clench. I do not ruin expensive headgear. And I am not presented with the artistic effect of a tear escaping from a pair of soft grey eyes."

He realised that, once again, he was clenching his teeth—his hands curled into fists. He carefully relaxed his toes, which had been eager participants in the clenching and curling manoeuvres.

"Well, Seb, it's true that in all cases not involving the Wentworths—more specifically Miss Amanda Wentworth—you are the voice of reason. I'll grant that you have impressive skills in winning the cooperation of all parties."

Henry paused to see how his audience received the qualified praise. The burgeoning and heavy silence boded ill. He prodded a little more.

"How did Mrs. Wentworth receive you? Was she in agreement with your arguments about the inadvisability and perceived impropriety of her daughters engaging in trade?" A fierce scowl answered him. He braced.

"Mrs. Wentworth, alas, was laid upon her bed, completely done in by the exigencies of the past few months. Mrs. Gladys Whiffletree, however, was in fine voice."

Henry covered his mouth as he tried to turn a guffaw into a cough. Sebastian scowled again and continued. "She gave me chapter and verse on how "the poor dear" had all but collapsed into her arms when she arrived. Without the stout—pun intended—help of La Whiffletree, she would have been flat on the floor. Only by great efforts, outlined in minutest detail, were they able to get her up the stairs and into bed. I trust I will never again have to endure such an experience."

Henry hooted.

Sebastian's glare succumbed to his lively sense of humor. His mouth twitched and he grinned. "To tell you the truth, Henry, I would have given something to see our Gladys achieve all she claims she did."

Just then the bell hanging over the front door jangled. While he hastened to attend to his customer. Henry made good his escape. He was woefully behind owing to the fire and the arrival of the Wentworths. Unfortunately, the paperwork waited and waited. Indeed, Henry had long claimed that a vigorous breeding program was in effect, for the papers multiplied at an alarming rate.

CHAPTER 7

"Thanks, Zeke. I'll check tomorrow to see if that special order has arrived." Bert had used care and craftiness in developing his current persona in Marcher Mills. His public demeanor was beyond reproach. He made a point of utilising the services of the local establishments. His prompt settlement of his accounts added to his consequence as a local businessman. He also made a point of never revealing more than necessary to any of them.

It had taken time and patience, but he had gradually established a bank account and a second identity in Toronto. At first he'd considered Hamilton, but it was too small. Also, he was too well known there in some quarters. His identity in Marcher Mills was that of a reliable, if not desirable, person who would follow through on assignments and ensure their speedy and efficient completion. Bert had nurtured this reputation slowly and cleverly. In fact, he was so clever that now his name occurred as a matter of course. It was almost time to let Marcher Mills know that he was the proprietor and president of Stiles Services Corporation.

His final goal was in sight: pay back Sebastian for humiliation suffered in school, disappear, and live well off the spoils of his deeds.

His ruminations lasted until he approached the Station Hotel. A beer would provide a logical reason for an apparent casual meeting with Al. Bert tended to discount the intelligence of others, and was secure in his knowledge that no one suspected that Al worked for him. Once free of this hick town, he'd indulge his palate with the fine wines he now enjoyed only when out of place or in the privacy of his room.

"This is the wine you ordered." The waiter slanted the bottle across the napkin on his arm. Bert nodded and watched as the cork was removed and offered for approval. He noted the degree of dampness, and passed it under his nose.

"Fine." A small amount was poured into his glass. He picked it up, swirled the wine gently, and held it to the light to assess the color. And nodded.

Soon that's the only *kind of drinking I will do. No more sitting in a common beer parlor.*

But a beer at the hotel, and occasionally a round for the usual layabouts, had frequently put him in the way of useful information. Currently he wanted to know more about the optometrists. Keeping his face still, he grinned mentally.

From what he'd heard, Miss Wentworth had won the right to establish her practice in the room off the pharmacy. She must be a force of nature. Apparently the settling-in period had provided much grist for the local gossip mills. The ladies of the town were divided in their opinions. Those who felt themselves confined by society's rigid rules cheered her on. The contingent who supported the status quo was appalled. But there was a history there he felt sure would stand him in good stead. Sebastian Montgomery's rigid ideas about a woman's place were common knowledge.

Gladys Whiffletree, an inveterate gossip, had been easy to pump. Miss Wentworth was not a servant. Neither was she a woman of lax morals. In her zeal to establish the Wentworths as desirable neighbors, she revealed that the two young women of the family would begin to offer examinations and eyeglasses the following morning.

He knew that once the Wentworths had settled in their new home, Gladys would discover an urgent need for some items at the general store. Bert, familiar with her routine from days gone by, carefully timed his own visit to that establishment. He encouraged her to share the results of her conversations with neighbours and friends. He would retain only that which was, or might be, useful.

✿✿✿

Henry shook his head. Sebastian, so strangely confrontational with Miss Wentworth, carefully placed a small container of pills in old Granny Banders hand, gently folded her arthritic fingers over it—as far as they would reach—and reassured her that these pink pills had a great deal more to recommend them than the white ones. He had compounded them especially for her, and she was to let him know how they worked the next time she was in town. Mrs. Banders smiled, patted his hand, and promised to do so.

As Sebastian returned from escorting the old woman to the door, Henry asked for a private word. As soon as they entered the back room, he closed the door and faced the culprit. "Those were sugar pills. I know, because I saw you make them up. Pink pills, indeed." He smiled. In spite of your inexplicable irritability with Miss Wentworth, you fraud, you're a soft touch."

"Nothing of the sort, Henry, and well you know it. I am a tough, focused, hard-headed businessman, with not one ounce of sentiment or softness in my entire body."

Henry snorted. He knew better than anyone the anonymous kindnesses that typified this supposedly tough and hard-headed businessman. Baskets of provisions frequently appeared in a mysterious fashion on the doorsteps of destitute or struggling families. The local doctor had a small fund to offset medicines and visits to those same families. Definitely not one ounce of sentiment or softness in Sebastian Montgomery.

Scanning the beverage room for a table with some privacy, he spied a table with several reprobates. Under the guise of civility, he greeted the men and asked what was new. Bert made a point of being approachable while simultaneously discouraging familiarity.

Anticipating that this would be one of the times that Bert would buy a round, they answered in boring detail about the recent fire. Hoping for information that would further his plans, he asked if they had heard of the new service for those needing eyeglasses. He received a large helping of fiction and a minute amount of fact about the "eye ladies".

"You don't want to see them women, Bert. They'll blind ya."

"Don't be so stupid, Johnny. They wouldn't stay in business if they did that."

"Hugh is right. They do tell you that you need spectacles, even if ya don't."

"You're an ass, Herb. The real news is that Montgomery and the older spectacles woman hate each other. They fight all the time." Nods of agreement from all parties around the table reinforced the statement.

These men were bone lazy; their main goal was to do as little as possible. There was small chance of them meeting the eye ladies, except in passing.

Amongst the chaff, Bert gleaned a small, but potentially important kernel of fact: Montgomery's reaction to the older sister had been out of proportion, even factoring in his views on a woman's place. Also, Sebastian had been seen squiring a luscious beauty around for the last while—ostensibly a cousin from Australia. The rumor mill suggested a possible romance, especially when it seemed the lady was a second cousin.

Why, if such a stuffed shirt was supposedly showing a keen interest in one lady, did he react so strongly to another? It might, he allowed, be simply the brashness Miss Wentworth exhibited in insisting on providing the contracted services, but Bert was doubtful. No, something else was responsible. He would find and twist it to his advantage.

Just then he heard the door bang against the wall and was unsurprised to hear “Bert, Bert” in Al’s embarrassingly loud voice. Taking a deep breath to avoid lashing out and alienating a necessary, albeit irritating, crony, he nodded, then jerked his head to indicate a table in the furthest corner of the room. He caught the eye of the proprietor and indicated he would buy a round for the table. Thanks were thrown over shoulders as the herd stampeded for the beer.

Al was not known for subtlety. No matter how many times he was told to keep his voice down, as his excitement grew so did his volume.

“I done it, Bert! I done it!” True to form, he endeavored to tell the room. “I couldn’t find you nowhere yesterday. Where was you?” As soon as he asked the last question he cringed. “Sorry, Bert, sorry. I know that’s none of my business.” Bert had given Al frequent and painful reasons never to question his actions.

Bert glared. “Quiet, you fool.” He softened the admonishment with an offer of a beer and flipped a coin in Al’s direction. “Get me one, too, but say nothing to anyone. This is our secret, remember? If you trumpet the information to all and sundry you’ll get no more jobs from me.” Since the threat was delivered from a face devoid of emotion, Al gulped, nodded, and scooted for the bar.

Al hurried to complete his task. With a “Sorry, Bert. I just got so excited about the news.” He placed two full schooners of beer on the table and took a seat.

“Well, that’s fine then. Let’s hear it—but remember to keep your voice down.” Al nodded and began his story in a whisper.

“I really done it, Bert. I watched the lady’s house, just like you said." He stopped for a satisfying pull and continued. "She and her sister was walking down the street--and it was just half-past six! I couldn't believe it!" He nodded as Bert made a downward motion with his hand and obediently lowered his voice to a murmur. "They went straight to the pharmacy—back door, of course—and Horace Mindley, you know, the cleaner, let them in."

He stopped. Finished his beer. Gazed mournfully at the few drops left in the bottom.

Bert sighed and resigned himself. He provided the funds for another beer with the comment that it was the last. Al grinned and made good time to and from the bar. Slurping the suds off his newest acquisition, he continued. "At first I couldn't hear nothin'. Then Henry Waters come in. I did hear him say hello to the wimmin. But the door snapped shut, and the walls ain't as thin as they might be for lissenin'. But you can be sure I heard both Sebastian Montgomery and the older lady when he arrived. He was furious that they were there. She claimed that he'd better let them do their job, or his name would be mud. She didn't use that word, but it's what she meant."

Once again Al addressed himself to his drink. Bert nodded encouragement.

"That's all I could hear, Bert. But I kept watch, and some people did go into that part of the store." Sighing, he sank back in his chair.

Bert knew Al wanted praise. He would have to be satisfied with beer and lack of abuse. He watched Al pick up his glass to drain it, then think better of the action when he realized that Bert was finished buying. He knew Al would nurse the last few gulps.

"That's all for now, Al." Bert watched as chortles of glee and crude razzing of players beckoned Al to a rowdy game of poker.

As he smiled and nodded on his way out the door, Bert turned, twisted, and rearranged the information gleaned in order to give him the greatest leverage.

He had designed his campaign with consummate care. A conflagration of monumental proportions would be his swan song. Every commercial building in which the Montgomery family had a financial interest would be torched. As would their home. Al would do for the preliminary work.

Bert already had names of people from Hamilton who would come in and do the final job. He wanted no connection to Toronto. Meanwhile, his plans to increase the monies received through blackmail proceeded apace.

CHAPTER 8

Elizabeth Wentworth sighed with pleasure because she stood on a surface that didn't move. She was free to cross the middle of a room, and not cling to the wall just in case the ship or train gave one of its mysterious lurches. She gave thanks daily for such a miracle. The sun was shining, beckoning her to visit her kind neighbor, Mrs. Whiffletree. Gladys, as she insisted she be called, had been so very thoughtful. The cup of tea she offered when the Wentworths arrived at their new home had been a supreme gesture of welcome.

Elizabeth's shock and grief at the loss of her dear husband, as well as exhaustion from the funeral and subsequent journey, were finally lessening. Part of her would always remain buried in England with her Amos, but this new life became more interesting by the day.

Essentially a strong woman, she enjoyed her feelings of increasing physical wellbeing. A cautious hope was growing. Their plans to open their business in Canada seemed to be falling into place, in spite of a few challenges.

She had not missed the tension between Sebastian Montgomery and Amanda. Presently their mutual attraction floundered under surface animosity, but such strong feelings denoted an equally strong chemistry. The participants had yet to discover that one reaction covered another. She planned to sit back and enjoy the fireworks.

Donning her cloak from the hook in the front hall, she adjusted the angle of her hat, checked that a clean handkerchief was in the reticule dangling from her left wrist, and smoothed her kid gloves. House key clutched firmly in her right hand, she was ready to venture outside.

Perhaps Gladys would care to join her in a walk, and then come in for a cup of tea. She locked the door, slipped the key into her pocket, and descended the front steps.

Those flower borders will certainly need some attention. I wonder if Gladys knows of someone to do the lawns and heavy digging.

The earth seemed to call to her, and she planned on responding as soon as she had some tools. The garden gate screeched, and she added oiling its hinges to her growing mental list for the gardener.

Imagine! No soot. No noisy cobblestones. No one shouting their wares. The silence practically has a texture. One can hear it and feel it.

Taking a deep breath of the wonderfully fresh, clean air, she unlatched the gate to Gladys' walkway. Same screech. These flower beds could also use some loving attention, but at least one could distinguish between flowers and weeds.

The five steps up to the porch had her puffing, so she took a moment to compose herself. She raised her hand to grasp the knocker, when the door swung open. Her neighbor greeted her with a big smile and a warm welcome.

"Mrs. Wentworth, please do come in. I've been wondering how you've been doing after that dreadful journey."

Elizabeth watched the smile fade as Gladys' remembered she was addressing a recent widow and tried to look suitably somber. Her emotions flitted across her face for all to see.

Once again Elizabeth thanked her lucky stars. *Such a kind woman, and how lucky I am that she is here.*

"I really came to invite you to accompany me on a short walk and then return to my house for a cup of tea. Will you come?"

Gladys beamed, her smile escaping once more. “I’d love to. Please come in while I put on my coat and hat.” Knowing that the fastest way to enjoy her walk was to do just that, Elizabeth complied. This was her first opportunity to see another Canadian home.

Its neatness and cleanliness spoke to the character of its owner. The furniture, while familiar as to function, was subtly different from its English counterparts. The deacon’s bench provided a seat and a place to store overshoes. It was quite comfortable. She had declined an invitation to wait in the parlor in the interests of leaving more quickly.

From her vantage point on the bench she had an excellent view of the parlor. Six chairs surrounded a round table covered with a velvet shawl. A painted globe lamp rested in the middle. The corner of a small side table, topped with a walnut tea caddy, peeked from behind.

“Thank you for waiting, Mrs. Wentworth. I’m ready now.” Gladys’ face was flushed with excitement. Elizabeth realised that her overture of friendship had been received with pleased surprise. The ladies determined that they would venture as far as the main street. Marshall’s Emporium would offer a chance to meet more neighbors. Betty Keppel’s store had loomed large in Faith’s conversations about her walks to work. And that interesting little shop was just a few doors away from Marshall’s.

CHAPTER 9

Phil Landers, Chief of the Marcher Mills Volunteer Fire Brigade and assistant chief, Steve Jones, left the June sunshine and entered the Station Hotel. They chose a table well away from any of the other occupants. Each man carefully centered his half pint in front of him, leaned forward, and kept his voice low.

"So, Steve, have you had any luck finding out about the recent rash of fires? I've really been hoping that your job in the mill would provide some clues." Phil's eyebrows rose alarmingly. He had an unusually elastic skin. This, combined with a hairline that began on the crown of his head, made for a remarkable countenance when he frowned or raised his eyebrows. Comments about Phil being known as Old Accordion Face were quite apropos. Steve often thought it was a shame that the superabundance of eyebrow hair couldn't be transplanted.

"The only rumors I'm getting are about how the fire department isn't doing much to stop the damage. Mind you, what they say about us is mild, compared to their abuse of the sheriff and his staff. I've invited Jeff Napier to join us. I deliberately did not extend the invitation to include that sergeant of his. Darwin Whitelock is after Jeff's job, and he doesn't care how he does it. I wouldn't put up with someone who constantly undermined me." Phil muttered a curse as he prepared to enjoy the first pull of his drink.

"You've sure read that right, Phil," Steve agreed. "That prick badmouths Jeff every chance he gets. Don't know why he hasn't been fired." He savored the fine flavor of the local brew.

"Well, I wonder if it's a case of giving him enough rope to hang himself. Jeff's a pretty sharp cookie. I have a feeling that Darwin will be looking at moving to another town if he wants to continue in police work." Phil could mix his metaphors with the best of them.

Just then the duo spied Jeff approaching their table. "You two look as if you're hatching big, bad plots," he observed with a grin that failed to reach his eyes. "I'm glad you've called this meeting." Jeff sat in the chair across the table so he could face both men and carefully centered his cup of coffee in front of him. He was meticulous about not drinking on duty. More than one member of his staff had been fired for imbibing before the end of his shift.

"Yeah. We think it's time to put our heads together. Have you noticed that each fire gets a little bigger, and has the potential to do more and more damage, even kill someone? We've never had anything like this in our town before, and I'm getting really nervous." He finished his coffee.

"My crew is top notch, but it's not as if we have a full-time staff. We all have to have regular jobs. It takes valuable time to assemble the men, not to mention the minutes required to get someone to sound the alarm."

"Absolutely, Phil. I couldn't agree more." Jeff hung his hat on the back of the chair and lowered his voice. "I've done a comparison of both the fires and the vandalism that we've had in the past few weeks." He removed a much-folded piece of paper from his shirt pocket and carefully smoothed it. His spectacles were retrieved from the opposite pocket. "My first date is March 31."

"Right. That was the fire set beside the Crofton's shed. Fred had been working on the front gardens, and if he hadn't needed a file to sharpen the hoe, the whole thing would have been gone." Phil was clearly worried.

"Didn't Fred say he thought that fire had started quickly?

While he didn't put it in so many words, the suggestion was that something had been thrown on the fire to make it catch and burn fast." Steve's face reflected his concern.

Phil nodded agreement. "You're right. I really didn't think of the fires and vandalism as being connected. Why do you think they are? They seem totally separate. The vandalism is a nuisance, but the fires could cost lives."

"What you're saying is true, Steve. I don't know that they are connected. It might be a coincidence, but in my business you get suspicious about coincidences." Jeff continued. "Also, between the fires and the vandalism my staff has been very busy. That's a great time for the local hoodlums to increase their activities. There's only so much we can do, and when you're stretched to the limit and tired, things can slip by you that wouldn't in other circumstances." His listeners nodded their agreement. Jeff continued reading from his list.

"April 6 is the next date." He looked up and grimaced when he heard the chuckles.

"While you might find humor in cut washing lines, let me tell you I was in danger of life and limb from those ladies. They had each just finished hanging the last of their white wash and returned to the house to get the next load. After the rain we had on April 5…." He could see that there was no need to continue. Both Phil and Steve were married. Laundry, especially white laundry, dropped onto wet grass or a muddy yard was cause for a man to take to the hills.

"April 15 is probably the next thing on your list. The fire at the public school was more than malicious. It was several feet from the building, and the principal, teachers, and some of the older students had it out in short order." Phil's anger had caused his voice to rise. Steve frowned and issued an imperative "Hush" from the corner of his mouth. Phil mouthed the word "sorry".

Jeff continued. "On April 21 some fool removed the lids from the garbage cans behind the Golden Star and stood on their rims. Whoever it was must have been damned quiet. Eddie Knowles was fit to be tied. He was stomping and swearing and waving that damned great cleaver of his until I was eyeing the door. When I finally got him settled down, I discovered that he'd put the garbage out as he does every Wednesday night, making sure the lids were on tightly." Jeff grinned. "Have you ever heard him go on about the wild night life in Marcher Mills? He swore that every cat, dog, racoon, and skunk in the county had a party in his back alley that night. We can smile now, but it really isn't a joke. Eddie serves a lot of chicken, and those bones can cause an animal to choke real easy."

The other men chuckled and nodded ruefully. Eddie's temper when anything threatened the smooth running of his establishment was legendary.

Steve piped up. "Would that make the April 28 outhouse relocations the next items on your list? I seem to remember that as being particularly nasty. My wife told me that each of the three outhouses had been shifted back little more than the width of the hole. Someone could have fallen in. While the fall probably wouldn't have hurt them, their chances of surviving the results of the fever they would get would be pretty slim."

"Doc Reddings is foaming at the mouth. I wouldn't want to be in the culprits' shoes if they're caught. He's threatened a near death experience if he gets within reach of them." Phil's countenance showed his lack of concern for the fate of anyone who would do something so despicable.

"Did you hear about the rocks placed on the front and back steps of the hotel?" Jeff queried.

"I'm not too sure how many people know about it, although it's no secret. I'm pretty sure it happened on May 4.

"Mary Blain had a large pan of peelings and such and was on her way to add them to the compost heap. Someone had placed several rocks, about the size of an egg, on each step. She stepped on one and fell. It took her more than a month to recover from a badly sprained ankle."

"My God, Jeff, she could have broken her leg." Steve was outraged.

"This has gone way past being a prank. We really have to do something about it." Jeff nodded agreement.

"I guess that means that the next thing was the fire at the Redding's on May 15. Now that we're discussing it, do you suppose it could have anything to do with the doc's threats? I remember that one well, as it was our fifteenth wedding anniversary, and Linda was a very unhappy lady when the fire bell started ringing just as we finished that bottle of wine." Phil's deadpan expression didn't fool the others. They had no difficulty whatsoever filling in the couple's aborted plans.

"That was really dangerous. The fire at the school was too small and too far away from the building to really pose a hazard." Jeff observed. "The others tended to fall in the category of nuisance and might even be put down to high spirits—probably liquid. But the Reddings—that could have ended in death or horrible injuries." He shook his head.

"Right, Jeff. That's the first time someone was in danger. For a while it was touch and go. If the wind hadn't shifted, we would have lost the house, too."

Steve piped up. "Apparently the Reddings' bedroom is over the porch and Lily Redding smelled smoke. I hear that she's a mess, jumping at the least little thing. My wife told me that Lily gets up about five times a night just to check for fires. Did you hear that she was expecting? According to the ladies, it'll be about Christmas." He soothed his anxiety with a large swallow of beer.

Phil was resolute in pulling his partner back to the matter in hand. Steve was a damned fine fireman, but he could be easily distracted—except at a fire site. Then he kept his mind on his duties until the official declaration that the fire was fully contained and out.

Jeff consulted his list. "The mill was next in line, apparently. That date was May 20. Whoever took the manure from the livery stable was canny. We estimate that it took two wheelbarrow loads to create the mound heaped in front of the employee's entrance."

"How the hell could they do that? Wheelbarrows are not noted for their silent running." Steve noted.

"Yes, and why didn't the horses raise a ruckus? And don't the stablehands take turns sleeping in the loft just to guard against theft or fire?" Phil's comment followed closely on Steve's.

"Well, according to what we discovered, the thief took the manure from the far side of the pile. The wheelbarrow we found on scene practically dripped grease, and thus operated with virtually no noise at all. They leave it outside, upended against the building. A large puddle of grease marked that spot.

"Also, if you plan your route, it's possible to use back alleys all the way from the stable to the mill, thus cutting down or eliminating any chance of discovery." Jeff waited.

He wasn't disappointed. Phil and Steve leaned half-way across the table in order to keep their voices as low as possible. Phil beat Steve to the punch by half a breath.

"We've verified that paraffin oil had been dripped over the front porch of two homes on Gilmour Street. You know the extent of the damage to each of the houses. A couple of my crew are still recovering from breathing too much smoke, as well as burns to their hands and faces. We were just damned lucky that no one was seriously hurt."

Jeff nodded. "Yes, that's next on my list—May 28."

"Right. Thank God that heavy shower came along in time to save what was left. No matter how hard we pump, we just don't have the ability to put out more than one blaze at a time."

Phil had appeared before the town council on several occasions, pleading the need for at least a skeleton full-time staff and more equipment. Marcher Mills fought its fires with gear that had been in use for more than twenty years. The town's population had increased by almost fifty per cent in the last ten years. Old, worn out equipment and volunteers as firefighters constituted a recipe for disaster.

"I know just what you're thinking, and you're right. We're on a slippery slope, indeed. The council needs to spend less time patting itself on the back because it will probably be the county seat, and more time assessing the needs of the community. Those stupid buggers don't realize that it has more to do with Marcher Mills' geographical location than anything they have, can or will do. It's too bad that somebody, or several somebodies will have to die before they wake up."

The three men regarded each other, their bodies tense with worry. "So, what do you see as our next step, Jeff? We know that it's only a matter of time before there's a death. Do you have any leads?"

"No solid leads, Phil, but plenty of ideas. Do you and Steve have any insights on these fires?"

"Like you, Jeff, ideas, yes, but no proof. You've given us lots to think about. Why don't we meet back here the day after tomorrow? Maybe considering a possible connection between the vandalism and the fires might give us some other avenues to explore."

"I'll see you in a couple of days. In the meantime, if you come up with anything, leave a note at my house." The men exchanged meaningful glances. There was no need to say more: they were all aware that information left at the his office could be "lost" or misplaced, if by doing so it would reflect badly on Jeff.

CHAPTER 10

Gladys checked the placement of her hat in the mirror beside the front door. It must be at exactly the right angle for her visit to Elizabeth. *Elizabeth, imagine that. She wants me to call her Elizabeth. And people say the English are so stuffy.* Gladys was very aware that her antecedents were much more humble than those of her hostess.

Satisfied with the placement of the hat, she smoothed her best black kid gloves over her hands, then draped her new and exceedingly smart reticule on her wrist. She had decided the best approach to acquiring social polish was to concentrate on one thing at a time.

Today her focus would be on her hostess' greeting, the taking of outer garments, and escorting her into the parlor. A notebook, purchased specifically for this purpose and well hidden from both family and friends, contained copious notes on table settings and food.

She admired the shine on her shoes, opened the door, and prepared to enjoy her afternoon—after the greeting and getting to the front parlor, of course. She was always nervous about her chosen area of study. Concentrating on the information she wished to acquire while seeming only to enjoy the occasion always proved difficult.

As she prepared for an afternoon of gossip and learning, she repeated her mantra: *Gracious. I must remember to be gracious. It costs nothing and makes everyone feel better.*

She descended the five steps from the front porch. The

appearance of her flower beds framing the short walk caught her attention. She made a mental note to speak to the yard boy about the slapdash way he had cut the grass. And trimmed the edges of the beds.

Once again he had forgotten to oil the hinges on the front gate. Their loud, high-pitched shriek caused her to flinch, then flush with embarrassment. Surely the entire neighborhood had heard that dreadful noise.

She approached the Wentworth home in a leisurely manner. She did not want to arrive in a fluster. It was impossible to remember important details if upset.

Their front gate opened soundlessly. Their flower beds, a riot of blooms, had no weeds. Their front steps appeared scrubbed, and not just swept. Gladys resolved to have her porch and its steps in a similar pristine state; the yard boy could certainly handle that chore, too.

Even the brass knocker on the Wentworth front door sported a glowing finish. She raised and lowered it three times in a measured beat. Head cocked to one side, she listened intently.

Elizabeth's footsteps approached. The door opened. Her usual charming greeting and honest pleasure were evident. The Whiffletree/Wentworth alliance exhibited all the signs of a strong foundation.

"Come in, Gladys. It's so lovely to see you. Let me take your cloak." Gladys surrendered the garment, making a point of stepping to one side in order to see into the parlor. While eager to receive confirmation of her good taste, she was also curious to see which tea set adorned the lace cloth covering the tea cart. *Ah, violets. That's different from the last time. I must make a note of this.* As she performed her side step, she ostentatiously resettled her new reticule.

Her hostess did not fail her. "Is that a new reticule?" She hung the cloak on the hall tree and continued. "Such lovely beadwork. Did you get it in town?"

Eager to expand on the acquisition of her newest treasure and hungry for approval, Gladys responded. "Yes. I just happened to be checking on the delivery of a skirt I've commissioned from Betty Keppel. It will be perfect with my new green jacket. While I waited for her to finish with another customer, I noted that she had a new shipment from Eaton's. The reticules and some other things were on the counter, as she had not yet had time to put them away."

Elizabeth slipped her arm through Gladys' in a friendly manner and escorted her into the parlor.

"Do sit down, Gladys. The kettle's on the boil, and I'll put the tea to steep. You might be interested in the latest *Godey's.* My sister-in-law kindly forwards her copies to us."

Gladys carefully eased the gloves from her hands and prepared to enjoy herself. Her hostess bustled towards the kitchen. Part of Gladys' mind followed the steps she knew Elizabeth would take: removing the damp cloth from the plate of small sandwiches, pouring the water over the tea leaves after she had warmed the pot. A tiered cake stand on a small side table promised toothsome treats.

Gladys continued her comments on Betty Keppel as her hostess appeared from the kitchen.

"She's also a good businesswoman. The invitation to be the first to see the latest goods resulted in a purchase, as we both knew it would."

This subject was dear to Elizabeth's heart. "I've also heard that she has one of the Singer sewing machines. They certainly take the drudgery out of straight sewing. My girls and I have discussed purchasing one."

How interesting. If the Wentworth family considered the

machine an asset, perhaps I should reconsider getting one.

She stopped stirring her tea, realising that her comfort in having her purchase admired resulted in too much enthusiasm. Her etiquette book emphasised the importance of moving the spoon gently and noiselessly in the center, avoiding any contact between the spoon and the side of the cup. It required a huge degree of concentration to continue a conversation and remember so many rules.

"Of course, when you think of it, the miles and miles of seams required for tablecloths and sheets and such could be done so much faster. I would much rather spend my time with embroidery."

The ladies sipped their tea and enjoyed the food, chatting comfortably about daily events. Finally, Gladys could wait no longer.

"Elizabeth, are you aware of the rumors of a possible marriage between Sebastian and his Australian cousin, Marianne?"

"I've certainly heard the possibility discussed on several different occasions. I believe there is to be an announcement when the senior Montgomerys return from England." Gladys knew that Elizabeth was willing to chat about their mutual acquaintances, but that she would not repeat idle or vicious gossip.

"The general opinion is that their future marriage is now a fact, and not just idle speculation."

Gladys had personally observed Amanda and Sebastian interacting with each other. Their behavior definitely betokened great interest—an interest that was all the stronger because neither would admit it. Instead, they seemed determined to argue at every opportunity.

"Well, Elizabeth, "Gladys gave a little wiggle, carefully placed her cup in its saucer, leaned forward and lowered her voice. "Well, Elizabeth," she repeated, "Marianne was overheard talking about her fiancé. And not only that, but in a manner that clearly indicated it was *not* Sebastian." She leaned back, raised the teacup to her lips, and waited.

Intent on the reception of this bombshell, she failed to realize that Elizabeth controlled her reaction by fulfilling her duties as hostess. "Forevermore! I had no idea. I wonder what she could have meant." She filled both cups and carefully placed the pot on its stand. Gladys waited. Elizabeth obliged.

"Are you sure? Is it just a wild rumor, or do you think it has some basis in fact?"

The tea in Gladys' cup was in danger of spilling. She caught her hostess' look of concern just in time to avoid a disaster. "Oh, I think it's true, even though Marianne and Sebastian have certainly fostered the idea of being a couple, I always thought the spark that indicated true interest was missing. I could be wrong, mind you, but I don't think so." She pretended to straighten her napkin and study the pattern in the lace tablecloth.

"As a matter of fact, Elizabeth, I think there is more spark between Amanda and Sebastian than ever existed between those two Montgomerys." She failed to see the success of her ploy. Elizabeth's napkin slid off her lap, permitting her to hide her reaction.

"Well, Gladys, I guess we'll find out. Now, do you have time to show me that crochet stitch? As you know, I have very much admired your black shawl, and would be glad to know just how you devised such a delightful pattern."

Gossip yielded to stitchery as the ladies settled side by side, crochet hooks in hand.

CHAPTER 11

May, even in the middle of the month, could be reminiscent of March. Tonight the cold, heavy rain beat mercilessly on the figure huddled in the dark shadows of a stand of lilacs. Mrs. Wilson had no idea that her love of its fragrant blooms would provide a lookout for a spy. Neither glow of cigarette nor hasty movement marked his presence. The watcher ignored the elements, his only concession to tip his head slightly to one side the better to slough off the drops falling from the budding branches which arched over his head. The footing was damp, but no puddle had formed. The roots of the bushes were slightly elevated from the level of the street, which served as a run off for the excess water.

Bert Stiles hunched his shoulders and curled his hands into fists as he shoved them deeper into his pockets. If he didn't move very soon he would start to shiver, causing the branches to rub against each other. Not only would this release the accumulated rain, but movement was the first thing to catch the human eye. No one must know he watched the house across the street, or even that he was in this part of town tonight.

He had used his usual guile when selecting a watching post. Ambling about the town in the late evening on seemingly aimless strolls had provided him with considerable blackmail opportunities. He knew every alley, path, and shelter. He chose his observation points with care and an eye to continuing his profitable anonymity. Because his scheme to ruin the Montgomery family was proceeding so well, he decided to apply his information-gathering skills to certain members of the Marcher Mills community.

He planned to disappear just after the final conflagration, and extra income was always welcome.

He never ceased to marvel that people seemed to be lulled into a false sense of security because it was dark outside. Candles and kerosene lamps shone through the windows where curtains or drapes had yet to be drawn. The actions he observed were often those that customarily occurred in the utmost privacy. Even when the husband of A was with the wife of B, the combination of open curtains and uninhibited actions offered surprising entertainment for those passing by. So abundant and profitable were the blackmail opportunities that he frequently struggled to live within his perceived income.

Blackmail, he knew from experience, was much better than extortion. For one thing, no one knew who he was. He smiled with satisfaction. Extortion had required much too much visibility in addition to the possibility of physical harm. Years of perfecting a menacing attitude, combined with a reputation as a dirty fighter, usually led to the victims handing over well-earned cash in exchange for remaining pain free. But once his blackmail scheme proved profitable, he had discontinued the extortion.

A considerable savings in travel expenses also resulted from his switch to blackmail. He had plied his so-called trade under a false name and in towns on the rail line for ease of transportation. He made sure to conduct his business at night to further muddy the trail. Naturally inquisitive, his schemes continued to develop and flourish.

A quick scan in both directions showed that no one could see him. He was alone. Cold and damp nights offered the best opportunities for information gathering. In this case, the final nightly routine of the house presently under observation would provide his next victims. Of course, he referred to it as contributions to his welfare fund, but whatever the name, the money spent the same.

Now it would be the Biltmore's turn, and their own fault, really. If they had only closed those curtains, they wouldn't be receiving one of his letters.

In the Biltmore's house, directly across the street from the lilac bush, lights began to wink out. The sequence was the same as it had been over the past six weeks. As clearly as if he had followed Stan Biltmore clutching his light and closing up his house, it told a story. First the parlor light disappeared, restricting the illumination to the lantern accompanying Stan. It disappeared briefly, entered the kitchen, then returned. He lost track of it as it ascended, then reappeared in an upstairs window. The routine never varied.

By clever and apparently aimless questioning of the delivery boy from the general store, Bert had determined that the house had a center hall plan. The lad had been so intent on proving that he could be a good detective that he proudly shared his knowledge of the interior of several of the houses on his route.

The light continued towards the only other illumination in the house—the parents' bedroom. The lantern's glow dimmed as it entered the bedroom Bert knew held the two boys. It stayed for less than a minute before brightening as it advanced to a room situated at the front of the house—the room belonging to the twelve-year-old daughter of the family. The light stopped. Pre-dawn ambles down the footpath that ran behind the houses had enabled him to glean this information.

He slowly drew out the watch he had placed in his coat pocket. Each movement had been carefully planned to offer the least chance of discovery from someone passing by or looking out a window at an inopportune moment. Holding the watch close to his body, he flicked open the glass cover and gently touched the hands to determine the time, then waited. Finally the light began to move again, this time towards the parent's room. A few moments later the building rested in darkness. Once again he touched the exposed face of the timepiece: twenty minutes had elapsed.

After checking carefully that he was still unobserved, he stepped smoothly from his shelter and turned towards the Station Hotel. Slipping quickly from shadow to shadow and street to street, he reviewed the knowledge he had acquired and now confirmed: the father was the last to retire, and the time spent in his daughter's room varied from sixteen to twenty-three minutes.

The six-month investigation had ended. Perseverance and intuition would pay off once again, and the Biltmores would receive some extremely disconcerting mail. This particular letter, addressed to Mr. and Mrs. Stan Biltmore—Bert did enjoy making it a family occasion— would reach them in time for their first donation to be on its way by the end of the week.

He remembered once hearing that English army officers prayed for "bloody wars and sickly seasons" in order to speed their promotions. His own thoughts leaned towards rain, snow, sleet, and hail. People clung to the warmth and comfort of their own, or others', hearths in such weather. The enforced idleness left plenty of time to participate in pursuits destined to increase his income.

✿✿✿

Bert smiled as he dropped the letter into the mail box which stood on a busy Toronto street. He extended his arms in a movement he thought of as particularly gentlemanly—shooting his cuffs. The brilliant white cuffs extending below the edge of the jacket sleeve made it easy to admire the gleam of his gold cufflinks. He frequently shot his cuffs when wearing his fine clothing, enjoying the satisfying feeling of being well dressed.

Being an independent businessman left his days free to attend to his affairs—except his research. Spying at night reaped many rewards. Of course, he couldn't entirely discount chats in the billiard parlor, livery, barber shop, etc. The barber's and billiard parlor provided fascinating information on the activities of men. He'd received many a lead there.

Surprisingly, given that both men and women frequented the place, the general store's regulars around the stove or on the bench in front of the big window had gifted him on more than one occasion. Their nuggets pertained more to families and the women, but any information included power over others.

Thus far he had kept his blackmailing activities confined to Hamilton. Living in Marcher Mills had proved very convenient, with its placement about half-way between Hamilton and Toronto. With his plans made and ready to go, Bert decided that Marcher Mills would also prove profitable.

To that end, he had begun instituting his blackmail strategy. The Biltmore family was destined to join the ranks of the plundered.

✿✿✿

The train permitted combining a trip to Toronto for recreation with avoiding possible detection through the presence of a local postmark on his early retirement correspondence—his own code phrase for blackmailing income. Sometimes he caught the morning train on Sunday morning and came back on Monday. At other times, such as today, he made the trip during the week to transact business, even though he planned to return the same evening.

Punctual, as usual. Plenty of time to go to his room and change into clothing more suited to his role as Bart Stone, entrepreneur.

A short time later he stopped in front of a store window to admire the fine figure reflected there. His brown sack suit, featuring a smart single-breasted waistcoat, contrasted well with his blinding white shirt and gold and brown silk four-in-hand. He raised his hand to enjoy its softness, congratulating himself that the colors in the tie complemented his suit perfectly.

Bert appreciated good clothing and knew he was attractive. Smoothing his moustache assured him that the wax applied several hours earlier added the finishing touch. *Yes, I was right. The bowler is perfect for my face and this suit.* He gently buffed his nails on the suit's lapels and smiled at the dashing and debonair reflection.

With the establishment of the persona of Bart Stone, he now had a room in an unremarkable residence. It provided him with an opportunity to change from Stiles to Stone. The many hours spent locating a rooming house that combined respectability with a mutual lack of interest in its inhabitants had paid off.

Bounding up the Post Office steps two at a time, he whistled softly. Time to check the mailbox registered in the name of the Jones Supply Company. Bert counted on his victims, in the unlikely event that they would try to discover the identity of the blackmailer, being confused by the fact that they were sending their funds to a company, and not an individual. He further muddied his trail by renting a mail box at this sub post office, and paying a fee to have all correspondence rerouted from the central branch.

"Mail for the Jones Supply Company, please." Over the years he had created an identity which portrayed him as the brother of the firm's owner.

"Certainly, sir, here you are."

Bert headed for the nearby billiard parlor, left hand covering the pocket containing the valuable letters. His right hand dipped inside his jacket to reassure himself that his bankbook rested in its accustomed place. As usual, he would visit the washroom at some point, open the envelopes, remove the contents, and shred the envelopes before flushing them down the toilet. Then, before he returned to Marcher Mills, he would visit his Toronto bank to make a deposit.

That bankbook was one of his most treasured possessions, worn limp from the hours of fondling while he dreamed of spending the funds.

Later, deposit made, a fine meal in his belly, and two dollars in his pocket from winning at billiards, the clacking wheels of the Marcher Mills bound train kept time with his favorite fantasy.

The house, surrounded by mature trees, will have beautiful gardens with two ponds and at least one fountain. The lights of the city disappeared, his reflection in the window invisible to his inward-turning gaze.

A porte-cochere—he rolled the words on his tongue, relishing their flavor—*definitely a porte-cochere. There was something so elegant about a drive that swept under its protection to let his guests—cream of the locals—arrive in comfort, no matter what the weather. The house, three stories high, plus an attic for the servants' bedrooms. Conservatory crammed with valuable and unusual plants.*

That part of the fantasy never appeared with satisfactory clarity. Bert had no idea what constituted valuable and unusual plants. He avoided investigating the subject at the local library. The Marcher Mills' grapevine's efficiency was legendary. Miss Wheeler appeared to be discreet, as did her assistant, but, as always, the best chance is no chance.

A large kitchen, with cook. Housemaid. Gardener. Faceless silhouettes flitted across his inner vision. *A dining room, parlor, and smoking room. Oh, yes, and a library. Must have a library.*

Bert enjoyed reading, so the library was certainly feasible. *Lots of history books. And travel books. Maybe even a few on archeology.* The train rocked and lurched. Bert's introspection continued undisturbed.

CHAPTER 12

Sebastian doffed his hat yet again. Surely half the county had chosen to promenade on the main street this morning.

"Well, here we are, Marianne, parading around downtown Marcher Mills, as you requested." Sebastian's tone did not encourage a flirtatious reply.

"Thank you, Sebastian. We are beset with chaperones, even though we're related. I wanted to have a private conversation with you."

He watched as Marianne twirled her parasol and nodded affably at two women whose sidelong glances took in every detail of the young woman on the arm of Marcher Mills' most eligible bachelor. Parasol twirling invariably preceded revelations he would prefer to avoid. He feared there was no escape. While her hand appeared to rest gently on his arm, he was well acquainted with the strength of her grip, if thwarted.

Politely he raised his hat and murmured a greeting. The ladies smiled and showed every sign of wishing to engage him in conversation. He pretended not to notice, and urged Marianne to increase her pace. As the women passed, he replaced his hat and ground his teeth. He had no difficulty whatsoever in interpreting the looks of avaricious interest on the faces of two of his customers.

"I gathered as much, dear cuz. Now tell me what's on your little mind?" Sebastian and Marianne were well acquainted. Their families had met in England for an extended vacation on three separate occasions.

"I'm sure you've been told why I've been banished to a land

far, far away from home. It's a ploy to separate me from my fiancé."

Aha. He was right. He knew she had a reason for wanting to be alone with him. He paused at the entrance of a small park to indicate his willingness to amble through its winding paths. She nodded, and their steps veered to the right. The fresh, young leaves on the trees danced in the breeze. Marianne continued her story.

"You are no doubt aware that my family does not approve of Durwood. I do not approve of their assumption that they, and not I, should select my bridegroom."

He sighed. This was worse than he thought.

"Marianne, my aunt and uncle are not unreasonable. Tell me what is really going on."

"It's true that they are usually amenable to logic, but in this case we seem unable to agree. Therefore, our compromise was that I would come to visit your family, thus removing myself from his presence." She used her old trick of pausing to view his reaction through lowered lashes.

"Yes, yes, I'm well aware of the shenanigans you've been pulling." An indignant gasp from his companion failed to stop him. "They feel that your poor, undeserving choice's eye is on the main chance. And having a beautiful bride isn't hard to take."

Sebastian was furious at this interruption of his day. God alone knew what That Woman and her sister would be doing to his pharmacy while he danced attendance on his difficult cousin. Henry, usually a stalwart support, was useless; he simply watched Sebastian fume and Amanda get her way. The fact Sebastian's discomfort amused Henry was the final straw.

"You are so right, Sebastian." Her voice brought him back to the present. "They absolutely refuse to see that Durwood is a man of today. Because he's passionate about 'new-fangled doodads', such as electric fans, they think his head is in the clouds." She smiled at a gentleman who courteously raised his hat.

"But they're wrong. Electricity is the way of the future. Marcher Mills has electricity. The market for electric fans and other electrical wonders hasn't even been tapped. Durwood really is a man of vision. His plans are based on solid research and a firm grasp of economics. He already has branches in Adelaide, Sydney, and Brisbane. Companies in Japan, New Zealand and several countries in South America are anxious to have access to his products. He'll be a great success."

She stopped for breath and to catch her skirt and raise it in preparation for crossing the street. The ice cream parlor was just across the way.

"Durwood, I'm sure, is a paragon, Marianne, but you are not yet twenty-one. Until then, your father can forbid your marriage."

Sebastian checked carefully to ensure they had enough time to cross the street safely. He slipped her hand from the crook of his arm and grasped her elbow.

"Now. Before those wagons are upon us and the dust is thick in the air." They entered the ice cream parlor just as the first wagon rumbled behind them.

Sebastian remarked mentally on Zeke Marshall's legendary ability to anticipate and provide those items which people wanted. He and his wife operated Marshall's Emporium.

Zeke was unique in that he listened to, and frequently acted upon, his wife's suggestions. One such suggestion was the establishment of a small ice cream parlor. Because the location required a short stroll down a side street, the rent was nominal. Zeke had a three-year lease on the property. If the ice cream parlor failed, he could use the space to store seasonal goods. In point of fact, the parlor was such a success that the Marshalls planned to serve hot drinks and sweets in the colder months.

Sebastian returned to his current dilemma.

"So far you've mentioned that Durwood sells electric fans and is a forward-thinking chap. Is Durwood his first or last name? And why, if he has stores in three major Australian cities, plus keen interest shown by overseas contacts, are your parents so much against him?"

He chose the corner furthest from the door and held a chair. She took time to place her parasol and reticule on the table and look around before sitting down.

"Perhaps I should wait until they bring our sodas so we won't be interrupted."

"Stop stalling. Our sodas are on their way right now." She sighed, resigned.

"Durwood is his first name. His surname is Bosworth. The Bosworths do not live in the best part of town, but not the worst, either. They do not move in the highest social circles. They are honest and hardworking, and have made considerable sacrifices in order to help their son in his chosen field.

"He graduated from a respectable school, then worked in the retail trade to learn how to run a business. He's also taken courses at the Mechanics' Institute to learn all he could about electricity. His reputation in his field is first rate.

"However, since he cannot keep me in a style to which I am accustomed, my parents have prohibited our marriage. Durwood is perfectly capable of supporting me in comfort, but not luxury."

She paused for breath. Sebastian braced himself for the worst, but Marianne appeared to have completed her defence.

"Very well, give me the word without the bark. What madcap scheme have you now concocted?" She glared at him. Straightened her shoulders. Inhaled.

"Durwood will meet me here. In Marcher Mills. Within the next two months. And we will be married. My birthday is in three weeks' time. No one can stop us." She braced herself, as if to withstand the firestorm her escort was sure to fling her way.

But he was quiet, his eyes focused on a distant point. And he was rubbing his chin—a sure sign of deep thought. He frowned; then smiled.

"Since you've been so honest with me, I'll support you in this madcap scheme. Or I'll do so until I meet this Durwood Bosworth. If, and only if, mind you, I feel he is a suitable candidate for your hand, I'll even help organise the wedding."

She glowed, took a dainty handkerchief from her pocket, and dabbed her eyes.

"But," his raised finger and serious expression showed his resolve, "if I *don't* think he's all you said, I'll do everything in my power to foil your plans." Her smile lit up the room.

One part of Sebastian's mind was on his precious pharmacy. Another part was mulling over the information his cousin had so obligingly supplied. A brilliant idea occurred, and he hastened to share it.

"You said that your Durwood would be here in a few weeks, right?"

Marianne stirred her soda slowly and eyed him with a look he recognized. He knew her mind was racing to determine what scheme he had just hatched. She nodded slowly. And waited.

"Well, it seems to me that we can help each other." She raised her eyebrows, and continued to stir her beverage. Sebastian knew he had her attention. Now to lay out his plan in the best possible way.

"How often have you heard me complain of the matchmaking mothers and their not-so-adorable daughters?" She raised an eyebrow.

"Well, if we pretend to be interested in each other, those busybody aunts providing chaperon duties for us and intelligence services to our parents will pass the word." She laughed and clapped her hand, eyes sparkling.

"You're right! That will keep you free from having to come up with fancy footwork to avoid an unwanted marriage and give me respite from those very same aunts. Do you know that I've had to rent a mailbox in Toronto in order to receive Durwood's letters?" She huffed at the indignity.

"We'll both benefit from the scheme, Marianne. You can have Durwood address his letters to me, with yours sealed inside. When I see his return address, I'll be sure to pass them on to you."

"Unopened," she stated, giving him a gimlet glare.

"Of course! And now I want to apologize to you."

"Whatever for?"

"When you asked me to promenade through the centre of town, I resented such a waste of time. And worried about what That Woman was doing in my pharmacy." He pulled his timepiece from his pocket, opened the case, and frowned at what he saw.

Marianne pretended to have something in her eye so that her handkerchief covered her smile. The phrase *That Woman*, or even *That Woman and her sister*, uttered between gritted teeth occurred with ever-increasing frequency.

"However, the time has been well spent. Now, if you've finished your soda let's go to the pharmacy. I'll have Henry take you home."

"No need to bother Henry. I'm dying to meet your nemesis. Then I want to visit the general store and the seamstress' shop. I'll enjoy a slow stroll home through a town that will be mine for the next while. Don`t worry about me. It`s perfectly respectable for a young lady to be unaccompanied during the day."

The cousins smiled at each other and rose. Marianne opened her parasol as they stepped onto the boardwalk, then nestled her other hand in the crook of his elbow. The parasol twirled slowly.

CHAPTER 13

Jenny Biltmore finished setting the table, then turned to check the pots on the stove. Just a few more minutes. The small sliced roast waited in the warming oven. *Time to call the children to get washed.*

Suddenly a draft slid across the nape of her neck. Probably one of the boys failing to latch the back door. She turned to remedy the situation and jerked to a halt.

"Stan, what's wrong? Are you ill?" She rushed toward her husband, dishcloth clutched in her hand. Framed in the kitchen doorway, his livid face and swaying body terrified her. Stan, six feet tall and two hundred pounds, customarily radiated strength and confidence. In their fifteen years of marriage she had never seen him like this.

"Here, lean on me." She placed his hand on her left shoulder. Holding it there, and slipping her right arm around his waist, she supported him to his chair at the table. He seemed totally unaware of his surroundings.

After assuring herself that he wouldn't fall, she hurried to the cupboard to get a glass and the whiskey bottle. She filled it to the half-way point, thumped the bottle on the table, all of her attention focused on her husband. She bent his fingers around the tumbler and guided it to his mouth.

"Drink. Drink it right now." Her voice was shrill with panic. Tears trickled down her cheeks. Her heart pounded. She had a sinking feeling that whatever had caused Stan's condition was sure to bring grief to their family.

Stan focused first on the liquid and then on his wife. He appeared unsure of his surroundings and puzzled by the presence of the beverage. His gaze seemed fixed on the table, moving from plate to cutlery to condiments and back.

"What's wrong, Stan? You're frightening me. What is wrong?" The volume of her voice increased with each word. Stan swallowed the entire contents of the glass, and shuddered.

"No need to shout, dammit, woman." He glared at her. "I'm not deaf, you know." In an automatic reaction to the release of unbearable tension, anger rushed in to replace fear.

"Why are you trying to pour whiskey down my throat? Usually you're whining that I drink too much." He slopped a generous two fingers of alcohol into the empty glass and polished it off.

"And no need to shout at me, either." Jenny, too, expressed her relief with sharp words. Her heart still resided in her throat. She panted and fought for breath.

"You stand at the door, pale as a ghost, swaying like corn in a high wind, let me help you to the table, hold the glass and guide it to your mouth, and then ask me stupid questions?"

The words flew from her mouth with ever-increasing speed.

"What could possibly have happened to make you do that? I've known you all your life, Stan Biltmore, boy and man, and I've never seen you like this." She used her apron to blot her tears.

"We got a letter." He pulled it from his pocket and watched in disbelief as it shook in his grip.

"So? We do get letters, you know." Relief was still making her voice sharp. An underlying anxiety refuted the relief that she should be experiencing. "What's so bloody special about this letter?"

Jenny seldom used rough language. That she did so when there was a chance that the children could overhear underlined the extent of her concern. She sensed that their lives were about to change, and not for the better.

"It isn't a letter from the family, Jenny. And it's not a letter telling us we forgot to pay a bill. It's not even a letter trying to sell us something." Stan rotated the glass in his hands before draining the last drops.

"Well, then, what is it? Stan, you're frightening me. What is it?" Jenny no longer worried about who might hear. She was terrified.

Stan opened his mouth, then closed it. He opened it a second time. Finally, he gave up and thrust the letter at her. "Here, you read it."

Jenny stared. She slowly reached forward and drew the fateful missive from his trembling hand. Stan. Trembling. She had never known her stalwart spouse to tremble in all the time she had known him. Chilled to the bone, she slowly and reluctantly removed the letter from his hand. Afraid. So afraid.

"Well, woman, read it. You won't know what's in it if you don't unfold it!" Stan reached for the liquor and poured another two fingers. Jenny groped for a chair, pulled it away from the table, and wiped her free hand on her apron. Then, ignoring the seat, she opened the letter and began to read.

Dear Mr. and Mrs. Biltmore

It seems that Mr. Biltmore has a problem. Every night on his way to bed he visits his daughter's room for an appreciable length of time. It takes but a minute to check on a sleeping child. What are you doing, Mr. Biltmore, for the rest of the time? Why don't you stop him, Mrs. Biltmore?

The Jones Supply Company feels sure that you would not wish this information to become common knowledge. And it can remain a secret. Starting this Friday, your payday, Mr. Biltmore, one of you will buy a money order payable to bearer and mail it to the Jones Supply Company, Post Office Box 3317, Toronto, Ontario.

Should you fail to do so, this information will be given to the mill's owner, Mr. Barry Masters. It will also, by some mysterious means, reveal its ugliness and horror to your community. The stain on your family would last through generations, and you will be pariahs wherever you go.

We look forward to receiving your regular weekly payment of two dollars from this point on.

Sincerely,

Jones Supply Company

Jenny saw the words, but they made no sense. Her knees refused to support her and she thumped down on the chair seat.

"What do they mean? How could anyone know that you tuck our daughter in each night? Stan?" Her voice rose to a shriek.

Stan reached across the table and backhanded her. "Shut up, you useless tit. Do you want the neighbors to hear?" he snarled. His face, glistening with sweat, had gone from white to red, a vein in his forehead pulsing rapidly. His voice, controlled with difficulty, growled. There was no resonance, just a flat, menacing sound.

Jenny rocked back in her chair, one hand cradling her reddening cheek, the other pressed against her stomach as if to control its reaction. "You struck me. You struck me! In all the years we've been married, you've never raised a hand to me, and you struck me!" Her mind could not cope with his action; it refused to contemplate the horror that would, from this time on, rule their lives.

"I'm sorry, I'm sorry. I didn't mean to hurt you, but no one must know." Tears were bathing his face, too. Jenny had seen her husband furious. Happy. Sad. But she had never seen him afraid, and Stan was terrified. He tore the letter from her hands, ripped off the section with the address, and quickly thrust the remainder into the stove, moving the potato pot aside in order to accomplish the task. "There, now no one will know except us."

"And the writer of the letter, Stan. Who do you think it could be?" Jenny's mind began to function again. "You've told me and told me that you haven't hurt our little girl. I believed you. Did you lie to me?" She held her breath as she awaited his response.

Jenny had often questioned Stan about the length of time he spent saying goodnight to Susie. But she never asked for specifics. In spite of his reassurances, a niggling doubt sometimes crept into her head, no matter how hard she tried to banish it.

Once again she forced herself to remember the many ways he showed his love for the children. She knew he would never hurt them. Any of them. And, while she had hinted and circled the subject with Susie, she never asked exactly what transpired in those lengthy good nights between father and daughter.

The children had never shown fear of him, unless they knew that a trip to the wood shed for indulging in forbidden pursuits was in order. Even then, and she examined her babies carefully, they were never marked with bruises.

"NO! No, dammit, I would never hurt Susie." He rubbed his face. "Why?" He regarded her suspiciously. "Has Susie said anything to you?"

"Of course not. I would have told you. But how could anyone know what goes on in our house? Who could it be?" Jenny's hands worked her apron, rolling her hands in it from the hem upwards, removing them, and smoothing it down, only to start again.

"I'll find out. I'll find out who the bastard is, and then I'll kill him." Jenny didn't doubt it. She had never seen that look on his face before.

"Oh, Stan, two dollars every week. How will we manage? That means no more savings. Two dollars a week is more than I make cleaning houses. We had planned such a nice Christmas this year." Tears flooded her eyes, streaking her cheeks.

"We'll have to manage, Jenny. What choice do we have? I

wonder if I could get another job on Sundays." Elbows on the table, he ran his hands up the sides of his face, tugged on his hair. "This is blackmail. It'll never stop. Worse, it will probably increase. We'll never know when the next demand will be coming." He covered his eyes to hide his tears from his wife.

She reached across the table. "Stan, we'll manage. We always have before. You just wait. I'm going to find out who's doing this. You'll see." Holding hands, she locked her gaze on his, refusing to acknowledge that his was filled with shame.

Rising from the chair, she prepared to put the supper on the table. She thought he probably had no appetite either, but the children would be hungry.

"You get washed up and I'll call the children. No one, absolutely no one must suspect that anything has changed." He rose heavily to do her bidding.

That night, while her husband snored, Jenny started a systematic mental review of each of the town's residents. When she realized the futility of such a huge task, she abandoned that avenue and determined to begin another. The best place to start would be with the letter. Jenny had done well in English, winning a prize for her composition in grade eight. There was something about that letter that bothered her. She fell into sleep trying to remember what it was.

✿✿✿

Marcher Mills had a very good chance of being appointed as the county seat. This meant increasing the administrative space in the town hall and the addition of one more jail cell. In order to accomplish this, the Marcher Mills Improvement Society had spearheaded several fundraising events in the community. Three of the five Society members had also contributed considerable private funds to the cause. The monies garnered facilitated the purchase of cement, wood, and other supplies necessary to achieve completion of their plans.

Because of recent pilfering, they had passed a motion to hire a night watchman until the project was completed to a stage where the extra materials could be kept in the building itself. This watchman would be selected from the men who had submitted their names for consideration.

The main door of the town hall was unlocked in preparation for tonight's meeting. Four chairs, aligned with mathematical precision, graced the vestibule. A note on one of them invited prospective candidates to be seated. The lantern on the table in the far corner of the room had not been lit and turned down to emit the least possible amount of light. Dark shadows lurked in the corners of the main room, its air stale with disuse. A faint glow through the doorway at the other end of the chamber indicated the location of the meeting room.

In his twelfth year, Bert's parents moved to another community at some distance from Marcher Mills. When he returned, he was a young adult. Well dressed, his source of income remained obscure. He did take on the occasional job for local townspeople, and his reputation was one of steadfastness and dependability. it appeared that he was well compensated.

Control, an integral part of Bert's nature, included matters of dress and demeanor, both nicely calculated to convey respect. Through keen observation and a gift for mimicry, his deportment was mannerly. He took care with the way he walked and moved. He knew better than to swagger or adopt an air of superiority. Once he discovered bullying was so much less effective than manipulation, he had the key to success. Crusher, his pseudonym while pursuing his extortion and intimidation career, was rumored to have been dispatched by a clever thief with an extremely sharp knife. Bert soared, phoenix-like- from the ashes of his former life in Hamilton.

He often boarded the train to Hamilton or Toronto, and did so with the air of a man with places to go and things to do. His company, Stiles Services Limited, had several solid customers in those two cities. He usually wore a suit on these trips, and dressed in the customary work shirt and pants when in Marcher Mills. Unlike the majority of workmen, his clothes were immaculate, pressed, and without hole or patch.

A stranger would consider him attractive and pleasant; helpful without intruding. But, in spite of his appearance and ostensible willingness to help his fellow citizens, he was not well liked. He knew this, and had made very conscious efforts to avoid raising the hackles of his customers. Marcher Mills was about to experience Bert the businessman.

✿✿✿

Thirty minutes before the meeting was scheduled to begin, Bert walked up the road leading to the town hall. Careful to keep in the shadows, his excellent night vision stood him in good stead. His point of observation hid him from the sight of all but the most observant. He knew movement attracted the human eye, and had developed an uncanny ability to remain still for extended periods of time. Information meant power.

He sneered as he watched the other candidates approach the building. The post was his. He had developed his plan when he discovered the identities of his competition. The customary posturing on the part of the committee members would ensue, but they really had no other choice.

Because it was very much to his benefit, Bert had every intention of doing this job in an exemplary manner. He shifted slightly and prepared to enjoy the show. Such a treat to see these lord high mucky-mucks twist in the breeze.

Zeke Marshall, chair of the committee, Henry Soames, and Reverend Peabody approached the building. Their hushed voices indicated an urgent discussion of various strategies. Bert knew that they were experiencing extreme pain at the prospect of awarding him the contract.

Al Anderson and Bernie Perkins trailed the first group of committee members. Bernie abhorred soap and water, for either his person or his garments, and had thus earned the nickname Putrid. A brisk breeze from the west assured that the reek surrounding him blew away from Al, who had long since learned to factor in wind direction.

An appreciable distance separated them from the next duo. Sebastian Montgomery and George Gillately meandered up the walk, their slow pace accommodating George's dependence on a cane. Bert barely controlled a snicker as he contemplated George as a watchman. He was seventy-six years of age and unable to hobble more than one or two steps without his trusty "stick". If his contribution to stopping the thieving amounted to more than an indication of which way the culprits ran, Bert would eat his shirt.

Of course, Sebastian, as one of the almighty Montgomerys, flaunted his good manners as he shortened his stride to accommodate George's stately pace. Bert sneered. *Just another way of currying favor with the locals. What an ass! One of these days, Montgomery, one of these days I'll wipe that holier-than-thou expression from your face and give you and your family the comeuppance they deserve.*

With control honed over a lifetime of accepting slurs and sly innuendos in order to focus on the main chance, Bert redirected his thoughts to the matter at hand. Giving the last two people time to reach the porch, he prepared to join the other three hopefuls.

The committee members' voices echoed as they made their way across the hall and into one of the smaller meeting rooms. His confidence in the final decision derived from knowledge of the various players. Its members would moan and groan, but they really had no choice.

Putrid's main claim to fame was his ability to occupy a chair until the beer ran out, and he could make a pint last all day. Of course, the effluvia surrounding him ensured that thieves would flee in fear of imminent infection. A grin tugged at the corner of Bert's mouth as he contemplated the probable scenario.

Al, an enthusiastic drinker of beverages supplied by others, relied on Bert or some other person with ideas. His propensity for staying warm and dry—and lubricated—made him a non-starter. Neither Al nor Putrid had read the advertisement. Instead, they had relied on rumors amongst their drinking companions, thus missing entirely the part which stated that the successful recipient of the position had to own property within the county. George, at least, met the requirement of being a landowner, but his tottering gait eliminated him from contention.

Henry Soames would have checked the qualifications of each applicant. Bert would like to be a fly on the wall to see the stunned expressions of the committee members at the revelation of his ownership of a farm which extended into Halton County. The majority of the property, situated near Valdeekerson's Corners extended northward, but the two acres which extended over the county line definitely qualified him as a property owner.

Of the chairs provided for the applicants' ease, only one was occupied. Putrid's usual ability to clear a space around him worked a treat. The others stood as far away as the confines of the room permitted. The four men listened to plodding footsteps approaching the vestibule. They indicated the imminent arrival of a man reluctantly determined to do his duty. Zeke, in his role as committee chair, opened the door between the vestibule and the hall and faced the group.

Bert could well imagine what Zeke saw when he looked at the candidates. Putrid swayed even as he sat, his eyes bloodshot. His miasma, containing equal parts of filth, body odor, and alcohol, filled the room. Al Anderson had shaved and put on a fresh shirt. Zeke would appreciate that this represented a considerable amount of thought and effort. George was his usual clean and tidy self, his cane shining from a recent polishing. Bert wore a suit, collar, white shirt and a natty four-in-hand. His shoes were shined, he was freshly barbered, and had obviously bathed before he came. His posture radiated humble confidence.

"Gentlemen, thank you for your patience. The committee has made its decision." He paused, then continued. "Al and Bernie, thank you for coming." The two rose and exited. Al's shoulders slumped, but Bernie appeared focused on making the best possible time to his favorite seat in the hotel's taproom.

"George, your willingness to serve your community, in spite of challenges which would discourage many a younger man, is admirable. My fellow members have asked me to thank you for your determination to serve the greater good." George rose slowly, his body straightening bit by bit.

"That's all right, Zeke. Bert, here, is a good deal more nimble than I am." With unimpaired good humor, George and his cane creaked out of the room.

At last, Zeke turned to Bert with the air of a man determined to do his duty, no matter how repugnant. His ramrod straight posture and backward leaning stance reinforced his distaste.

"Bert, the committee has decided to use your services. Please come with me so that we may discuss the details." Without waiting for a response, or even checking to be sure that Bert followed, Zeke turned and led the way.

They entered the meeting room. Zeke took his place at the head of the table and addressed his fellow committee members. "Gentlemen, as you know, we've asked Bert Stiles to meet with us to discuss the details of guarding the building materials. We estimate that his services will be necessary for approximately four months."

With this introduction, Bert was given a seat at the table. Hours, wages, and record keeping were outlined at some length. He confirmed he would appear an hour early on the following night in order to review the accounting procedures with the site foreman. The Council was satisfied that he had the necessary intelligence for the job. The recommendations of two of their members as to his honesty and work ethic were reassuring. But he was still Bert Stiles.

Later that evening, over a snifter of brandy worthy of the Montgomery table, Bert gloated. He would hire Stan Biltmore to be his relief on Sundays. Danny Tomlin would be glad to cover for him on those nights when he wanted to expand his knowledge of the actions of his neighbors. At eighteen, Danny's absorption in his own plans, combined with the thrill of doing something of which his parents would not approve, ensured his cooperation. *Yes, all's right in my little world. As soon as I nail that insufferable, overbearing, prick Sebastian Montgomery and his holier-than-thou family, I'll assume my Toronto identity, and build my funds to even greater amounts. Then, when I recreate myself again, I'll have the kind of home that's worthy of me and be an important part of my new community."* He reached for the bottle and splashed a generous measure in the crystal snifter.

CHAPTER 14

"Now remember, you promised to be calm and collected when discussing the terms of our agreement with Sebastian. You know that Henry is on our side. The papers he signed on behalf of Mr. Montgomery are in your reticule. There is no need for you to convince anyone of anything. It was all settled before we came. And Henry also promised to be there today." Amanda could feel her sister's admonitory glance.

Amanda, forgetting that she was taller than Faith, increased her pace as they approached the pharmacy. Her entire concentration centered on the very important meeting with Sebastian.

I was right to insist we wear black. It emphasises our recent loss.

Until now they had added small touches of white or gray to their ensembles. This met the criteria of exhibiting a proper respect for the death of their parent, while lessening the impact on their customers.

"Of course I'll be calm and collected. Why do you think it necessary to mention such a thing? There is no reason not to be calm, and my thoughts on the subject are certainly collected. I really can't imagine why you would be the least bit concerned. Any discussions with Mr. Sebastian Montgomery that become in the least heated are always instigated by him. You know that Faith, so there is no need to worry." She pretended interest in the shop windows as an excuse to permit her sister to catch up.

"We have the figures to prove that Sebastian will benefit not only from the rent we will be paying from this point onwards, but that he will also reap increased profits from the number of people who come into his shop. It's not often that his till doesn't ring before they leave." Amanda's rate of speech matched her footsteps. Faith was hard pressed to keep up. Three inches difference in height meant a much shorter stride.

Just as they reached the back door of the pharmacy, Henry stepped out, held the door, and flourished his arm to invite them to enter. The preparation room offered both privacy and a line of sight to the front door. It was an ideal location for the meeting.

Sebastian rose courteously and greeted the ladies with a pleasant "good morning". Amanda noticed he had positioned himself at the head of the table. This gave him the double advantage of a position of power and the ability to monitor any early customers. His message was clear: he was in control. The lines were drawn.

She narrowed her eyes as he invited them to take a seat. Henry poured and served coffee, punctilious in the observance of the amenities. She noted that he and Faith had the same expression, combining equal portions of hope, despair, and determination.

Amanda cannily and adroitly took the high ground. Deliberately arranging the folds of her skirt, she timed her speech to catch Sebastian just as he was about to ask Faith if she would like some sugar.

"Thank you for agreeing to meet us so early, Mr. Montgomery—Sebastian, I should say." Amanda's jaw trembled, but she resisted the urge to grind her teeth. She had capitulated to his oft-repeated request that she should use his first name solely as a way to further her cause. "It is most kind of you to spare us the time. Of course, it's really just a formality. My sister and I have both commented on the number of people who now come into your premises. It is certainly much greater when we arrived. We are delighted that you have benefited from the additional custom we have generated. How gratifying that you will now have our rent as well to add to your profits.

"I'm sure as a successful entrepreneur, you insist your investments show the best possible return." She observed the results of her speech with satisfaction.

Sebastian, caught off-guard by such a pre-emptive strike, froze, the sugar bowl suspended in line with Faith's nose. She deftly removed it from his grasp, helped herself to two spoonsful, and pretended great interest in stirring her coffee to conceal her expression.

Amanda watched Faith wince. No doubt her mental comments centered around what she amusingly referred to as a juggernaut tactic. Regardless of the terminology, every one of those occasions inevitably centered around persons who either tried to discount her abilities because she was a female, or weasel out of an agreement.

Henry reacted by trying to drink coffee that was much too hot. The resulting coughing spell required him to use his handkerchief to cover his mouth. She knew that he was probably covering a smile.

Sebastian nodded, and calmly asked Faith if she would like cream for her coffee. She smiled and refused. If his insistence on playing the good host seemed a little stiff, he persevered. He was then free to turn the full force of his attention to his antagonist. Henry, instead of pouring oil on the roiling waters, was giving a remarkable imitation of a hole in the wall.

"Miss Wentworth, Amanda, I should say," he would not be bested in the matter of conciliatory gestures, "you have made some extremely interesting observations. While your comments about the financial arrangements made with your *father* before your arrival are correct, they do not necessarily apply to the current situation. Even you must agree that having a business run by two women is a far cry from having one operated by a man, with female assistants." He eyed his opponent with interest. She glared. Her chin rose a notch. She looked ready to explode, but took a deep breath, and prepared for a shot across his bow.

"Perhaps you have forgotten that the agreement was made with Wentworth Optometry Services, not with a particular individual. I notice that you have not responded to the comments about your increased income from a rise in foot traffic through your store. Nor have you acknowledged the fact that the document *signed in good faith with Wentworth Optometry Services* has already raised net profits to the pharmacy. This increased revenue, I might add, costs you nothing, and permits some semblance of truth to your claims of providing the best services in Halton County." Flushed with triumph, she graciously yielded the floor to her opponent.

"Amanda, Sebastian, perhaps we could keep our attention focused on the payments for the lease. It is, after all, the purpose of this meeting. If we could concur on the points already arranged; that is that the lease will be honoured as originally presented, with payments to be made quarterly starting with the next quarter, we could then open the doors to the customers. I see that there are two women at the front door already." Sebastian did not always appreciate Henry's adroitness in using his years of experience as a man of affairs to his advantage. But Henry ignored his silent message, and continued.

"Amanda, do you agree to the terms as outlined in the original agreement? And Sebastian, do you also agree to these terms?" Silence. Inimical glares from the two combatants. Finally, Amanda broke the stalemate, her voice and attitude blending to a nicety reasonableness and condescension.

"Of course, Henry, if Sebastian initials and dates the original agreements—his copy and mine—I have no problem. Indeed, this seems to be somewhat of a storm in a teacup." She knew she was being deliberately provocative, but couldn't resist the opportunity to turn the knife.

Sebastian ground his teeth. Audibly.

Faith raised her empty cup to her mouth in order to hide her grin. Henry refused to meet anyone's glance.

"Naturally, Henry," Sebastian managed to grind out. "We'll just use the pen and ink you so cannily provided. I'm sure that Amanda has her copy with her, as I do mine. Then I can get on with the important parts of my day."

The expression on Amanda's face did not change, but the sparks shooting from her eyes promised retribution.

Sebastian saw Henry wince, obviously cognizant of the fact that the truce was fragile and probably temporary. He would speak to the coward who had so adroitly slipped through the doorway and into the shop. His excuse was the necessity of opening the front door.

✿✿✿

"Jenny, Jenny. I have great news!" Stan's smile threatened to split his face in two. He flung open the kitchen door and looked for his wife.

"What, Stan? Tell me." Jenny wondered what could have caused Stan to smile. Or even stop frowning, for that matter. Neither had found much cause for joy since the arrival of the fateful letter. Christmas plans had been scaled back to the bare bone. Jenny desperately looked everywhere for more housework, or for any work that would provide extra income. She and Stan had scrimped and saved for years in order to have three months' income in their bank account, just in case. They were determined to do everything they could to keep those savings, and not lose them to the blackmailer.

"Bert Stiles has hired me to cover a guard shift on Sundays for the next four months."

"Bert Stiles? Guard shift? What on earth are you talking about?" She wondered if the pressure of their situation had caused Stan to become confused. "What would you be guarding? And why Bert?" A tiny spark of hope refused to be doused, no matter how much common sense she poured on it.

Stan grabbed her in a bear hug and swung her in a circle. "It's the material for the additions to the town hall. Apparently there's been some pilfering and they've decided to pay for a watchman for the next two months or so. Just to give them time to get far enough along so they can store the remaining stuff inside." His arms tightened.

Jenny could feel her face redden as she fought for breath. She struggled to release his hold. Sometimes he didn't know his own strength. He loosened his grip slightly, but refused to let her go. She gasped and smiled at his joy.

"Because it's only for a short time, and because it's on Sunday, the pay is more than usual. I'll be earning three dollars. That means that we'll be able to put some ahead." His face lost some of its joy as he finished his sentence.

With the ease of a spouse, she watched as the realization that they would have to keep paying two dollars every week washed over him again. And there was no guarantee that the amount would not increase.

"What a relief that we now have some time to plan. I'm going to find out who this bastard is." Her face and posture reflected her resolve, even as she patted his arm. Stan gawped.

"Now, Jennykins, don't you be rash. How do you think we could possibly find the bastard? Where would you even start?" Fear for her safety warred with hope. "If he blackmails, then I'm sure that he'll protect himself and his income. Really, all he has to do is collect the money."

Jenny had no intention of letting Stan know her plans. Indeed, she didn't know them herself. But there was something in that letter that bothered her. A word? A phrase? The handwriting? She knew she would protect her family, no matter what it took.

"That is fantastic news, Stan. What a relief to know that the next few weeks are taken care of. I'll keep looking for more housework. Or maybe I could set up as a small laundry. Whatever it takes, darling, we'll manage. We always have, and we always will."

Straightening the contents of the spoon caddy provided an opportunity to hide her face. Experience had taught her that while Stan's intentions were good, he had a real gift for putting unpleasantness on a back burner. Once again she kicked herself mentally for letting him destroy the letter. But she would remember. And save her family.

"Call the children. I'll lift the dinner." Meals, laundry, housework, and children needed taking care of, crises notwithstanding.

✿✿✿

"Amanda, Amanda. Why must you always push for something else?" Elizabeth's voice reflected her concern and frustration. "The arrangements for our occupying the space in the pharmacy are ironclad. You said it was worth the money we paid to Henry Soames for his legal opinion. In addition, Sebastian agreed to an extremely reasonable rent for the space." She put the teacup into its saucer with considerable force. Fortunately neither cup nor saucer cracked. She dropped her hands to her lap to hide their shaking.

Amanda was a wonderful daughter; caring and considerate, but not calm. When Amanda got an idea, it was lodged for life. When she was very young, Elizabeth could distract or out-talk her, but no longer.

Amanda was right when she insisted that "they who pay have the say," but she frequently failed to recognize that often the quickest path from one place or person to another was not always a straight line; it meandered from the straight and narrow. Elizabeth had managed her husband for years on this premise.

Amanda, on the other hand, refused to "pander to male egos" and insisted on being treated as an equal. Elizabeth sighed. She tried again to convince her daughter that negotiation indicated strength; not weakness.

"Amanda, just listen to me. The community is coming to recognize Wentworth as the name of the people who take care of eyes. Why is it so necessary to have a sign—a large sign—proclaiming Wentworth Optometry Services?"

Amanda took a deep breath and prepared to explain the facts of life as seen through the eyes of a business owner. "You are right, Mother, when you say that Wentworth is recognized as the name of the ladies who take care of your eyes. But the sad fact is that very soon Wentworth will simply be the name of the women who work at Montgomery's Pharmacy. Wentworth will sink into the general mass of products and services offered by Sebastian."

Elizabeth drew a deep breath, ready to leap into the fray once more, but her daughter, experienced in these conversations, thwarted her.

"Please understand that we must identify ourselves as a totally separate business and service. It is convenient for the community—and for us—that our valuable service is easy to access. That works to both Mr. Montgomery's and our benefit. Currently, our standing is that of a valid member of the commercial section of the community, not an appendage to one already firmly established. And another thing," she once again forestalled her mother's attempt to jump into the conversation, "our job is doubly hard because we are women. Right now we're the only business in the community that is run by women, other than traditional ones, such as sewing, laundry, etc." Elizabeth seized the opportunity provided by her daughter's need for breath.

"I'm not suggesting for one minute that we should forego recognition as the purveyors of services which are necessary for the wellbeing of our new community. Nor am I at all willing that people regard us as an adjunct to the other services offered by Sebastian. What I am saying is that there is more than one way to make a cake." She raised her hand in the universal signal to stop.

"That old adage about catching more flies with honey than vinegar contains a great deal of truth. Yes, we should mention the sign. I just don't think we should hit Sebastian over the head with it."

Elizabeth really wanted all these problems to go away. Her husband had always handled business matters, and she had little interest in the day-to-day running of the operation. Her world centered on family and home.

Amanda gritted her teeth. Elizabeth knew she desperately needed the support of her family. They must present a united front, and Amanda wanted to invite Sebastian for Sunday dinner. Then, when he was replete with a magnificent meal, in the parlor of a widow and two daughters draped in funereal black, she would deftly slide the matter of the sign into the conversation.

Sebastian, Amanda insisted, stiffly observant of the social mores, would find it difficult to be his usual obnoxious and obstructive self. During their initial confrontation, he had stated loudly and clearly that Wentworth Optometry Services would *never* be partners with Montgomery's Pharmacy. Amanda meant to use his own words against him.

Her real goal was his agreement to acknowledging Wentworth's Optometry Services as a separate entity. She would be very careful to avoid any discussion vis-a-vis size. Her bureau already concealed a modest sign that she would hang in the doorway leading to their portion of the building.

Elizabeth had shuddered when she learned that an order for a much larger sign, similar in size to that which decorated the outside of the pharmacy, needed only a word to have it delivered.

The agreement was that no work would be done on it until she said so. Then, sign ready, the next time Sebastian had to leave to attend to business at one of the factories, Amanda would arrange for its installation.

Elizabeth, lips clamped over her disagreement, poured another cup of tea. It gave her an excuse not to look at her daughter and to acquire control over her own expression and feelings. She watched while Amanda fidgeted.

She picked up her shawl. Put it down. Adjusted the ties of her bonnet, took a deep breath, and continued. "Mother, you know I value your ideas and opinions. May we continue this discussion tonight, when Faith is here, too? She agreed to go ahead, as we have two people picking up their spectacles this morning." Elizabeth offered her cheek for a kiss and sighed as the door closed behind her wilful daughter.

CHAPTER 15

"Henry, how is the Sanderson family coping, now that the machine shed is no more. Their house is close to their business, and I wonder if they can still live there."

"They can still live in their house, but Marv must be devastated. He had just put up that new building. Keep your ear to the ground. If he has trouble getting a mortgage from the bank, perhaps we could help."

"Absolutely, Sebastian. And I presume this will be through a third party. That's your usual style."

"I have no desire to play Lord Bountiful, as you well know. Neither does my father. If you bruise a man's pride and make him feel grateful, that gratitude can often turn to resentment."

"How many times have I heard those exact words come out of your father's mouth?" Henry smiled. "Anticipating your reaction, I've already put the wheels in motion."

Sebastian snorted. "One of these times you'll get your nose caught in the door, and then what will happen?" But Henry was already out the door; he knew an empty threat when he heard it.

✿✿✿

Phil and Steve, representing the fire department, had arranged to host the meeting with Jeff Napier. Jeff's own office provided no privacy, and possible ramifications from internal politics made it politically advisable for this particular gathering to take place where confidentiality was guaranteed. The avowed reason for meeting in Phil's office was the planning of a presentation to the town council for a more modern pumper truck. A fresh pot of coffee waited. No one mentioned the undeclared and underhanded campaign being waged by the deputy sheriff.

Darwin Whitelock, keen contender for Jeff's job by whatever means, was happily and officiously reviewing the vandalism reports to see if he could come up with a different approach. That approach would reveal his superior administrative and planning abilities.

The sheriff's duplicate copy of the information he planned to discuss today rested in a safety deposit box at the bank. Joshua Croft, bank manager, had agreed to seal, date and sign the outside of the document. He did so without comment, and with a knowing gleam in his eye. Joshua's mouth always seemed to be clamped shut. His customers gave enthusiastic references to his ability to maintain confidentiality. Jeff had noticed for some time that important papers and information mysteriously disappeared if left unattended in his office.

"Well, gentlemen, do either of you have new information, or a different point of view on the vandalism and fires?" Jeff waited for a response. Playing poker with Steve was like taking candy from a baby. As his excitement grew, he went from rocking back and forth in his chair to bouncing up and down. Steve considered himself canny and stone faced. His control over his facial muscles was superb, but he had no idea his rocking and bouncing gave him away every time. Steve's bounce was in its early stages—barely perceptible except to those who knew him well. He was dying to present his point of view. Phil would let him speak first, then offer his own observations.

"I'm absolutely convinced that the fires and the vandalism are connected. It's just too well planned. As soon as you're called out because of some shenanigans, we're called to a fire." Steve didn't pause for breath until he finished the thought. As he inhaled in preparation for another verbal marathon, Jeff headed him off at the pass.

"It just so happens that I agree with you. When we had our last meeting, I started to see a real pattern."

Phil was ready to contribute. "I noticed that the first couple of vandalism incidents could be passed off as high jinks, which they might well have been. However, as time went on, and not too much time at that, they escalated from silly and somewhat predictable to vicious and life threatening."

Steve continued. "Right. I've made a note of what happened and the date on which it occurred." He consulted his list. "For instance, on March 31, the cutting of the washing lines was annoying, but it in no way interfered with the response to the fire in the Crofton's garden shed. We've already discussed the fact that we suspect the use of kerosene. I've checked with all the possible places in town, without any luck, then expanded the search to other towns and villages close, but not too close, to us."

"The next occurrence was two weeks later, on April 15. The lids were left off the garbage cans at the Golden Star. This was potentially dangerous to pets, but more a nuisance and guaranteed to get Eddie's goat. He's known for that temper of his. However, the fire that accompanied it, while not presenting a danger to the school building, had scope for more serious injuries from children thinking they could put it out. Any danger to children is always a sure bet to get everyone up in arms."

Steve couldn't hold his tongue. "My God, Jeff, you're right. It looks as if these were well planned." His bouncing caused his buttocks to leave the seat. In spite of the seriousness of the subject, Jeff wondered if he would stand up and sit down in his excitement and enthusiasm.

"I couldn't agree with you more. Also note that on April 28 we had the next incident."

Phil interjected, "There was a definite rise in the danger level on that date. Doc Redding let anyone and everyone know how dangerous it might have been if relocating the outhouses caused someone to fall into the waste pit. He made it very, very clear that such an occurrence could result in death. It's not often you see Doc getting really mad, but he sure was that time."

Steve was in danger of bouncing off his chair. The height of each rising had not increased, but occasionally he teetered a bit when he sat down. "Thank God we had those heavy showers or both the Gilmour Street houses would have been lost. You remember that their porches were doused with coal oil. And who knows how much farther it might have spread? That was quite a wind driving the rain." His anger and anxiety caused an already ruddy complexion to flush even further. "Both the men suffering from smoke inhalation and facial burns lost time at work. Their wives are now waging a campaign to have them resign as volunteers and find another way to help their neighbors."

"Hard to argue with that." The sheriff consulted his notes once again. "So far we've had three events occurring at two-week intervals. Then, on May 4, just one week later, we had The Big Stink." All three men grinned, and Steve remained anchored in his chair. "I had no idea Barry Masters had such a loud voice. I swear they could have heard him in the next county."

Phil nodded. "Well, he had a point, Jeff. A four-foot high pile of ripe horse manure blocking the main employee entrance to the mill was bound to get a lot of attention—especially on a day which decided to give us a preview of just how hot summer could be. It provided interest, amusement and frustration."

"Yeah, well the fire at the Reddings was far from amusing. Lily Redding is pregnant. She's now so nervous that she gets up several times a night to check the doors and windows. The worry and lack of rest might cause her to lose the baby."

"I wonder if that particular fire had anything to do with Doc Redding's remarks about possible fevers from falling into waste pits? It followed pretty closely on his letter to the editor—just two days after it was printed." Jeff played host. He refilled their cups, put the pot back on the stove, and consulted his list once more.

"Did you notice that it was three weeks before the next incident? By May 4 my men had almost healed from the Gilmour Street fires. The town had settled down, and the *Clarion* started to focus on other things in the community."

"How's Mary Blain doing? I heard that she won't be able to walk or even stand for a month. She can prepare vegetables sitting down, but cooking's a very physical activity. Putting those stones on the step could have caused her to break her head, not just sprain her leg."

"She's a tough old biddy," Jeff responded, "I hear they got someone in to help her, and the orders and complaints are fast and furious." There were smiles all around the table. Mary Blain seemed determined to single-handedly support the theory that cooks were cranky.

"But burning the new equipment shed will cause Marvin Sanderson and his family a lot of grief. Of course the community will come together to help him put up a new one, but I heard he had to take out a mortgage to build the replacement. Joshua Croft's a good guy, and I know he'll do his best, but…."

No one spoke. The silence lengthened. "You know, we've talked about the timing of the vandalism and fires, but we haven't discussed *why* they might be happening. Do you have any ideas?" Jeff waited. Silence.

This time Phil refilled their mugs and stoked the stove. It promised to be a long meeting.

While it was helpful to have the opportunity to look at the situation with others, all three men were tense as they waited to see if more fires would follow. Once again Jeff was grateful for their cooperation in delivering communications to his house, and not the office. Was it just a coincidence that the fires, vandalism and infighting had combined to make his life more and more difficult?

✿✿✿

"Goodbye, Mama. I'm off to the dispensary via the library. I have the books you wanted to return, and I'll leave your list with Miss Wheeler." *My path to the library will be via a long and winding route, but no need to mention that.*

Faith had devised a perfect way of learning about Marcher Mills and enjoying some freedom from constant surveillance. Well, realistically she knew that people were watching from windows and doorways, not to mention those she met on the streets, but, overall, she loved being able to ramble on her way from home to work. Almost invariably she and Amanda returned together, which meant straight home and no detours. But unaccompanied rambles were a secret and cherished delight.

The names of the various Canadian towns, villages and streets were so intriguing that she had started a list in her journal. If she also discovered the meaning of the name, she recorded that, as well. For instance, the name Punkeydoodles Corners led her to the library. Mavis Wheeler, the head librarian, knew just where to put her hand on a fascinating history of the tiny hamlet.

Toronto, she discovered, meant "where the trees are standing in the water", and came from the Mohawk word, Tkaronto. Niagara Falls, which she hoped to see on her honeymoon—should she ever have one—meant thundering waters. Or the neck, which referred to the portage between lakes Ontario and Erie. Its origin, too, was Mohawk. She was still trying to get a definitive answer, which meant yet another trip to see Mavis

Moose Jaw. *Moose Jaw.* So far it was her favorite. One of her rules was that she couldn't consult a map or atlas, or ask directly for odd or unusual names. The information had to be acquired in a more subtle manner. Lemon Drop Lane smacked of home and hearth. Moose Jaw, on the other hand, brought a vivid mental picture of a weathered bone sitting on a prairie. Or found amongst a pile of rocks. Or washed up on shore. Moose Jaw provided the impetus for Mavis to find reference material on this intriguing name. Mavis' enthusiasm for the project was unfeigned.

Faith's supervision of the gardens on her routes was unknown to their owners. She mentally moved clumps of flowers, rearranged shrubs, pruned, repositioned or discarded any number of bushes and enjoyed the fruits of her mental labors. Various addresses were etched in her memory.

The sadly overcrowded plots lining the front walk at 42 Berkshire had been dug up and a tasteful arrangement of perennials and annuals substituted. Dandelions covering the lawn at 12 Tupper Lane started as a robust green, blossomed to a glowing yellow, and then lifted fragile globes to the breezes. She wondered that the neighbors hadn't had a party to rid their neighborhood of the pests. Of course, without dandelions, the chickweed, which seemed to comprise the rest of the lawn, could and would spread untrammeled.

So occupied was Faith with her inspections and musings that the front door of the library seemed to appear in front of her as in a dream. She entered the building and looked for her friend.

"Good morning, Faith. Do you have a new name to check?" Mavis seemed to enjoy her conversations with the youngest member of the Wentworth family. In spite of the years between them, they were forming a fast friendship.

"Moose Jaw, Mavis, Moose Jaw. What a name! I'm on a search for the origins of this newest addition to my list." Her friend smiled. "I need to know where it is and how it got its name. You showed me a picture of a moose, and it *seemed* to be from a legitimate source, but I'm still in awe that such an animal can exist. But the biggest puzzle is why one of its body parts would be used as a geographical reference."

"You're right, Faith. Until you came to town and started investigating the origins of the names of various streets, towns and cities, I had just accepted that Moose Jaw was Moose Jaw. I will tell you that it's in the west. Perhaps when you've satisfied your curiosity about Moose Jaw you'd be interested in Kicking Horse Pass."

"Mavis, you wretch. You know just how to keep me on my toes—especially since, according to the rules of my game, I must finish with Moose Jaw before sampling the joys of Kicking Horse Pass."

"Kicking Horse Pass? Moose Jaw? Why do Canadians remark and marvel about billabong or kookaburra?" A feminine voice with a definite Australian twang joined the conversation. The two ladies greeted the newcomer with smiles.

"This is Faith's project, Marianne, so I'll let her explain while I help Margaret shelve some more books. Just let me know when you're ready. I'll stay in sight of the desk." She scanned her little kingdom and trotted off to help her assistant with the never-ending task of shelving books—and straightening and sorting those which had been shoved anywhere, regardless of their content.

She and Margaret had often marvelled at the inability of the library patrons to read the numbers on the book spines. If they could read, they knew the alphabet, but the general public appeared addicted to the pick-it-up-here-and-put-it-down-anywhere system. Mavis had an appointment with the Superintendent of Education to request an opportunity to speak to the high school classes.

"Hello, Marianne. It was lovely to see you at church and the Spring Social. Your idea to add a Touch and Take table to the event raised some much-needed money for the missions."

"It was nothing. We always have one of those tables at home. It's such fun to see some of the same horrors reappear each year. It took my mother five tries to get rid of the ugliest vase you've ever seen."

"We had just such a horror on the table. Have you ever seen such a botched attempt at embroidery as was on those pillowcases? It would definitely ensure bad dreams." She adjusted her glasses and peered at her watch. "Is that really the time? Amanda will wonder where I am!"

"Do you mind if I walk with you to the store? I hear that Betty Keppel received a shipment of goodies yesterday." With a wave to Mavis, they headed out the door.

A brisk walking pace didn't preclude chatting. "I see that you have Sebastian whipped right into shape and dancing attendance on you." Faith pretended to brush a speck of dust from her skirt as she monitored Marianne from the corner of her eye.

Marianne laughed, obviously very much at ease. "Sebastian and I have a very brother-sister relationship, didn't you know?" She lowered her voice and continued. "Please don't tell anyone, but due to some personal issues—my personal issues—Sebastian has agreed to appear to be courting me. I do the same in return. That way he's not hounded by every hopeful in the county. Being the most eligible bachelor in town is not unalloyed pleasure, he assures me."

Faith, riveted by this confidence, hastened to reassure her new friend. "I won't tell anyone, Marianne. You may be sure your secret is safe with me." Promise notwithstanding, Faith was convinced she could convey Sebastian's actual availability to her sister. Of course, she first had to get her sister to hear and understand her message. Sometimes Amanda could be incredibly annoying with her "I'm older so I know better" attitude.

She and Sebastian had got off to a bad start with misconceptions on both sides. The energy between them was so strong that people moved aside or retreated slightly when they were together. Nothing Amanda could say would convince Faith that Sebastian's charms were invisible. She and Henry Waters had conferred on more than one occasion about the possibility of smoothing the waters sufficiently to permit the combatants to acknowledge their fierce mutual attraction. The purpose of the discussions was fairly equally divided between goodwill toward the two determined people and a strong sense of self-preservation.

CHAPTER 16

This was the morning! Having gained a reluctant nod of agreement from her mother, and the staunch support of her sister, Amanda promised them they would hear no more about identifying Wentworth Optometry Services.

Arrangements to have the large sign completed and hung on the outside of the pharmacy were conducted in greatest secrecy. *No, not secrecy,* she assured herself, *just respect for Mother and a fervent desire to spare Faith the subterfuge. Well, not exactly subterfuge, which sounded much grander than sneaky, but...well, she knew what she meant, and that would have to do.*

Her first choice had been to blazon Wentworth Optometry Services over the doorway leading directly from the street to their premises. It was interesting to see just who entered from the street, and who wafted through the communicating doorway from the pharmacy. Women wafted more often than men, but there were exceptions. Spectacles, while necessary, were not fashionable. Ladies, especially, seemed to regard them as shameful.

The men professed not to care, but it was amazing how many edged through that same convenient entrance. In either case, the approach was never in a direct line. Instead, intense concentration on the contents of the shelves which bracketed her doorway occupied the reluctant entrants.

Because the pharmacy's sign was centered on the front of the building, she had decided to make use of the space between the window and the door that permitted direct access from the street into their section of the store. In view of the lack of traffic through that particular door, initially it seemed to be an odd location. Amanda, however, was clever enough to realise that it could be read with ease while passersby feigned great interest in the objects featured in the conveniently-placed pharmacy window. The pedestrians could enter directly through their doorway, or elect to come through the pharmacy entrance.

Two smaller signs were ready to go over the interior doorway that allowed an easy flow of customers between the pharmacy and their premises. It had taken all her powers of persuasion, plus a hefty bonus, to arrange for a *very* early morning installation.

The front of the building looked wonderful when she stopped to admire her handiwork. Key at the ready, she transferred the cloth bag—necessary to hide the signs at home and on her way to work—to her left arm. Grasping the doorknob in her left hand, she concentrated on the slight tug-and-turn necessary to unlock the rear door. Engrossed in her manoeuvres, she failed to hear the hurried footsteps approaching from the street.

"Amanda, what have you done? Does Sebastian know about this? Are you trying to give him apoplexy? Do you have *any* consideration for my continued wellbeing." Henry's voice, weak with desperation, reached her ears.

"Of course I care about your wellbeing, Henry. Why on earth would you ask such a question?" She entered. "Are you talking about the signs? I mean the one on the front of the building. Rather handsome, don't you think?"

Initially she had planned to be settled in her space, drawing it around her like armor, before the questions from Henry, and verbal vitriol from Sebastian, began. Apparently that was not to be. Sebastian's subsequent raging and ranting could at least be postponed until his return from the business trip which allowed for the admittedly surreptitious achievement of her goal.

"Now, Henry," she said, trying to calm him, "as an astute business manager, I'm sure you fully appreciate the value of identifying services clearly. Plainly. Avoiding any confusion on the part of the customers."

He had failed to remove his hat. *Oh, dear, he really is upset.* She hastened to resume her arguments.

"I've merely protected the independent identity of Wentworth Optometry Services." She increased her rate of speech. Henry appeared to be ready to explode, so she hastened to forestall such a painful experience.

"While it's true that Sebastian has been generous in letting us use that part of his premises which had lain vacant for some time, it's also true that he benefits from our presence. And the rent. And the increased traffic, not to mention similarly increased sales as people find excuses to put off entering our part of the facility."

She watched him drop his head in his hands, then discover he was still wearing his hat. He snatched it from his head, turning to hang it on its usual peg. His arm waved in the general direction of the rack, but the hat remained in his hand. Amanda rushed on.

"You see, we'll identify that this entrance leads to Wentworth Optometry Services. Wanting to be scrupulously fair," she grabbed his sleeve and drew him, unresisting, into her part of the shop, "we'll put *Montgomery's Pharmacy* put up on this side. Thus, each business is assured of equal status."

She waited.

Nothing.

Henry's mouth opened and closed, opened and closed, but speech appeared to be beyond him. She gently removed the hat from his hands, and placed it on its usual peg.

Still nothing.

"Come with me. I'll put on the kettle and we can talk about this over a nice cup of tea." Obediently, he followed. She heard some wheezing noises, but chose to ignore them.

"Sit here."

He sat.

Mute.

"Mother made some of her raisin oatmeal cookies, so we can have a treat with our tea." Thank goodness she managed to have the work done when Sebastian was away. By his return, the major part of the gasping and gossiping of Marcher Mills' residents should have died down.

Two cups of tea and three cookies later, Henry appeared to be recovering his equilibrium. He cleared his throat.

"Amanda, why didn't you discuss this with me? I know why you didn't discuss it with Sebastian, but I thought we had a good business relationship." Amanda winced.

"Well, Henry, to be perfectly honest, I didn't think there was the least chance of getting Sebastian's approval. As a matter of fact, I thought a world war would probably cause less commotion." She industriously filled both their cups again.

"Part of me regrets that I was less than forthcoming about the plan." *But not much.* She took a sip and carefully placed her cup in its saucer. "But you know very well that it's easier to get forgiveness than permission."

Henry inhaled in preparation of entering the fray. She held up her hand to stop him.

"I'm under no illusions that said world war still isn't imminent; however, given that everything is in place, and that Sebastian's out of town for a few days, the first wonder should be worn off before he returns. I'm counting on that. You may be very sure that both Faith and I will be diligent about pointing out the Montgomery's Pharmacy sign and praising Sebastian's modern ideas."

Henry choked. He glared at Amanda, who had the grace to blush slightly.

"You're dead right about that world war—and maybe *dead* isn't such a bad choice of words. I cannot agree with your methods, much as I'm afraid the forgiveness and permission part of your explanation has rather more truth than I would like. Usually. With time, we could have got Marianne on side."

Amanda's jaw dropped. Was she hearing correctly? Henry's words did not radiate wholehearted agreement with her decision about the signs, but he hadn't ordered her to take them down. And what did Sebastian's cousin have to do with supporting anyone against Sebastian? The rumor mill was more and more adamant that they were secretly engaged. Her heart jerked, her pulse raced. *He's free. He isn't getting married. And why do I care?*

Still trying to grasp the import of his comments, she almost missed the rest of his remarks. *Was Henry proposing to support Wentworth Optometry Services?*

"Sebastian isn't out of town. He'll be here this afternoon. The trip was put off until next week."

"Not out of town? Here this afternoon?" She gave thanks she was already seated. Felt herself sway slightly. Clutched the edge of the table for support. Whatever would she do? She had not even told her mother and sister of the surprise.

The days of Sebastian's absence, in addition to letting the initial gossip subside, had been allotted to smoothing Faith's feathers at being excluded from the end of the project, and to getting her mother's approval. Well, if not approval, then at least not active resistance.

"When do you expect him to be here, Henry?" She prayed that her nemesis would not appear until just before closing. Preferably after closing, so she could be safely off the premises.

Just then the bell over the front door chimed. Henry excused himself to greet the first customers. Quickly tidying up from their early morning tea party, she brushed her skirts to remove any errant crumbs, checked the pins in her hair, and hastened toward her desk. Incipient panic did not preclude a slight hesitation at the doorway in order to admire her handiwork.

Bert inspected Al's appearance with grudging approval, and noted his directions had been followed to the letter. Obviously he had had a bath. His cheeks glowed from a recent shave. Hair, still wet from his ablutions, lay straight and flat against his head. His clothes were clean and almost new. Even his beloved battered boots had been replaced by shoes which had received a cursory swipe of a cloth. They were free of manure. They exhibited no signs of having traversed mud puddles. The laces hadn't been mended with knots because of too much pressure being placed on them. Although, given the infrequency of their use, it was amazing that the laces suffered from anything other than old age. Al had done himself proud. He was almost standing at attention. Bert expected a twirl at any moment. Since the grooming met with approval, Bert progressed to the meat of the matter.

"Now, Al, are you sure you understand just what it is you are to do? God knows it's not much." He waited for a response.

Al, always willing to perform dirty tricks, showed little evidence of even average intelligence. He had a certain native cunning which lent him the ability to think of things he'd like to do, or trouble he'd like to cause certain people, but he was hopeless at designing schemes that would permit him to do so without detection.

"Sure. I'm not stupid, you know," he responded indignantly. Bert bit his tongue.

Al, taking advantage of a rare opportunity to voice his thoughts, continued. "Now you're one of the mucky-mucks and not just a plain guy. Today you're telling Zeke that the watchman you agreed to provide for the building materials for the addition to the court house and town hall will be me."

Bert inhaled, ready to elaborate on this information, but Al, on a roll, beat him to the punch.

"And I'm your new employee. I'll be in charge of guarding

the site every night, except Sunday. You said you would get Stan Biltmore to do that one. I even remember that you'll cover the day shift on Sunday." He paused for reflection, then hurried on before Bert could correct him.

"No, wait. I forgot—you'll cover Sunday night, and Stan will cover during the day." He rocked back on his heels, anticipating seldom-heard praise.

Bert was impressed. This was a rare, almost unprecedented, example of Al's ability to remember instructions.

He slid his left hand into his trousers' pocket and fondled his brand-new business cards. He rejected the customary term "trade card". His mind showed him a picture guaranteed to please anyone, but especially a man whose very real business acumen and abilities had been discounted or ignored all his life. He had thought long and hard about the image he wanted to portray, finally deciding on an impressive multi-story building. Several horses and buggies were tethered to the rail in front of the building, indicating a prosperous establishment. A locomotive trailing a plume of smoke added a feeling of hustle and bustle.

The locomotive, however, was a personal joke: Bert's plans to destroy the Montgomery's enterprises and escape retribution for his actions depended on a timely exit from Marcher Mills. The train would do just that.

"Right, Al. We'll go into Zeke Marshall's store. I'll do the talking. Don't forget that part. I'll explain the arrangements I've made to have the site guarded and tell him how I'll manage it. Your job is to stand there and be quiet. And to look as if you're paying attention." He ignored Al's sigh. "Do you understand?"

"Yes, Bert, I've got it. Stand still and shut up." His expression failed to denote any pleasure in the upcoming exercise.

"Right. When we're done, we'll have a beer at the Station Hotel." Al's face lit up. It was a well-known fact that there wasn't much he wouldn't do for a beer.

Bert took a moment to admire his reflection in the store window. A good suit, sparkling white shirt, stiff new collar, and a tie with a perfect knot all proclaimed a person upon whom respect, even deference, would be bestowed automatically. The black bowler completed his ensemble and portrayed just the right image. He smiled with satisfaction as he heard the bell over the door announce his presence. Finally, finally, he would make these backwoods clowns sit up.

There was a new game in town. Well, not exactly a new game, as he had been operating *sub rosa* for some time, but now he would be acknowledged as a legitimate businessman. *Right, and what they didn't know wouldn't hurt him!*

He savored Zeke's expression of amazement as he and Al sauntered up to the counter. Zeke seemed unable to take in their sartorial glory. His mouth opened. Shut. Opened again. Shut once more. He finally greeted his new customers.

"Hello, Bert. Al. What can I do for you?" Confusion caused him to blurt, "are you going to a party? Did somebody die?"

Bert controlled his laughter. He heard Al snicker, and carefully nudged him with his foot. They were close enough to the counter that Zeke would not be able to see the action. Al cleared his throat and fixed his gaze on his shoes.

"Hello, Zeke. I'm here as a courtesy, and as the owner of Stiles Services Limited. I want to tell you about the arrangements I've made for guarding the building materials."

Once again, Zeke's mouth opened and closed. His struggle to assimilate this new information was so obvious that Bert could almost hear his thoughts. *Bert a businessman. Bert telling him that he, not the committee, would organize security on the site. Al in clean clothes. Shaved. And where did Bert get that suit? And hat? Not from Marshall's Emporium.*

"You know Al Anderson. He's the Stiles Services Limited employee who will be guarding the site every night, Monday to Saturday."

Bert realised that the repetition of his company's name was excessive, but it just sounded so wonderful, the syllables rolling off his tongue like beads of gold, that he couldn't resist. Zeke's head swiveled back and forth as he gazed at the two men.

"Stan Biltmore will take over from Al on Sunday morning. I'll cover Sunday night, and hand off to the foreman on Monday morning."

Zeke's head continued its metronome-like action, gazing first at Bert, then at Al, repeating the action again and again. Bert bit the inside of his cheek to control his laughter. *Take that, you son of a bitch. And show some respect.*

"Here's my business card, Zeke. My name and address are on the reverse. Since Marcher Mills is so small, I haven't bothered with a map. My customers all know me. Of course, as a local, you are aware that you can leave messages at the Station Hotel. If you wish to be more formal, send a letter to my post office address." If Zeke didn't speak soon, Bert was sure he would guffaw in his face.

"Uh, thanks, Bert." With a dazed look, Zeke took the card, looked at the picture on the front, and turned it over to see the back. "This is some trading card. Most people have more of a picture on the front. And some of them are even in color." He appeared grateful to have something to discuss.

"I prefer to call it a business card, Zeke, because I use it in all my business transactions. Black on white is much more distinctive than gaudy colors." *And cheaper, but no need to burden others with too much information—after all, what others didn't know invariably benefitted him.* Zeke raised his head from contemplation of the sparse information on the back of the card and stared.

"All your business transactions, Bert? What business transactions? You're available to do some things around town, but this is the first I've heard of a business." Zeke was recovering from his shock, and had more to say.

"And what's this *Stiles Services Limited*? Since when do you have a company? Or is this someone else's company and you share the same last name?"

Bert found it prudent to take out his handkerchief and brush some imaginary dust from his sleeve to hide his expression. Zeke's questions and comments were so predictable that he might have been reading from a script.

"Oh, I've had the company for some time, Zeke. And my business is my business, but I assure you I do have customers." Again he waited for a reaction.

"Well, I don't know about this. Do the other members of the committee know you're now a so-called businessman?"

Bert controlled an urge to grind his teeth. "There's nothing so-called about it. It's quite true. A little support for local-boy-makes-good seems to be in order."

Zeke's jaw dropped. It was clear he was not accustomed to having his actions criticised. Especially from a source formerly known as the town's bad boy.

"I just wonder what you would do or say if, for instance, Mr. Sebastian Montgomery presented his card to you. I'll just bet you'd gush like a river after a thunderstorm." He felt his temper rising and hastily reached in his pocket for more cards to give himself time to control his reactions. Six cards were now carefully aligned on the counter.

"Here are a few more cards, Zeke, for the other members of the committee and a few extra, as well. Be sure you tell them that Stiles Services Limited is available for a variety of projects."

Not for anything would Bert use the word "jobs". Projects had substance. Projects took time. Projects were for businessmen, not odd job people.

"Now, I'm going over to the site to introduce my employee, Mr. Al Anderson, to the site foreman." Out of the corner of his eye he saw Al's chest expand when he heard himself so described. "Stiles Services Limited does things properly and professionally, as I promised to you in the interview. Good day."

He spun on his heel, jerked his head to indicate that Al should follow him, and walked out of the store. It took all his control not to slam the door shut. It would serve that bastard right if he had to replace the glass. But it wouldn't be good for business. Or his stature as an up-and-coming presence in the community.

CHAPTER 17

Bert eyed Stan and prepared to lay out the rules. "You'll be here at 6.45 am on Sunday morning. I'll probably drop in once or twice during the day, but don't plan on going home for a meal. You'll have to bring your food." Stan nodded, obviously concentrating on remembering the instructions.

"The coffee in the tin is mine. Don't touch it."

Again Stan nodded. Bert could see Stan knew what happened to those who touched his things—mysterious fires, dead pets dropped into wells, animals let loose, garden produce destroyed.

Bert eyed his new guard and relented enough to assure Stan that he could use the stove if he needed warmth, or brought his own tea or coffee. The irony of receiving two-thirds of Stan's Sunday wages in blackmail made it difficult not to smirk. *Planning, planning, planning—it always paid off; this time in both cash and satisfaction.*

The tour of the site, records of materials on hand, and the irregular schedule of patrols occupied the next half hour. Stan stood in the doorway of the guard hut with the look of a man who hopes he's understood all his instructions. Bert headed toward the Station Hotel. He had earned a respite with brandy and a book.

✿✿✿

Sebastian hurried down the street. A crowd was gathered around the auxiliary door of his pharmacy. *Had an accident occurred? Had someone fallen? Had something happened to Amanda?* Forgetting his usual irritation with That Woman, he rushed forward. As he got closer, he noticed that heads turned, first toward the door, then to a neighbor. Voices exclaimed in wonder. The back and forth motions from door to neighbour continued. Questions were being asked. Answers or denials of knowledge offered. It made no sense whatsoever.

His trying day continued unabated. Late last night, he received a telegram cancelling his main meeting in Toronto, as well as two other appointments connected with the first meeting. This resulted in a complete rescheduling of his time. The morning had been filled with sending telegrams, tendering apologies to various and sundry persons, and suggesting alternate dates. Then he had to wait for the replies. All in all it was frustrating, made even more so by several small but irritating problems in the factory.

In the normal course of events, Henry would take care of them, but, because he had planned to be out of town, his general manager was in charge of overseeing the pharmacy before checking on various other matters. He could be contacted, but only in the case of an emergency. If the problems were not addressed immediately, a great deal of production time would be lost. Unfortunately for Sebastian's peace of mind, frustration did not equal emergency, and he was left to deal with things in order to avoid a crisis.

As he reached the edge of the group, the reason for the hubbub became clear. Crystal clear. *That Woman* had struck again. How dare she put up a sign on *his* building without so much as a by-your-leave? He was under no illusion that the timing of its placement and his proposed absence coincided.

Before he could edge away from the group, someone noted his presence and exclaimed.

"Mr. Montgomery, how very clever of you to have this sign placed beside the door that leads directly into Wentworth's shop." *So now it's the Wentworth's shop and not the pharmacy.* He could feel his polite smile fading.

"And generous, too, as he's made Wentworth Optometry Services stand out so clearly," one of the Great Unwashed confided to anyone within earshot.

"It certainly lets a person have more privacy when they need a service," said another in a complacent tone.

"Quicker, too. So often if you go through the pharmacy you get caught in several conversations. Can't be rude, but it can take a chunk of time." Several mob members nodded sagely.

"It's cheaper, as well. I always seem to find something in the pharmacy that I had no idea I needed." An anvil chorus of "Yeah, that's right," "I've often said just that," and "always trying to get our money," followed.

Sebastian had not been blind to the fact that those who feared either the optometry's services, or their neighbor's comments should they be seen using them, favored an oblique approach to their actual destination. They could always pick up a little this or that before getting to the connecting doorway.

Extricating himself from several invitations to chat, he decided against entering from the street in favor of slipping down the alley and in the rear entrance. An additional benefit would be the very solid door between the back room and front of house. A man could exercise a considerable degree of his lung capacity and still not be overheard. Suiting actions to thoughts, he escaped his vociferous neighbors and hurried down the lane.

Henry had just finished serving a customer. He turned to survey the store and frowned when he saw Sebastian, then consulted his pocket watch. Sebastian motioned him to approach, which he did, but with great reluctance.

"You know whom I want, Henry. Bring her in here. I don't care if she has the half of Marcher Mills that isn't outside gawking at that soon-to-be-removed abomination which is defacing my building. Just get her here before I explode." Henry headed for

Wentworth Optometry Services.

Sebastian watched as Amanda approached with an air of wariness. Her posture indicated knowledge of what was to come. The tilt of her chin meant battle was about to be joined.

"Well, madam, what do you have to say for yourself?" He was disappointed to see that she showed no signs of nervousness.

"Hello, Sebastian. It's nice to see you, too. Have you heard from your parents?" He watched as her chin went up another notch—a fighting stance that betokened a deplorable willingness to dig in her heels. He ignored the jibe.

"You know damn—er—very well what I mean. The sign. The one about which you have said nothing. The one that is defacing the front of my premises. The one that is giving me indigestion."

"You are really going to have to do something about your temper, sir. I have been given to understand that it is a source of great concern for your family and very few friends." His eyes narrowed. Undaunted, she continued.

"You are flushed. Your voice has risen to unacceptable levels. And you appear to be unable to speak with reason and good judgement." Her voice remained calm and well modulated. She had yet to put her hands on her hips or tap her foot.

He circled the room and took several deep breaths. Well did he know her methods. She had an absolute gift for putting her finger on a sore spot and digging it in. He *hated* her power to make him lose his temper. Over and over he had vowed not to let her get the upper hand. Time and time again he failed. He clasped his hands behind his back so he would not be tempted to shake those slender, feminine shoulders, and tried again.

"That isn't worthy of you, Amanda. If you weren't so aware that your actions were indefensible, you would answer in a straightforward manner." Her chin rose yet again—she would soon be staring at the ceiling—and she glared. Her hands now rested on her hips. One foot tapped an irritable, almost menacing, rhythm.

"Very well then, *Mr.* Montgomery. You are the reason why I have been forced to act in this manner. Your contract with Wentworth Optometry Services states that it will provide optometry services to Marcher Mills and its environs, operating from the premises of your pharmacy." Her breath control was amazing; she did not pause, but sailed right on.

"Wentworth Optometry Services is a business within its own right. Yet nowhere in your store, inside or out, have you made provision to so identify us. Therefore, it has fallen to us—to me, actually—to rectify the situation."

He exerted every ounce of his self-control and remained silent. Let her continue to dig her own grave. He would be happy to assist her with the first step.

"Because of your unreasonable and short-sighted behavior, I was forced to act in a manner which I find repugnant."

He was appalled to hear himself growl.

She remained undaunted by his implied threat.

"You are right in thinking that I waited until you would be away for a period of time. Better, I thought, to let the community get over its first amazement and settle down before you returned. You see, I knew how you would react."

The growl increased in volume. And still she spoke.

"Therefore, this morning the sign was attached beside the door which leads directly to our premises. I assume you are unaware that there are two more."

The growling stopped. The woman was crazy. *Three* signs? Was she intending to paper the walls? The irritating voice continued.

"When you have had a cup of tea or perhaps a stronger composer, you will notice that the other two are over the doorway between our two shops. Your side says *Wentworth Optometry Services;* ours proclaims *Montgomery's Pharmacy.* Equal representation."

A pause—finally. She must be concocting another insane tale. But no, it was simply to replenish her lungs. By the time he had determined just what was happening, she was, once more, talk-talk-talking.

"I trust this explanation is sufficient. Now, even if your side is bare of customers, mine is not. Good day, sir."

A deft twirl, a dextrous turn of the door handle, and she disappeared. The door closed softly, firmly and irrevocably. In his face. He was alone with her explanation and his temper.

CHAPTER 18

Jenny Biltmore put her hands in the middle of her back and straightened slowly. As much as she appreciated the chance to earn money towards keeping their nest egg safe from the blackmailer, she could not deny the fact that she ached from top to toe.

The back porch, loading dock and stairs of Marshall's Emporium were as clean as soap, water and elbow grease could make them. Her next task was to make a list of all the items in the storeroom, but only after she made sure the shelves in the front of the store were full.

Zeke's wife, Charity, rounded with their sixth child, had apparently had some spotting. Strict instructions for complete bed rest meant the Marshalls were forced to hire outside help. Their oldest boy, Ephraim, was only twelve years old. He, Daniel and their sister, Lorna, ten and nine, respectively, could run errands and be of considerable assistance. The others were too young. However, Zeke and Charity both considered education a priority, which meant hiring someone to help—at least until school ended, and probably until the baby was born and its mother had regained some strength.

Jenny headed for the front of the store, first turning her apron clean side out. Awareness of her outstanding good luck ensured that she would do everything possible to earn those precious funds. On her way she noticed that someone had knocked over several articles from one of the lower shelves that lined the outside wall.

Boots for men and boys. I'll just get a clean rag and wipe the shelf before putting them back. The promise of getting off her feet, even if it meant kneeling right where anyone might see her, gave her energy.

Damp rag in hand, she knelt to clear all the merchandise before starting her cleaning. Her posture made her invisible to anyone not standing in her aisle. She soon discovered it provided a perfect location for eavesdropping. Women's voices—she recognized Gladys Whiffletree and that old bat, Elvira Wheeler—were enjoying a good gossip. She started to jump up to serve them, but forgot that her head was still under the shelf. The resulting impact caused her to sit down abruptly. As she began to rise again, this time more carefully, their conversation caught her attention.

"Have you heard about Mr. Johnny Jump Up?"

That must be Elvira. She always has a sting in her comments.

"Bert Stiles is claiming to be a bona fide businessman. With customers, no less. Have you ever heard anything so ridiculous?" Elvira snorted.

"Ridiculous or not, Bert has a way of backing up his statements."

Gladys might enjoy gossiping with the best of them, but she was not vicious and refused to repeat that which she did not know to be true.

"I remember him as a young boy, often with a book in his hand. He'd try out his high-falutin' language on anyone he could get to listen. If an adult laughed at him or told him not to get above himself, he'd sneer and turn away. But, if another child did so…."

"You're right. He did some serious damage to one of the Wilson children—Barry, I think it was. Bert had called him a parry…no, pariah, that was it. Barry told him 'right back at you'. Apparently Bert went berserk."

Jenny froze. *Pariah—that was it.* The very word that had tickled the back of her mind after Stan had burned the letter. Bert Stiles must be the blackmailer: no one else she knew used that kind of language.

Gladys, never at a loss for opinion or rebuttal, replied. "People like Sebastian Montgomery might have a great deal more education, but Bert has loved reading and words forever."

Jenny's shaking knees refused to obey the commands of her mind. Her head felt light. She lowered herself to the floor and wondered if she would faint.

Hearing footsteps approaching the end of the aisle, she rolled to her knees, shoved her head under the shelf and began to straighten the boots, all thoughts of shelf wiping forgotten. Realizing that the arrangement made no sense—tall, short, small, large—side by side, but not in pairs, she drew a deep breath, and started over. Gradually the discipline required to ensure that the sizes matched, and the small sizes were at the front, soothed her.

Slowly she regained her ability to think. Her shoulders slumped, then stiffened. *That bastard. I'll make him pay. Somehow.* Anger surged through her, replacing fatigue. Suddenly she wasn't tired. When she found herself almost banging the boots in place, she forced herself to calm down. Catching such a clever man as Bert Stiles meant a great deal of careful planning.

What method could she use? He was stronger than she, and she had really no reason to approach him.

Must be careful not to give myself away when I see him. Have to remember that he's Stan's boss.

Shelf emptied, then refilled with boots marching in orderly processions across its length, she rose. She had no idea that she had performed this task three times, but had forgotten to wipe down the shelf.

First I have to make Zeke realise that I'm a valuable addition to the store. She rose, brushed off her apron, and set the first part of her plan in motion.

"Zeke, do you have a paper and pencil? It seems to me to be more efficient to make a list of those items that need replacing before I start cleaning. Then I can clean and restock all at once. Also, while I'm getting the articles from the storeroom, I can count what's left so you'll know what to order."

Zeke smiled and nodded. He ripped a piece of paper from the roll on the counter and handed her a stubby pencil.

"Makes sense, Jenny. Thanks." He also agreed that before she stocked a particular shelf she should wash it down. The Marshalls prided themselves on clean premises. They made a point of letting all and sundry know that all their personal food—meat, vegetables or fruit—came from the store.

Still riding the wave of energy that followed her lucky discovery, Jenny began listing those articles that needed to be replaced. But the major part of her attention was contemplating ways and means to destroy Bert.

List complete, she returned to the back yard pump and filled her scrub pail with fresh water. The bar of soap had dried, so she tucked it in her apron pocket. Grabbing a cloth from the ample supply provided, she prepared to work and plan. Or work and think, first. There were many, many decisions to be made before she could plan specific actions.

First and foremost was how could she kill Bert? She had neither a gun nor access to one. And even if she did, she had no idea of how to load, aim or shoot. Her father, as was the custom, had a rifle, mostly to kill varmints. Nor did she know what a handgun looked like, let alone where she would get one.

And ammunition—what would she do about ammunition? No, no: much better to think in terms of poison. There she *did* have some knowledge and ability. Her mother had been very skilled with herbs, and had passed her knowledge on to each of her daughters.

But wait—who knew of her skill with herbs and their properties? Stan and she had moved to Marcher Mills shortly after their marriage. They had had no acquaintances, let alone friends, when they arrived. Not only that, no stage coaches or trains had a route that took them through, or even particularly close, to her old home. Now she had one possibility, but better to have a choice.

"Jenny. Jenny, **Jenny**." Startled, she looked up to see Zeke smiling at her. I've been calling your name, but you've been working so hard you didn't hear me." She nodded, rag in hand and a puzzled look on her face. "It's time to go home."

"Already?" She checked the large clock hanging beside the front door. "Oh my goodness. I had no idea." She picked up her bucket and wrapped the soap in the rag. "Will you want me back tomorrow, Zeke?"

"Yes, please, Jenny. You're an outstanding worker. I'll be able to assure Charity that we'll manage just fine. Please come every school day." He paused, then continued. "Could you come in on Saturday? It's our busiest day. Even with the children's help I won't be able to manage by myself."

CHAPTER 19

Hamilton, nestled in a protective bay, sometimes flaunted its beauty. On fine days families picnicking on the beach enjoyed the view. Sun sparkled on whitecaps; sloops, yachts, tall ships with a host of smaller vessels punctuated the sapphire of the water and deep blue arc of sky. So much for a sunny day and admiring gasps from those who climbed the local mountain to enjoy the scenery.

The guts of the city remained as memory painted them. They had kept all their dirt. And damp. That same location on the shores of Lake Ontario, so beloved of its admirers, ensured fog in copious quantities. The bowl, formed by a small plain confined by high hills, trapped moisture, and smoke as well as encouraging noxious odors to linger.

Bert's footsteps rang out with assurance, their pace steady. He was familiar with the streets in the underbelly of the city. During his youth they represented home. If they had not also represented security, love and all the claptrap so beloved of the bleeding hearts, they had at least given him the skills he needed to survive and thrive.

As he travelled the well-known route, he made minor adjustments to his gait, stance and clothing which transformed him from a man of respectability to a streetwise predator. His hat, repositioned, shadowed his eyes and gave him an air of menace. He raised his coat collar, thrust his hands into his trousers' pockets, and adopted a swagger. Without uttering a word or making a threatening gesture, he cleared a path. People moved closer to buildings or stepped out into the street. Shoulders hunched, gaze focused on their feet, they sneaked sideways glances and increased their pace.

Light from the pub fought to reach the street through its filthy windows. Regulars of the Dog and Duck—porters, longshoremen and general dogsbodies—shared its amenities with less savoury patrons. The criminal element, tolerated with wary respect, demanded and received excellent service. Bert acknowledged greetings from several drinkers with a curt nod, and selected a place at the back of the room. It had a clear line of sight to the door.

The three who occupied his chosen table took one look at the man standing beside them and quickly moved to another location, drinks in hand. They stood close together, their furtive glances proof of their interest and fear.

The clean and comely customer attracted the attention of an eager barmaid. Well able to judge the quality of his clothing and his personal cleanliness that put him above her usual clientele, she hurried over. Her pendulous breasts almost escaped their flimsy covering and grazed his arm as she bent to take his order.

Bert wasted no time looking at what he didn't want and would not have used for any price. "Beer, and fast." When she failed to hasten to fetch his order, he gave her the benefit of a threatening glare. "I'm not interested in old, dirty meat, so get your ass out of here and the beer on the table." She whirled and flounced away, but at speed. "Dirty, arrogant bastard, you probably couldn't get it up anyway," she muttered.

Keeping his eye on the traffic in and out of the door, his beer remained untouched. He knew, all too well, that the mugs were simply refilled and delivered to the next customer. The proprietor was often heard to spout his own particular theory on such a ridiculous and unnecessary practice as cleaning, especially tankards. "Soap and water cost money to procure and wages for staff to wash and dry them between customers. Best leave it to them who can afford it." Acquaintances for many years, Jubal Lican was respected in the criminal underworld as a safe intermediary for payments or information.

Bert ground his teeth. When forced to visit establishments frequented in his youth, shame warred with disdain. Once, having enough money to buy a beer at the Dog and Duck represented success. Now, it was all he could do to remain in the room.

Just then the door opened. Soft caps, handkerchiefs tied around their necks above collarless shirts, shapeless trousers and jackets permitted the two men to blend seamlessly with the usual patrons. But the fact that there were no patches on the garments and that those garments were relatively clean sent a different message. To those familiar with the social levels of this area, they were successful in whatever they did. Appearance and attitude indicated that any job they took would cause trouble and pain for someone, and profit for them.

They glanced around the room, then headed unerringly for Bert's table. No greetings were exchanged as they pulled back chairs and sat without invitation. "What's up? You got something for us to do?" The taller man spoke for both of them.

"Yeah. I'll let you know when. I need a few buildings fired on the same night, and in the same town. I've been using a local, but he won't be available." Two grunts greeted Bert's statement.

"You want us to give people enough time to get out?" The second man picked at a hangnail.

"No concern of mine."

"How big are the buildings? Can we use slow fuses?"

"Do it whichever way suits you and avoids detection."

The two exchanged glances, hangnail forgotten. "We charge by the building. Big buildings are extra."

Bert reached into his pocket and removed a hand-drawn map. "Here're the locations and approximate sizes of the targets. The location is Marcher Mills." He kept the folded paper between his body and the table, flashing it briefly. One of the men snorted.

"Targets? We don't use no guns to set fires." His companion snickered.

Bert ignored the byplay. His steady, unsmiling look wiped the smirks from their faces. "With the exception of one house, they're commercial establishments. Are you in?"

"Don't you want to know our fee?"

"I wouldn't be talking to you if I didn't know your fee. You'll see that the buildings are numbered in the order I want them fired. I've made arrangements for Jubal to hold the funds for you. He'll advance you money for the train tickets. When you've completed the job, I'll tell him to pay you the rest."

"You helping?" Bert's mouth contorted into a half smile.

"Oh, yeah. I'll be helping the volunteer fire brigade fight the fires."

The two ruffians goggled at him.

"It's none of your business. Just be there when I say. Do the job, take the money, be sure you have an alibi, and forget you ever saw me. I don't know you after you get your pay. Got that?"

"Yeah, yeah. Don't try to teach your grandmother to suck eggs. How'll we know the date?"

"A message will be delivered here for you two days before I need the fires set. Begin checking for it next Wednesday." He caught and held the eyes of his temporary confederates. "If the job isn't done to my satisfaction, you'll be hearing from me. Any more questions?"

They appeared unimpressed with his threat. "What about the cost of the materials we'll need? That stuff don't come cheap, you know."

"I'll provide supplies. Details will come with the message." Bert waited for a confirming nod from each of them, stood, and left. Heads swivelled to watch him. As the door closed, the conversation resumed, animated, loud and thirst-producing.

✿✿✿

Gladys, Elizabeth, and Faith approached the front door of the Montgomery mansion, anticipation apparent in their demeanors. The ladies sported their Sunday best. They were a walking advertisement for Betty Keppel's good taste and keen eye for fashion, as well as her astuteness in matters of dress. Gladys' hat, Elizabeth's shawl and Faith's reticule had all been purchased at her shop.

Invitations to call at the Montgomery's home were few and far between. They were cherished, savored, and talked about for years to come.

"I see that Betty Keppel has done well from the three of us." Elizabeth smiled and adjusted her shawl. Gladys snorted.

"I saw that shawl, Elizabeth. But the dress I had made for this occasion," she smoothed the fabric and removed an imaginary bit of lint from the sleeve, "would not have done well with black." She paused, and added, "but it looks charming with your outfit. Just the right touch."

Elizabeth smiled. She knew shawl envy when she heard it. Wentworth Optometry Services' reputation for quality work had spread faster than a flood. She and Faith had been the delighted recipients of new clothes on the occasion of their birthdays. Her remonstrance with Amanda resulted only in the comment that they could well afford a splurge for such an auspicious occasion.

"I could say the same about your hat. It's exactly the right style and colour, both for you and that lovely gown." Faith smiled. There was nothing like a little fashion jostling to liven up a rather dull walk.

"And I'm very pleased with the beadwork and fringe on my new reticule." She adjusted its position on her wrist and admired, once again, the final, crowning touch to her ensemble. But the older women had moved on to another topic.

"I wonder what china Marianne will use. I've always particularly admired that violet set of yours, Elizabeth. It will be interesting to see what the Montgomerys have chosen." Gladys failed to mention that the china pattern, whilst interesting, came second to a close, but polite, inspection of the décor and ornaments of her hostess.

"I'm so glad you like that set. It's a particular favourite of mine." When no response was forthcoming, she continued. "Do you think that Sebastian will make an appearance? I understand that he and Marianne are becoming quite close." She kept a watchful eye on her neighbor to measure her reaction. The strength of the interactions between her older daughter and Sebastian betokened a strong interest. And protest though they might, the interest was not *negative.*

Faith stifled a giggle. True to her word, she had told no one of Marianne's confidence. Let the town wonder about a match between her friend and Sebastian. She knew better. Amanda protested a little too much when confronted with the fact that she always knew where to find Sebastian if they were both in the store. From her position at the rear of the group, she piped up.

"I think they have Limoges china, Mrs. Whiffletree. The Chantilly pattern." She controlled her grin as Gladys smirked with satisfaction.

"Mother, let's not forget that Marianne and Sebastian are first cousins." That was as close as she could come to keeping her promise to Marianne while offering comfort. The ladies' steps slowed as they checked the condition of the flowerbeds lining the path and flowing over the rims of the urns that marked the beginning of the steps to the front door. Meanwhile Marianne prepared to move from her vantage point in the parlour and to open the door herself. Her head buzzed with questions and observations.

Must remember to mention Mrs. Whiffletree's dashing hat and admire the obviously-new shawl that Mrs. Wentworth is sporting. Mourning or not, she has a real eye for fashion. Darn, Faith got that reticule I had my eye on.

I'm sure that Faith has kept her word. I wonder if she's as ingenuous as she seems? I hope so, because I really like her. Her sister is keeping Sebastian on his toes. She grinned. *And just what plans do you have, Elizabeth Wentworth? I'm sure you realize the strong attraction between your daughter and my cousin. Will you try to come between Sebastian and me to ensure her happiness?*

The group had virtually stopped, their enthusiastic conversation obviously pertaining to the flowerbeds and urns. Marianne acknowledged that they were well worth a little admiration.

Gladys is somewhat of a dark horse. I know that she and Henry went to school together. They seem to be getting closer. Gladys, she knew, ruled the Methodist Ladies' Aid with benevolence. In spite of her status as a widow, she knew exactly what transpired in the Men's Bible Study Group. Henry, also a Methodist, was a faithful churchgoer, even though he failed to march lock-step with his church's view on wine and spirits. She had heard a couple of stories about his extreme bonhomie whilst imbibing the forbidden grape or grain.

Before her guests could reach for the knocker, she swung open the door in welcome. After the bustle of initial queries re health and comments on the weather, the group proceeded in a stately manner from the hall to the parlour. Gladys' head looked to be on a swivel. Elizabeth and Marianne kept up a flow of social nonentities. Faith brought up the rear. Each member of the group had an inner dialogue.

Faith was right. It is *the Chantilly pattern. And just look at the beautiful things they have. I'll never remember them all. Never mind, I'll just note the most affordable ones.* Gladys concentrated on her self-imposed task.

I don't believe those rumors about Marianne and Sebastian being so close. There's no glow or consciousness about her at all when his name is mentioned. Elizabeth relaxed and prepared to enjoy the visit.

Why is Marianne so willing to go along with the engagement charade? She doesn't act at all like someone in love. Or rather, she's in love, but not with him. I wonder what plans she really has? Faith stopped worrying about her sister and contemplated the name of her latest geographical search: Peepabun.

I can't believe that Faith is anything but what she seems: an attractive and honest young woman whose word is her bond. I'm so glad. Marianne smiled warmly at her new friend.

The discussion of a particularly delicious square ended with a promise to give the recipe to Elizabeth and Gladys. Various church matters of community concern received close attention to every detail. Company manners remained intact, but the chitchat descended from the rarified heights of fashion and religion to the mundane and fascinating.

"What do you think of Bert Stiles getting the security contract for the building materials? It just doesn't seem like the Bert we've all known and silently despised."

"What do you mean, 'silently despised', Gladys. I thought the council put out the word and that four applicants turned up," Elizabeth queried.

Gladys rarely made disparaging remarks about anyone. Elizabeth, Faith, and Marianne were all mystified. As newcomers, they were still feeling their way through the long and winding trails of Marcher Mills' gossip.

"Bert lived here until he was twelve, then moved to Hamilton with his family. He had a well-earned reputation as a bully."

"Lots of children are guilty of bullying when they are young, but grow out of it." Elizabeth was curious at the strength of feeling in Gladys' voice.

"Very true, but Bert's form of bullying went beyond the usual schoolyard stuff. He has a nasty temper, and he's strong. When Barry Wilson taunted him about using 'high falutin' language', Bert injured him so badly that he still suffers." Her audience gasped in horror.

Marianne, feeling it was the duty of the hostess to smooth the waters, or at least paddle the boat into a quiet bay, asked. "I remember Sebastian being displeased at the outcome of that meeting. He attended in his father's place," she explained. Her guests gave her their undivided attention.

"He said Mr. Stiles was the best of a sorry lot." Gladys nodded her head sagely. She agreed with Sebastian's sentiments.

"He was right. Al is a fool, Putrid's a drunk and poor George must depend on his cane to move more than two or three steps."

Marianne continued.

"I'd never heard his name before that, and I've been here almost three months."

"That's longer than us. I've heard the name, but only in passing."

"I have too, Mother, and usually in conjunction with another name, Al Anderson. No one is ever specific, but there are significant glances and downturned mouths."

Gladys had more news to share. "Whatever Bert is doing will benefit him and hurt someone else. Did you hear that someone saw him walking up and down residential streets in the middle of the night? No one knows what he's doing, but I can assure you, it isn't looking for an opportunity to perform a good deed."

Elizabeth shook her head. Faith and Marianne kept their fascinated gazes on the speaker as they determined to enjoy this cornucopia of local lore.

Marianne cleared her throat. “I understand that the security contract’s conditions were site security at night, from seven to seven, Monday to Saturday. One man could certainly handle that, but there’s all day Sunday and Sunday night. What’s happening then?”

“Bert has all the corners covered. He’s hired Stan Biltmore to cover Sunday from morning to evening. Al Anderson takes care of the weeknights. Bert will guard the goods on Sunday night.”

Elizabeth felt compelled to move the conversation forward. “Do any of you know Danny Tomlin? I overheard quite a heated argument in Marshall’s last week. Apparently he’s been seen on the streets in the middle of the night. I wonder if there’s any connection with Mr. Stiles.”

“That is strange. I could see a father running for the doctor, or even a problem at one of the Montgomery businesses or the mill that might constitute an emergency. Stiles and Tomlin. Let me think. They’ve both been seen, at night, in town. A connection doesn’t seem likely, but with Bert Stiles, who knows?”

“Who is Danny Tomlin? Why does he have ideas above his station? Is it because he wants to go to university?” Faith asked, placing her cup on a small side table.

Gladys, as the Marcher Mills’ native, offered, “Danny is a local lad. His father works in the mill, and naturally wants his son to follow in his footsteps. But Danny wants to become an engineer. I can’t understand where he got such a ridiculous idea, or how he thinks he could pay for it. The Tomlins aren’t poor. They insist their children have as much education as the town offers, but they certainly couldn’t, and wouldn’t support Danny in this pipe dream. Where does he think to get the money for such a venture?

“Now, about both Bert and Danny having been seen on the

streets in the middle of the night." She continued, "I can't see the connection, but mark my words, there's something funny going on if our Mr. Stiles is involved. You may be sure that whatever it is will come out in the wash." Gladys often invoked "mark my words" when she felt particularly strongly about something.

CHAPTER 20

"Henry, That Woman will drive me mad. No, she does drive me mad. Just look at what she's done! She puts up signs without a by-your-leave, steals my plants and generally causes havoc. A mule is a model of cooperation compared to her."

"Now, Sebastian, calm down. Look at this with the logic you so admire. What are a few plants? She did offer to return them, and you refused."

"Well, what could I do as a gentleman? It was their first day here. I had to let her have them." He frowned. Henry smiled, then addressed what would surely be Sebastian's next point.

"Let's consider the signs. I don't think I've ever seen you so incensed. Ever. And to this day I'm not sure just which thing caused you the most grief. Was it the crowd outside? You know you didn't appreciate the remarks about always buying something in the pharmacy when they used that route to Wentworth Optometry Services." He deliberately used "Wentworth Optometry Services" just to see Sebastian's jaws clamp shut. It was a wonder, really, that the man hadn't cracked his teeth.

A cup of tea might help. It couldn't hurt, and the Amanda Discussions, as he had come to think of them, tended to go on and on. And on.

"Those comments had no basis in fact. I have never forced anyone to purchase goods from the pharmacy. If they choose to browse and buy, then we both benefit. They have something they needed, and I have their money." He brushed his lapels, and continued. "Besides, you know the pharmacy offers a valuable service to the community."

Henry ignored the weak rejoinder. "Or was it because she had the sign put up on the front of your building?" No answer. The jaws remained clenched. Henry smiled and continued to watch his friend squirm. He wondered what would happen if Sebastian realized his reputation was one of compassion and caring. The minute anyone criticised Amanda's conduct or business practices, Sebastian mounted the ramparts in her defense.

"Or the fact that one sign wasn't enough, and she added two more." Still no response. He decided to give the knife of truth another twist. Carefully placing the kettle on the stove in the pharmacy's back room, he poked the coals and added fuel to both fires.

Pretending to ignore the signs of an imminent eruption of the volcano of Sebastian's wrath, he continued. "My personal favourite was when she backed you into a corner fenced with logic. Her reasons were absolutely correct. And *that's* what you found hardest to bear." Cup, saucers, spoons, sugar and milk graced the table, with a plate of cookies anchoring the arrangement. Promising sounds started to come from the kettle.

"Henry!" Sebastian stopped, cleared his throat, and started again. "I beg your pardon. I didn't mean to yell." Henry hid a smile by scratching his upper lip.

"As I meant to state, there was no disputing the logic and sound reasons behind Miss Wentworth's argument." A flush suffused his face. "But, it's her. Miss Wentworth. Amanda, I mean." He started to pace, and Henry prudently cleared his path.

"She doesn't ask. She doesn't discuss. She just charges ahead like a very feminine bull in a china shop." Once again Henry addressed his upper lip. The revelation of unstated and unacknowledged feelings in "feminine bull" came as no surprise to him. Sebastian, on the other hand, would have been staggered to hear that he was very attracted to That Woman.

A steady plume of steam announced water at the boiling point. Henry spooned tea leaves into the pot, and added the water. He had time to make another point before it had steeped to a rich mahogany hue. "Well, Sebastian, I'm waiting for an answer." He retreated to the far side of the table as his friend's pacing had increased in speed.

"You're right, though it galls me to admit it. It's just that the degree of rage is about equal." He paused, considering. "I can't make a decision about her and then follow through in a calm, rational, courteous manner when we meet. It doesn't make any sense at all. Is it just because she's a woman? No matter how angry I became when negotiating with a man, I would never act as I do with her." He paused in his pacing, obviously deep in thought. A frown creased his brow as he started to pull his hair.

Henry observed these signs of extreme mental anguish. When Sebastian got to the hair pulling stage, the situation was dire. Even so, revealing the bald truth to the sufferer was not the way to go. In this instance, he had to arrive at that particular destination himself.

"I don't know what it is about her, but she can make me lose my temper faster than anyone else I've ever known. Even Bert Stiles."

"Did you hear yourself? How could you possibly compare Amanda Wentworth to Bert Stiles in any way whatsoever, even in their ability to tickle your temper." Henry was torn between laughing at Sebastian's frustration and ignorance of his attraction to Amanda, and his own umbrage at linking Bert and Amanda in any way whatsoever.

"Uh, well, I just compared their gift for tickling my temper, as you so delicately put it. Nothing else. Really. Miss Amanda Wentworth encompasses all that is a lady." He poured more tea into his cup, which now relied on surface tension to keep the contents from escaping over the sides. A cookie joined the two resting on his plate. He remained oblivious to the fact that any attempt to lift the cup would result in disaster. Or that he was collecting cookies, but not eating them. "It's just…just…damn it, Henry, she has a gift for doing just what she knows will irritate me. And then looks at me with those big eyes. Or her hands on her hips." A fourth cookie crowded the others.

Henry kept his eyes on his hands. The more Sebastian spoke of That Woman, the softer and more reflective his voice became. He picked up a spoon and began to stir his tea with vigor, ignoring the waves that rose over the rim and began to fill the saucer. Henry was hard pressed to keep his countenance. Sebastian often held forth on his own personal theory that tea was tea, not some kind of slop addled by milk, sugar or lemon. The tempo of the spoon increased. His litany continued, unabated.

"But her ultimate weapon is tears. I *hate* when she does that. I know it's just a ploy, but it works. Then I become even angrier." His expression changed from wistful to wrathful. His spoon splashed into the saucer-moat, and his posture changed from upright to rigid.

Henry guffawed. "Sebastian, put that aside for now. It is really immaterial whether or not Miss Wentworth papers the building with signs. It's done. Public opinion is overwhelmingly in favour of her additions. Leave it." He noticed that the furrowed brow had smoothed, the tea stirring ceased, and wondered how Sebastian would address the matter of safely moving an overfull saucer of tea from table to sink.

"Now, do you wish me to have Miss Wentworth join us, or not?" He knew the eye of the storm had passed.

"No, thank you. We'll leave it for now. Perhaps I need to think about this a little more." He regarded his cup and saucer with distaste, fetched a tray onto which he gingerly placed his cup before carrying it to the sink. A clean cup in one hand, he reached for the teapot with the other.

"Let's go over that list of problems and puzzles you have." His customary good humor restored, he grinned. "You know, Henry, the one that never stops? Just moves on to another sheet of paper?" Situations wholly free of the taint of That Woman, or of any woman, offered a welcome change for both gentlemen.

CHAPTER 21

For the third time in five minutes, Bert consulted his pocket watch. The designated time for his meeting with Al had not yet arrived, but he was anxious to complete the arrangements. Finally he could see the different parts of his plan coming together. The Montgomerys would soon know the strength of his hate and the scope of his proficiency in destroying that which he deemed unworthy. The very best part would be their inability to keep their commitments for delivery of goods. Old Man Montgomery had a real bee in his bonnet about that. On-Time-Every-Time-Montgomery was a byword with his customers.

Just then he became aware of someone approaching his table. He flipped a coin to Al and jerked his head in the direction of the bar. No words were necessary; Al returned with two brimming schooners of the local brew.

"OK, Bert. I'm here. Why all the hush-hush? I was just tellin' the guys… ."

"Shut up and listen." Bert reminded himself that Al, who had no idea of his final goal, must remain oblivious of its existence. But he still couldn't force himself to be polite.

"It should be obvious, even to your limited ability to understand practically anything, that it's time to escalate the fires and other things." Bert knew that "vandalism" was far, far beyond Al, and hastened to explain "escalate." "Escalate means to increase, or speed up."

Al grinned and nodded. Anything that promised skulduggery and more beer money would always get his complete attention.

Bert continued.

"This time, we're really going to hit them where it hurts. This time you're to loosen one of the wheels on the pumper."

His companion scratched his head, puzzled. "Why just one wheel? Why not loosen all the wheels? Or at least two of the wheels. Should I do a front wheel or a back wheel?"

Al was warming to his theme. Bert inhaled deeply, prayed for patience, and prepared to explain. *Honest to God, village idiot is* much *too complimentary a term for this jackass.*

Ignoring the question, he asked one of his own. "Do you have any idea why I want you to do this?"

Why do I even bother? Al required more time than anyone except Putrid to work things through—and usually arrived at the wrong conclusion.

"To cause an accident? Make them late to get to a fire?" *Well, that was better than I thought he could do. He can't have had too much beer, yet.*

"Yes—to make them late to a fire." Al beamed. Praise for any of his actions or ideas occurred rarely.

"OK, Bert. When do you want me to do that?"

"I'm not finished. You will also cut *almost all the way through* the traces." He was concerned that giving Al two things to do created a great deal of room for error. He also knew that there would be just one opportunity to tamper with the fire equipment. Phil Landers was not only a good fireman, but conscientious about his responsibilities to the animals and equipment.

"We want to let the horses get a block or two from the station. It doesn't matter if they don't break apart the first time they're used after you cut them. As a matter of fact, it would be even better if they didn't." Al frowned—always a bad sign. Bert tried again.

"Listen, tonight you'll loosen the wheel, *but make sure they can get the rig out of the building,* and cut the traces. Here's a tin of boot black. Don't forget to rub that on the cuts to make them harder to find." He made sure his hand, hidden from public view by the table and Al's body, would allow a smooth transfer.

Al accepted the tin and held it up to the light. He started to pry off the lid when Bert kicked him, grabbed his wrist and dug his fingers into the tendons. Al winced and dropped his hand to the table.

"I don't want the world to know you've got that. They know the closest you've ever come to it is passing it on the shelf at the general store. Put it in your pocket. Now." The venom in his voice guaranteed quick compliance. Al hunched his shoulders and lowered his head.

"When you cut the traces, be sure you do it on an angle, and from the top towards the bottom. *Think, man.* That way the cuts will be harder to find."

He waited for Al to process these very involved instructions, took a deep breath, and hoped for the best. Utilising the condensation on the table, he drew a rough sketch of the placement and depth of the cuts. "Now, repeat the instructions to me."

Al, face screwed into a position denoting extreme mental pain, did his best. *Miracle of miracles, he got it right.*

"Good."

Al's expression indicated disbelief at the compliment.

"So, now we've made sure the pumper will be useless the next time they try to respond to a fire. The day after you loosen the wheel and cut the traces, you'll set your next fire. And don't forget to rub some dirt over any bright spots left by the wrench on the wheel." Al nodded and smiled; here was something he enjoyed and did well.

"Now for the fire. I want you to put a pile of straw against the back door of the pharmacy. Make sure it's damp, so there'll be lots of smoke. Someone will smell it and sound the alarm." He could see the question coming, and hastened to provide the answer.

"Take a small bottle of gasoline and a handful of dry straw to start it." He waited for Al's nod. Bert's smile, meant to reassure, evoked terror. He adjusted his expression to indicate its usual painful forbearance when dealing with Al, and continued his discourse on the results of the sabotage.

"They'll harness the horses to the rig and have no idea that trouble is just waiting to happen. When the wheel falls off, which will occur soon after they leave the station but before they've gone very far, they'll have to unharness the horses. Terrified of the dragging rig, they will try to escape. If you've done a good job on the traces, they'll come apart and the horses will leave the rig in the dust."

Al's nod had a tentative quality which indicated agreement, but little comprehension.

"Do you understand?" A blank look greeted his query.

Bert sighed and prepared to explain. "Now they'll have to wait for enough men to assemble to push and pull the rig. Always supposing they can get the wheel back on and fastened, which I doubt, valuable time will be lost as they try to find a way to fix it. With any luck at all, the horses will have bolted because the traces have ripped."

This time Al's nod and furrowed brow represented hope that he understood his instructions.

"But, but… ."

"I'm still not finished. If the pharmacy goes up, so be it. Those thrice-damned Montgomerys can afford it." Bert took a large swallow of his beer. He'd earned it.

"But boss," Al finally had the chance, and the courage, to speak. "If the pharmacy burns, then those nice ladies will be out of business. I was planning on getting a pair of spectacles with coloured lenses. For protection against the sun." He beamed in smug contemplation of such sartorial magnificence. "I really fancy a pair of them glasses. I'd look prime."

"A prime ass, you stupid bastard. And if you're so damned set on coloured glasses, there are many places in Hamilton that can meet your need."

"Really, Bert? Where?" He leaned forward, eager to discover more. His companion sneered.

"Just do as you're told. Keep your mind on what's important." He nodded a greeting to one or two of the patrons, threw another coin to Al, grabbed his hat from a hook near the door, and left.

CHAPTER 22

"Go home. Your headache is so bad that you can't even focus. Any decisions that have to be made can wait." Faith was right.

Closing her eyes helped, but the lure of her bedroom, drapes pulled to create a soft and shadowed interior, was a siren's call to her throbbing skull. It would take all of her resolve and remaining strength to walk the few blocks between work and home without collapsing.

"All right, I'll go," Amanda whispered. "You're absolutely correct. I can neither see nor think, so I'm of no use here." *And now I sound like a cranky little girl, pouting because she can't do what she wants.* "Thanks, Faith. Feel free to close up early. We don't have any appointments, after three o'clock."

She silently cursed the hat pin necessary for her headgear, and wished fervently for a parasol. Anything to keep the light as low as possible. The special blue glasses Faith had devised would help, and also be an excellent advertisement for what they hoped would become a standard part of everyone's wardrobe: men, women, and children.

The distance between Wentworth Optometry Services and her home seemed endless, but eventually the familiar garden gate came into view. Opening it the least possible amount in case it should creak, she closed it with equal caution and climbed the few steps to the porch. So great was her pain that she failed to enjoy the beauty of the flowers bordering the path.

In case her mother was napping, she inched open the door, almost sobbing with relief at the gentle dimness and silence that greeted her. Not quite silent, she realised. The murmur of conversation came from the parlor. She sighed. There was no getting around it; she would have to be polite and greet the guest, but nothing on this earth could force her to remain. The murmur changed to individual words as she came closer to the open parlour door.

"And now, Elizabeth, let me tell you the latest about Sebastian Montgomery and his cousin, Marianne." Gladys' voice carried clearly. Neither she nor Elizabeth noticed Amanda's presence, or the look of shock on her face.

"Georgina Turner told Betty Keppel that she distinctly heard Pearl Murphy tell Miranda Knowles—her that married what's-his-name's younger brother—that Sebastian Montgomery and his cousin, Marianne, were definitely a match. Wedding's supposed to be in two months' time."

Elizabeth was obviously struggling to connect the names to various members of the community she had met. She had often commented on Gladys' ability to spew sentences of inordinate length without every losing her place. Gladys leaned back and waited for a shocked reaction. Amanda felt the room lurch. She clutched the door frame.

"Of course, that makes no sense. The senior Montgomerys won't be back for another three months. And what about giving the bride's parents and family time to get here? Why, the bride might even want the wedding to take place in Australia." She paused to sip her tea and savor the impact of her news.

"Good afternoon, mother. Mrs. Whippletree." *Was that really her voice? How could she speak, when breath and vision had deserted her?*

"Amanda, what are you doing home early? Are you ill?" Elizabeth began to rise from her chair. Gladys leaned forward, determined to hear the answer.

"Not really ill, just one of my bad headaches." She raised a hand to her head and closed her eyes. "I'll lie down for a while. You know how they are. I'll be fine shortly."

Please, God, get me out of here. Why do I feel as though I've been beaten with a large stick? Instead of a shock, this should come as an interesting, and yes, juicy, bit of gossip. Not a body blow.

Unaware of her daughter's internal dialogue, Elizabeth excused herself. "Please don't leave, Gladys. I'll get Amanda settled, and make some fresh tea."

Gladys appeared torn between enjoying a comfortable chat over a major piece of news, and rushing out the door to report Amanda's unexpected reaction. Her good nature prevailed.

"I'll put the kettle on, Elizabeth. Amanda, you are as white as a sheet. Now, don't you worry about me. I'll bring you a cup of tea as soon as it's ready." Gladys was genuinely kindhearted, but seemed to doubt that Amanda's condition was caused solely by a headache.

"No, thank you, Mrs. Whiffletree. I really couldn't swallow anything." She swayed, and tightened her grip on the door jamb. "Rest and sleep will do the trick." Just the thought of Gladys' energetic good will caused more pain. She really couldn't bear all that enthusiasm.

Releasing her grip on the door jamb, she took two steps across the hall and seized the newel post. *Just let me reach my room without throwing up.* Before she reached the top, she sensed her mother behind her and knew she would have a glass of water and medication in her hands. The drapes would be drawn, the bed turned down, and the glass of water with two aspirins resting on the bedside table while she removed her dress and shoes.

It's because my head hurts so badly and I feel as if the chamber pot should be at the ready. That's why I'm so upset. It's the only reason. Refusing to think, she took the pills, slipped under the covers, and prayed for sleep's combination of oblivion and curative powers.

✿✿✿

Later that evening she went downstairs for a cup of tea. The worst of the pain had subsided, but there was a dull throbbing in the area of her heart that filled her with dismay and confusion. Why should she be reacting to news of Sebastian's imminent formal engagement and marriage? The man was like a mosquito, persistently droning and threatening to dart in and draw blood at the least sign of her relaxing her guard. He was undeniably handsome, but that had nothing to do with his character. *And why should I care about his character, except as it pertains to business?* Reaching the bottom of the stairs and a decision at the same time, she resolved to put the pesky person out of her mind and enjoy her tea.

"Oh, there you are, dear. I've just now put on the kettle. Would you care for a bit of dry toast? You know it will help to settle your stomach." Her mother's cosseting was just what she needed.

"Faith and I have been in the parlour with our knitting. Why don't you come and join us?" Tea, toast and mothering—what could be more perfect?

✿✿✿

"Are you sure you don't want me to invent a headache or upset stomach for you?" Faith, Amanda knew, realised that she had heard the "Marianne and Sebastian" rumors.

"Of course not. And let's get this out so we don't have to worry about it. Yes, I heard the gossip that Sebastian Montgomery will marry his cousin. No, it doesn't bother me. Why should it? It couldn't possibly matter less. Sebastian Montgomery is nothing but a thorn in my side." *Liar, liar. It* didn't *matter until you heard it was true. He's nothing to me but a very troublesome business associate. Instead, of fretting, I'll enjoy the first carefree social outing I've had in some months.*

She moved the curtain to one side and glanced out the parlour window. "Here's Marianne. You take the smaller hamper with the drinks, and I'll manage the one with the food. I hope we have enough."

"We've enough to feed a troop. Stop worrying—about anything."

"Come in, Marianne." Faith smiled at her friend. "Amanda is once again checking to be sure there's sufficient food for half of Marcher Mills." She rolled her eyes and grinned. "I know Betty will be ready when we call." Marianne smiled at her friend.

"Don't forget your parasols. The blankets are in the buggy. After we collect Betty, it's off to enjoy this beautiful day."

Marianne had told Faith more than once how much she missed her friends. Amanda had agreed that a picnic with the four of them would help to fill that gap. She vowed that Faith would never know what it cost her to welcome Marianne's company. She hadn't understood herself until presented with the fact.

She liked Marianne. Enjoyed her company. Admired her free spirit and determination to do what she wanted. It was her own emotions that troubled her. The inner turmoil started the day she overheard that Sebastian and Marianne would unite their two branches of the Montgomery family. *Enough, finish checking the lunch, enjoy the afternoon, and stop fretting over what can't be changed and shouldn't cause concern.*

"Ready, ladies. Sorry I took so long. Just making sure I hadn't forgotten the napkins and cloth." *A lie, but all in a good cause.* She had needed those few moments to ensure her composure would not waver.

Laughing, the three ran down the porch steps and headed for

the buggy. Marianne assured them that her aunt and uncle insisted she treat it as her own.

A short time later, Betty chatted about who lived in which house. She interspersed her remarks between the necessary directions to Marianne. As the Marcher Mills' local representative, she had been tasked with choosing the location and bringing a dessert. Marianne provided the transportation; the Wentworth girls, the food and beverages.

Blue skies, fluffy white clouds, a gentle breeze, and lively companionship promised an afternoon of fun and relaxation. Because the Anglican service started at ten and finished by twelve, the remainder of the day was free to pursue other appropriate Sunday activities. They realised they would be the cynosure of all eyes until well out of town, and were on their best behaviour until it disappeared behind them.

"Why didn't we think of this before? Fantastic weather, delightful company, and no chores—it couldn't be more perfect." Eager agreement supported Betty's enthusiastic statement. "There, just by that big tree on the hill. The creek is at the bottom on the other side for water for the horses, and the grass is sweet and tender."

Marianne smiled. "And even if it weren't, I brought nosebags and oats. The horses should picnic, too."

Soon they reposed on blankets and pillows. Faith offered to read from Lord Byron's poetry, but the others refused. Instead, the conversation turned to various local personalities. Animated discussions and speculations about imminent and not-so-imminent births segued into speculations about who was behind the recent rash of fires and vandalism. Plans for future endeavors led to a spirited agreement on the place of women in present-day Marcher Mills and Canadian society. Betty, notorious for her occasional social ineptness, broached the topic which continued to fill Amanda's mind.

"So, Marianne, I understand that you and a certain well-known young man in Marcher Mills are hearing wedding bells." Faith gave her customary little wriggle that presaged rapt and undivided attention. Betty waited expectantly. Amanda stopped breathing.

Marianne smiled knowingly. "Marcher Mills' gossip certainly is creative. I have no idea what you're talking about. I'm merely here on a visit to the Canadian branch of my family."

It's true. It's true. You may deny it all you wish, but that knowing smirk says it all. Marianne and Sebastian will be married. Why do I have such a pain in my heart? Appalled to realize that her eyes were full of tears, Amanda whipped out her handkerchief. She pretended to sneeze, surreptitiously ensuring no outward evidence of her inner turmoil was visible.

Exclamations at her denial abounded, but Marianne remained steadfast. It was gossip. She was merely here on a visit. Then she adroitly changed the subject and focused the attention elsewhere.

"Why don't you tell us the latest Canadian place name to catch your fancy, Faith? I enjoyed hearing about Moose Jaw. What have you learned about Kicking Horse Pass?" Creative suggestions about the origin of the name came fast and furiously, and Amanda gave thanks that the conversation had moved on to other, less dangerous, areas.

At dinner that evening, Faith was full of their afternoon's activities, but Amanda found herself strangely reluctant to participate. Her thoughts swirled in shifting eddies. Nothing seemed to make sense. She would start to think of one thing, then find herself wondering about something else entirely. Pleading exhaustion, she escaped as soon as possible to the welcome sanctuary of her room. As she climbed the stairs, she heard Faith' animated voice regaling their mother about the Australian driving club for women. *Thank God they aren't discussing the forthcoming wedding.* In spite of her best efforts, sleep was a long time in coming.

CHAPTER 23

Bert was fuming. He made a point of being seen with Al as little as possible. Now, anyone in the town who might choose to walk by the construction site would see them together. Summer nights meant visibility for long periods of time. When Bert gave an order, he expected it to be followed to the letter. There was no excuse for shoddy workmanship. If he didn't keep up the pressure, the sheriff and fire chief would have too much time to think. They weren't brilliant, but they were far from stupid.

He strode angrily up and down the aisle created between timbers cut for floor joists and bags of plaster covered by tarpaulins. In his opinion they were tempting fate to have the plaster outside for one minute longer than necessary. But if the fools didn't have basic common sense, they could just put up with the results. He grinned. And egg on the faces of that high-and-mighty Montgomery bastard would be extremely pleasing. Just then he saw his quarry approaching. Hands in pockets. Whistling. No sign of hurrying to please. Bert stomped to the midway point of the aisle and snarled.

"Why the hell haven't you done what I told you? There hasn't been a fire for over a week. Or anything else, come to mention it. Are you totally lacking both brains and imagination?" *Stupid question. Of course he is. That's why he's often good at following orders.*

Bert's expression caused his henchman to hunch his shoulders, lower his head and retreat out of striking range. For the first time, Bert saw signs of a backbone. Al's body language indicated fear, but his words did not.

"Because I haven't been able to sneak into the fire hall." Al was still careful to stay outside of striking range, but his attitude was far from subservient. "I've got the straw, all right, and I keep it damped down enough to smoke like an entire building. But that damned fire chief won't get his ass out of the building long enough for me to get in and do what you want. Do you know that god damned Phil Landers is *sleeping* at the station?"

Bert was incredulous. Not only was the worm starting to turn, it even continued to bitch and whine.

"How the hell am I supposed to do what you want when it's either full daylight or that bastard is snoring up a storm? You know that horses don't like me. Can you just imagine the noise they'll make if I try to creep in there?" Bert drew a breath to verbally slap him down, but Al didn't give him a chance.

"And not only that, it seems that I get to do all the dangerous and dirty stuff, and you just swan around."

"You get the jobs you do, Al, because you can do them well." Even in the middle of his rage, Bert realised that a little honey should be mixed with the vinegar of his wrath. But this had gone far enough. *Time for a little discipline.*

He stepped forward until his footwear nudged Al's. It galled him that ugly workman's boots were required when he was on duty guarding the building materials. His closet in Marcher Mills contained shoes worthy of a man of business; the closet in Toronto featured shoes, and clothing, fit for an up-and-coming tycoon. He stared down at Al. Bert knew the advantages of superior height, and used every weapon he had. He lowered his voice and infused it with menace.

"In order for the plan I outlined to work, I must be observed as being above reproach. That means not taking any chances." He clenched his teeth over the rest of what he wanted to say. *You are pushed to manage what I* do *give you, and the assignment at the fire hall is a case in point.*

"If you're having a problem, tell me. I plan for all eventualities. You should know that, by now." Al swallowed and eased back. Bert tended to be frightening at any time, but more so when he lost his temper.

"OK. I'm sorry, Bert. I was trying to do just what you said, but I couldn't." Al's usual not-quite-cringing attitude had returned. Bert gritted his teeth, but forced a smile. Al blanched.

"Now, if you need to get Phil Landers out of there, I'll arrange it. Come back tomorrow, same time, and I'll have everything in place." *Somehow. How in holy hell am I supposed to get him out of there at night.* But in the back of his mind, Bert knew that stress and obstacles sharpened his brain. He had every faith that by tomorrow night he'd have a plan in place.

By seven the next morning when his shift had ended, he had revised some of his plans. If it took longer than he thought to put in place, he had only to notify the men in Hamilton of the changes. It might even work to his advantage to take more time. Several cunning ideas about combining ever-escalating vandalism with small fires lodged firmly in his brain. The idea of increasing dangers of one while lowering the other would throw the sheriff and fire chief off their stride. And anything that caused them confusion worked to his advantage. He would contact Al this afternoon and begin his adjusted timetable.

✿✿✿

Jenny found the time walking to and from work invaluable in planning how she would take care of Bastard Bert. She was still mulling over ways and means of disposing of the devil, but felt, overall, that using her knowledge of herbs would be best. Water hemlock was particularly powerful, but getting it into her target might provide some problems. Wolfbane was another very potent plant, but it, too, had a strong, bitter taste. She didn't want to harm anyone else. Her steps slowed as she continued to ponder alternatives.

✿✿✿

The joint meeting of the Inter-Faith Ladies' Guild produced an impressive volume of noise. At the sometimes reluctant behest of their various ministers or priests, the ladies were there in support, grudgingly given in many cases, of their priests or pastors' wish to organize the annual Inter-Faith Prayer Meeting and Picnic. In Marcher Mills, inter-faith meant protestants, and not just protestants, but "approved" protestants; i.e. Anglicans, Presbyterians, Methodists and Baptists. The Baptists were dangerously close to exclusion, mostly due to their lack of support of local dances given for various benevolent causes. And their exuberant and excessive singing. None of those idol worshipers or holy rollers was included. Baptists stretched the Christian tolerance of a good many participants.

The official part of the function was followed, as usual, by tea, cookies and gossip. The tea lubricated throats, the cookies provided energy, and the gossip rolled on tongues well oiled by speculation and imagination.

Elizabeth and Gladys stood at the end of the table. Plates and platters, now a hodgepodge of crumbs, covered most of the surface. Trays of tea and coffee issued forth from the kitchen in an unending stream. Each tray had a glass of spoons, a bowl of sugar and two pitchers, one each of cream and milk, as well as cups of tea or coffee.

Jostling for the right to carry the trays had been vigorous. Most nestled in the hands of those claiming a keen interest in their community. The corresponding interest in the various activities of its inhabitants, while unspoken, was understood.

"So, Elizabeth, what did you think of the meeting?"

"It certainly was interesting, Gladys." She thanked the lady passing the tray and exchanged her empty cup for a full one, shaking her head at the offer of sugar or cream. "Do you think the proposal to have joint services once a month is viable?" Just then she noticed her neighbour's attention directed towards a group of three women. The ladies murmured, looked at her, put their heads back together, and murmured again.

Gladys checked her hat pin, straightened her best summer shawl, grabbed Elizabeth's wrist, and advanced on the group with blood in her eye. Giving thanks that the full cup was in her other hand, Elizabeth quickly put it on a table in passing. She had no idea why Gladys' advance reminded her of soldiers marching to war. But she knew she would soon find out.

"Instead of hissing together, why don't you ask Elizabeth for her opinion?" Challenged, the group fell silent. Finally one of them, braver or more foolish than the others, spoke. "Gladys, so glad to see that your manners have not changed a whit. Why don't you and your friend join us?"

Undeterred by the gleam of malice or falsely-sweet words, Gladys prepared to carry the battle into the enemies' camp.

"Thank you, Noreen. We'd be delighted to do so. I believe you were speculating on possible upcoming marriages, especially those involving the Montgomery family. And, if I'm not mistaken, a member of the Wentworth family was mentioned, too."

She introduced Elizabeth to the three women. Two of them, while nervous when confronted by such a worthy foe, failed to indicate a desire to leave. Noreen Valens, known, if not lauded, for her propensity of discovering and sharing embarrassing facts about her neighbors, showed no signs of giving ground. She focused on Elizabeth.

"Mrs. Wentworth, we were, indeed, discussing possible upcoming marriages in our little town. Your daughter, Amanda, was mentioned. It seems as if, Marianne Montgomery's presence notwithstanding, she has a keen interest in the person and activities of our most eligible bachelor." Her gaze resembled that of a hawk on the trail of a particularly juicy and helpless rodent.

Elizabeth, an old hand at squashing upstarts, engaged the enemy head on. "Thank you for your kind words, Mrs. Valens. They show a remarkable ability to scrutinise, misinterpret, then speculate, on the actions of others. Given the level of intelligence thus displayed, it's no wonder you got everything wrong."

Gasps greeted this carrying of the banner into the other's court. Gladys, hands clasped at her waist, subtly extended her elbows to increase the jousting space for her principal.

"But I am absolutely in awe of your zeal for interfering in that which is really none of your business. Gladys, I think I see a friend by the door. Good bye, ladies."

Crisp diction accompanied her best English accent and the barest inclination of her head. It was all she could do to restrain herself until she and Gladys sat at her own parlour table, a pot of strong tea centered between her very best china cups.

"How long has my daughter been fodder for common gossip, Gladys? Do you know who started the rumors? Why is someone trying to soil her name? If she acquires the reputation for chasing men and Sebastian Montgomery in particular, Wentworth Optometry Services will be ruined."

"Now, Elizabeth, I think you are making much too much of this. Noreen Valens has no respect for anyone. On several occasions she made things up from whole cloth, just to see what would happen, or to even a score with someone she feels insulted her.

"It was very unfortunate that those seeds were sown in such fertile ground, but all is not lost."

✿✿✿

A silent and darkened house greeted Amanda and Faith. Neither their mother's cheery greeting nor delicious smells of dinner were evident.

"I'll check this floor, Faith. You see if Mother is resting." The girls rushed to their assigned tasks.

"I've found her, Amanda." Faith pattered down the stairs and whispered. "She's lying on her bed and insisting that nothing is wrong. 'Nothing' has produced a pile of sodden handkerchiefs that she tried to hide under the pillow. What do you think is the matter? Is she ill? Does she have a fatal or life threatening disease?" Faith was frantic. Amanda barely heard her as she rushed upstairs.

"Mother, what happened? Are you ill? Do you have a fever?" She ran back to the top of the stairs and directed Faith to make tea. "What can I get for you? Should we call the doctor?" As she bombarded her mother with questions, she shook out the afghan resting on the bedside chair and covered the weeping figure. Only once before, just after the death of her father, had she seen her mother like this. The absence of sound as the tears coursed down her cheeks terrified her. She made sure the window was open. Elizabeth was a firm believer in fresh air in a sick room.

Her mother's hand emerged from under the cover and grabbed her wrist in a strong grip. Amanda felt some of her fear recede—anyone with a grip that strong was not at death's door.

"Don't talk. After we've had some tea we'll be able to discuss what is wrong." A faint murmur of assent was the only response. Amanda helped her sit up and arranged the pillows at her back.

Just then Faith appeared with a tray bearing tea for three and some plain sugar cookies. They would be easy to digest and were Elizabeth's favorites. She refused the cookie, but cradled the cup in her hands, obviously savoring the warmth. After inhaling the aroma of the beloved beverage, she began her tale.

"As you know, I went to the Inter-Faith Ladies' Guild with

Gladys." Nods greeted her statement. The girls had encouraged their mother to reach out to the community. "The meeting had finished, and we were at the tea and cookies stage. And gossip."

Her eyes narrowed. She flung back the afghan and swung her legs over the side of the bed, groping for her house slippers. These were her precious daughters. She was fearless in their defense.

"Gladys grabbed my elbow and led me to a group of women. I could tell by the speed at which we crossed the floor that she was angry, but I had no idea why. Then I received the shock of my life." The light of battle faded from her eyes as once more tears began to run down her face.

"We're ruined. Whatever will we do? Wentworth Optometry Services is all that stands between us and starvation." She groped for a fresh hanky.

Amanda and Faith looked at each other in consternation. They sat on either side of their mother, surrounding her with their love. This was not the mother they knew. That mother was the hub of the wheel of their family. That mother's love for her children was so strong that she left her husband's grave in England and turned her face to a new life. That mother had mourned; indeed, still mourned; but the bedrock strength her girls counted on remained.

"Mother, please stop crying. We have no idea what you're talking about." Amanda put her arm around Elizabeth's shoulders; Faith replenished her tea.

"I'm sorry, girls. Tears never solved anything. As soon as I've finished my cry, I'll be fine, and we can create a plan of attack."

"'Plan of attack' sounds as if you're ready to wage a military campaign." Faith' attempt to lighten the atmosphere failed. Elizabeth straightened, blotted her tears, downed the entire cup of tea in a series of gulps, and confronted her children.

"Let me up. We have to make a plan and execute it. Immediately. Those women, those contemptible women, indicated that

Amanda was making a fool of herself over that Montgomery man. And here I thought he was so kind when he brought you home that first day." She pummelled a pillow, all but throwing it back on the bed.

"They said that Mr. Montgomery and his cousin, Marianne, will soon have the banns read. They say that Amanda is chasing him. And claimed that they wouldn't be surprised if, since she lost the most eligible bachelor in Marcher Mills, she started to chase every man in town. We'll be ruined."

The effect on her daughters was electric. Faith took the cups and saucers from her mother and sister, and plunked them firmly on the tray.

"Come, Mother. Let's have one of our councils of war in the parlour."

Amanda seethed. "The allegations are ridiculous. I have *never* chased any man, and I'm not about to start. War it will be." Amanda's jaw firmed as she folded and replaced the afghan.

"Do you need help, Mother? I know you can see the possible, no probable, negative effects on our business as well as I. It's time to fight with every weapon in our arsenal."

✿✿✿

"Here you go, Jeff. Hot and fresh—just the way you like it. Oh, and strong; did I mention that? I made sure it dissolved the spoon when I stirred." Jeff grinned and accepted the coffee.

"Thanks, Phil. This is a great idea to have a meeting right out in the open. Even better when we can sit in the sun and watch the world go by. Just two public servants shootin' the breeze and wastin' the town's money."

Both were aware of the unsettling absence of fires or vandalism. Convinced that the ominous quiet was a precursor to more violent and serious problems, they used every source of information and trick they could to discover the perpetrator. Chairs tilted back against the wall of the fire station, the men adjusted their hats to shade their eyes.

They had a panoramic view of the main street; from Nat Bodkins' blacksmith shop at one end to Marv Sanderson's livery at the other. Main Street traffic was an open book. Phil cleared his throat, a sure indicator he considered what he was about to say particularly significant.

"I have a really, really bad feeling that the next thing that happens will be the final hurrah of the maniac threatening our community."

"Villain, not maniac. I only wish I could argue with you, but I fear you're right. At first I thought that something would happen to those building supplies Bert Stiles is supposedly guarding."

"Absolutely, but, much as it galls me to admit it, not one thing has gone missing or been damaged on his watch."

"Maybe so, but leopards don't change their spots: once a conniver; always a conniver."

"Yep. And *that* makes me wonder what we might have missed."

"Right—or what's been put in place that could explode right in our faces."

"Wish you hadn't used that word, Phil. Given what's been going on, and given that dynamite isn't all that hard to come by…."

"Yeah. I hear you." Phil brought his chair forward so that all four legs rested on the boardwalk. "Want a refill?"

"Guess so, since we haven't really talked or planned, just bitched." Fresh coffee in hand, the men settled down to some serious plotting of ways and means.

"Do you think that this is aimed at a single person or family? Or the town as a whole? Or the men who've ponied up the money to buy the building supplies? Or am I desperate and talking nonsense?" Phil eyed his friend over the top of his mug. He wanted to hide his chagrin if Jeff thought him a fool.

The sheriff leaned forward and rested his elbows on his knees. Casually turning his head left, then right, he surveyed the main street before answering. “No, I don’t think you’re crazy. There is too much evidence of planning behind all these things suddenly happening in our formerly sleepy little town. Not just planning to ensure that the guilty son of a bitch gets away, but a careful escalation of incidents. We noticed that when we made our list of the events leading up to that meeting.” He took a mouthful of coffee, then continued.

“What do you think of the notion that we have two people involved—a planner and a doer?” He cradled the cup in his hands, monitoring his friend’s reaction with a sideways glance.

Phil’s chair thumped as he leaned forward. He used his hat to beat his pant legs, first one, then the other, as a ploy to check for traffic on the street. Satisfied that no one could hear them, replaced his hat and leaned forward.

“I think you just might have something, Sheriff.” He grinned. “And just what duo springs to your mind?” A snort of derision greeted his question.

“Damned if I know bugger all about that.” Bugger all referred, as they both knew, to Bert and Al. “If they aren’t, I’ll eat my hat.”

“Not very tasty, but you know you’re safe. Now, how will we catch them? Or otherwise prove our theory? Al’s thicker than two short planks. Bert is bright and capable. He was a nasty bully when he was young. Now he’s just an older, smoother bully.”

“You bet. And slippery, too. It’ll take some planning to prove he’s behind this. I think the key is to discover *why* he’s so hell bent on…really, when I think about it, this almost smacks of revenge. What do you think about revenge as a motive?”

“Before he left Marcher Mills for Hamilton, Sebastian Montgomery beat the crap out of him. They were both still in school.

Sebastian is two or three years younger than Bert, and that would stick in Bert's craw until he could get a payback."

"Knowing he's a conniver, bully and probably as crooked as a dog's hind leg isn't enough. He's also very, very smooth. Never a cross word—or a cuss word, come to that. Polite. Well spoken."

"And the fine work he's done on guarding the supplies has not gone unnoticed, especially by the older businessmen. They were adults when Bert and Sebastian were in school. They would have known about Bert's temper and vicious streak, but not in the same way that his classmates did."

"Right. We're faced with a smooth-talking bastard. Maybe his weak point is his far-from-intelligent sidekick."

"Al's lack of brain power is well known. So is his willingness to serve Bert. Hell, serve anyone, for that matter, as long as they'll buy him a beer."

"Oops, here comes Al right now. Let's finish our discussion later. In the meantime, try to think of some way we can prove our theory—*before* something else happens." The duo nodded to Al, picked up their chairs, and disappeared inside.

CHAPTER 24

Bert strode down the last row of building supplies. The new addition was almost complete. It was time to put the final parts of his plan in place. The failure of his scheme to damage the fire equipment worked in his favor. The delay allowed an opportunity to refine and add exquisite details to his cold and satisfying dish of revenge.

"OK, Al. You've been moaning and bitching about not having any fun. The time is ripe for the new plan, so pay attention."

"But Bert, we ain't done nothin' for ages. I thought you forgot about it." Al's expression indicated that his interest in creating mayhem had lost some of its fire.

"That's right." Bert clenched his teeth in frustration. He often thought how satisfying it would be to have someone with whom he could discuss plans. *Ah, well, the life of a mastermind is obviously a lonely one. Good thing I could get hold of those men in Hamilton and tell them to wait for the word to start. And that plans might change.*

"Now listen, and listen carefully." He waited for Al's nod. Because this meeting would take some time, they had moved inside the shack at the construction site. Out of sight was out of mind, especially with the idiots in Marcher Mills. September nights could be cool—a welcome relief from the often relentless heat of July and August. A fire was a waste of fuel except to make coffee. Bert merely increased his pace when patrolling the site, which took care of any discomfort related to the lower temperatures.

"I hope it's a doozy. My elbow practically forgets how to bend far enough to get the beer to my mouth. Can't drink without money." For Al, that was a hint of exquisite subtlety.

"You'll get money, don't worry. Some of it tonight, just for you, and some to be put aside until needed." His companion, obviously hearing only the first part of the sentence, grinned in anticipation.

"I repeat: listen carefully. Very carefully. You're going to kidnap either Marianne Montgomery or Faith Wentworth. The Wentworth chit will be easier to capture." Al's mouth dropped open. Bert held his gaze and continued.

"Miss Faith often takes rambling walks to work, and she doesn't always start first thing in the morning. If her sister leaves before she does at the end of the day, she rambles on the way home, but not so much. One of her favourite routes is past the library." Al's mouth had closed, but his expression still reflected amazement and confusion.

"Here's a bottle of chloroform." He passed it to Al, its long cork firmly in place. Have you ever used it?"

"No, but I sure heard about it." He failed to reach for the small glass container. "Haven't people been killed with it?"

"Indeed they have, which is why you will be careful to pour just enough on the cloth to put one of those women to sleep for a short period of time." Al scratched his head. Bert waited. "And here is the cloth. Wrap the bottle in the cloth and put it in your pocket. Tell me how you'll use it."

"Uh, I'll pour it on the cloth, hold my breath, and hold it over her nose."

"That's almost right. Try holding your breath first, and then dampening the cloth. Be very careful not to breathe it, and don't put it on the cloth until just before you use it. Got that?"

"Yeah, yeah. But *when* do I do this?" Bert held onto his temper with iron control.

"What did I just tell you about her taking walks?"

"She takes them to or from work, and likes to go past the library."

"So where do you think you might do this? Are you just going to walk up to her and push the cloth into her face? After standing in the street in plain sight and pouring the liquid onto the cloth?" Al's face registered disgust and anger.

"I know I'm not the smartest guy in town, Bert, but even I know she mustn't see me putting the stuff on the cloth."

"Very good. Obviously you've figured out that you need to be able to hide until you're ready to make your move. Which of the places I mentioned has some good cover?" But that was asking too much. Al scrunched his face and looked into the middle distance.

"The library, dammit. The library. The bushes by the library. You're right about not being the smartest guy in town, but right now you sound like the stupidest." Bert reined in his temper. If he rattled Al too much, he'd have to start all over again.

"Now, let's review. You see Miss Faith coming down the street. *By the library. The library.* You hold the bottle in one hand, and the cloth in the other." Al nodded. "You're hiding in the bushes." Al nodded again, this time with more confidence.

"The cork is quite long for a reason. Pull it out with your teeth, pour the liquid on the cloth. Drop the bottle and cork, and kick some dirt and leaves over them." Another nod, this time with a smile. "The chloroform will last for a few minutes, so you have time to do this as soon as you see her coming toward you."

"Can we just practice with the bottle and the cloth and the cork? It seems like a lot of things to do in a hurry." Manfully supressing a strong urge to kick Al on whichever body part he could reach first, he nodded. Al carefully put the bottle in his right hand pants pocket; the cloth in the left.

"OK, Bert. I see her coming down the street. I think I should wait until she's about a block away." He looked at Bert for confirmation. The nod of affirmation encouraged him to go on. "I quickly take the bottle and cloth out of my pockets and pull the cork from the bottle with my teeth." He proceeded to do so, inhaled in preparation for his next sentence, and promptly keeled over. Bert moved quickly to rescue both bottle and cork. Al recovered in a few seconds. "What happened?"

"I believe the instructions were *not to breathe* when you removed the cork. Right?"

"Did I breathe? I guess I did, but I don't remember." Seeing signs of a painful reprisal, he hurried on. "I sure won't do that again, Bert. Promise." Bert glowered and dropped some coins into Al's hand.

"Here, take this and buy us a pail of beer. I'll take another tour around the site and we can keep discussing our plan." Pleased, Al promised to return quickly.

"Don't, for God's sake, tell anyone why you're buying the beer or that you're going to share it. It's none of their business. Do you hear me?"

Since the last question was really a threat, Al nodded again and left. Bert could almost see the wheels turning. Al might be dreading punishment for stupid behaviour, but mostly he would think of how great that beer would taste.

✿✿✿

Where is that flibbertigibbet? She really couldn't wait any longer. "Learning to know her new home town" was *not* an acceptable excuse for Faith' constant tardiness. Especially on a morning when they planned to hang up a print showing the development of eyeglasses through the centuries. It promised to generate interest in town, including animated discussions in the barber shop and general store.

Faith or no Faith, she was determined to have it in place and ready to go before the first customer arrived. She thrust the handle of the hammer into her waistband, and put the nails between her lips. Three meant she had an extra if one dropped. Or bent. Really, they seemed to acquire a mind of their own, as soon as she started to apply the hammer. A small towel over the seat of a chair protected it from dust and dirt; the picture propped on the seat and rested against its back. She was ready.

Using the eyeball method so beloved by those who preferred not to spend half a morning measuring, she hammered the second nail into place, firmly convinced it was equidistant from the imaginary centre and in perfect alignment with the first. Success—no injuries and no bent nails. Really, the picture-hanging gods must be on her side. Carefully maintaining her balance, she hooked the wire into place. She stepped off the chair and retreated a few feet to admire her handiwork.

How on earth did I manage to get it on such an angle? I must have been leaning far to the left.

For what she fervently hoped was the last time, she rose again to the height of her morning's ambition. Adjustments made, she concentrated on stepping off the chair and failed to hear Sebastian enter.

"What in the name of all that's holy do you think you're doing," a voice roared.

The hammer flew out of her hand as she tried to grab the back of the chair in an attempt to keep her balance. No need to ask who was there; Nemesis Montgomery was striking again.

Frantic groping notwithstanding, she felt herself falling. Using a vise-like grip at her waist, Sebastian swung her to the floor. Disoriented, she staggered, and clutched the largest thing in sight in an effort to remain upright. Her arms now circled

Sebastian's waist.

He, also thrown off balance by the sudden embrace, put his arms around her back. Two pairs of eyes met. Two bodies seemed to suffer from lack of air. They panted and stared at each other.

Amanda fought to maintain control. She felt particularly fragile. Feminine. Proected. Knowledge she didn't want, tried to ignore, and refused to accept demanded attention. Ever since the picnic, she found herself thinking more and more of Sebastian as a man. A man to whom she reacted strongly. In spite of best efforts to the contrary, the wretch insisted on intruding on her most private moments. Protection from a vital attraction through anger was no longer available.

She had always thought that his shoulders were impressive. But how could she have missed that lush lower lip, or the intriguing mix of green and brown in his eyes. She had no idea that her own light-brown hair and blue-gray eyes were the subject of intense scrutiny. Nor that the softness of her breasts against Sebastian's chest was having a very noticeable effect. She wondered at the hard bump pressing against her abdomen. She inhaled carefully, savoring the unique scent that was his.

Suddenly she was free. And appalled. She had embraced a man. In the middle of the store. Why did she keep thinking *embrace*, a word that implied affection? And why did the location matter? Nothing mattered except the horrifying fact that she had embraced a man. And not just any man. A man who was practically a husband. He belonged to Marianne. He was not on the market, so to speak. And her interest in Mr. Sebastian Montgomery or any other man was non-existent.

As her thoughts whirled, she, too, retreated. Her lips parted as if ready for speech, but she had no idea what to say. Was her face as red as his? *Oh, the poor man. What a fool I am. He saves me from a bad fall and I clutch him like the last spar in a shipwreck.*

Whatever must he think?

He cleared his throat. "Are you all right, Amanda?

"Yes. Thank you." Surely that wispy voice wasn't hers. She watched his mouth in fascination as it came closer and closer. Her eyes started to close. Abruptly she found herself with two feet of space between them.

His voice rose from what had almost been a caress back to its familiar roar.

"How could you be so stupid as to climb on a chair? Were you trying to kill yourself? You know you had only to ask Henry or me. We would have been glad to help you."

Amanda's emotions switched from gratitude and wonder to embarrassment and anger. "Oh, yes? And just who was it who bellowed at the top of his lungs? Who caused me to lose my balance? Who was mortified when I quite naturally grabbed for a support? An unneeded support had you spoken in a polite, conversational voice."

✿✿✿

Sebastian ground his teeth. What was it about this damn fool woman? He was footloose and fancy free. Thanks to his cousin's plotting, he could remain that way for some time longer.

But that didn't explain why his heart leaped into his mouth when he saw That Woman teetering on a chair. Holding a hammer. With a picture at her feet—a picture that contained glass. The hammer might fall and strike the glass, creating dangerous shards that could scatter in all directions. They might fly up and hit her in the face. Or the eye. Or sever an artery in her arm. Or leg. Or fall on the floor, waiting to pierce the sole of her shoe. He couldn't remember if the foot contained an artery, but with her ability to cause the greatest chaos with the least effort, her feet probably had two arteries each.

It also failed to explain why he had yelled—he knew better

than to startle someone on a ladder, or in this case, a chair. And not a sensible kitchen chair with a plain wooden seat. Oh, no, she had to teeter on one with a soft, squishy, rounded cushion. Precisely the way to increase the danger, not to say probability, of creating just such a situation as he now faced.

Why had he clasped her waist, when a hand extended in a gentlemanly and socially correct manner would have done? And pulled her against him? Straight elbows, for God's sake, straight elbows would have kept her at her distance and avoided an inappropriate physical reaction.

Why, when all that soft femininity had grabbed him, had he responded in kind? That had been totally, completely, and wholly unnecessary. Simply maintaining his grip, elbows *not* bent, on her tiny, tiny waist would have allowed her to regain her balance. It must be her scent, which had driven him mad from their first meeting. It was uniquely hers – feminine and exciting.

Why, damn it, he had been about to kiss her?

Because he had.

And to top it all off, his body now sported proof of his undeniable attraction to the minx. He hastened to check that his suit jacket was buttoned properly. Thank God it was a sack suit. At least its length provided some camouflage. He just needed a few minutes to calm down, and all would be well. And socially acceptable. Such an automatic, involuntary reaction to an unexpected event, while embarrassing, was understandable. Especially by other men.

He inhaled mightily and surveyed the scene. The picture still rested on the chair seat. *Seat, yes seat. If I just bow slightly, in a most gentlemanly manner, the camouflage would work better. Then she'll be out of harm's way—and mine.* "Just have a seat, Amanda...Miss...just have a seat. *My God, I sound like an idiot.* "I'll be right back with a glass of water." She suddenly and silently sat on a chair.

Wonder of wonders, she did as she had been told. Too bad she did it so fast. I could have made good use of the extra time. The look on her face was one of amazement. She kept staring at him, wreaking havoc with his "calming down" plan. When had her eyelashes grown to such lengths? Her lips, slightly parted, invited kisses of comfort, et cetera. Especially et cetera in all its ramifications. *Water, get the water, for God's sake. Down, not up, is the goal.*

He turned, intent on getting a glass of the freshest damned water in Marcher Mills. That meant, of course, running the tap long enough to ensure the best possible results. Today there would be none of his usual complaints about how long it took.

Even better, he could chip some ice from the block in the cooler, conveniently located off the back room. That would add another minute. Or so. And if he went through the back room instead of the store, no one would be the wiser.

He found himself face to face with Henry, who had obviously enjoyed the latest in a long line of contretemps. The bastard was grinning openly, savoring every nuance of his employer's dismay.

"Would you like me to fetch that drink, Sebastian?"

"No, thank you." With precise diction and clenched teeth, he continued. "It's the least I can do. Why don't you stay with Amanda? I'm sure she's quite shaken by what has just happened." Henry's grin was quickly replaced by a look of mock concern.

"Oh, I can tell that *Amanda* is just fine. Her smile assures me she has suffered no ill effects." Sebastian looked at Amanda and pretended to frown. "It's you I'm more worried about. You're as pale as a ghost. You almost look frightened. Is it something you've just remembered? Or realized?"

Sebastian's glare would have slain a lesser man. A strategic retreat was a valid military tactic, permitting a regrouping of forces. He informed his fascinated audience that he would return immediately to deliver the promised beverage. What his departure lacked in dignity, it more than made up for in speed. Thoughts of baptizing Henry with the water, instead of giving it to Amanda, crossed his mind.

✿✿✿

Faith breezed into the shop. Her cheery greeting died on her lips when she sensed an atmosphere so thick it seemed tangible.

Henry stood to the right of the doorway, definitely positioned as an onlooker. Amanda, on the other hand, walked back and forth, her hands and arms in constant motion. Faith recognized the repetition of a series of familiar but meaningless gestures revealed extreme agitation.

She brushed imaginary lint off her skirt. Removed and polished her spectacles. Checked to ensure that no stray tendril of hair had escaped its anchor. The most telling part of the ritual was the momentary grasping of the back of her neck, as if for comfort and support, before her hands dropped to her sides, only to begin again. The neck clasp preceded a quick, sideways glance at Henry before checking the doorway one more time.

He alternated stroking his chin with rubbing a finger across his upper lip. This meant he was enjoying whatever had just transpired, but felt it prudent to hide his mirth. Something significant had happened.

Faith concentrated on removing her gloves slowly, easing the fabric off each finger, then smoothing the material, while darting quick glances at her companions. Finally, with gloves precisely aligned and placed in her reticule, she cleared her throat. The others maintained their silence, apparently struck dumb either by what had just occurred or her presence. She did what any caring, concerned and curious sister would do. She pried.

"Amanda, you appear to be quite flushed. Are you ill?"

No response.

Biting her lip, she turned her attention to the room's other occupant.

"Henry, what happened? And don't bother denying it, because both you and Amanda are hiding something. Something I intend to discover."

Henry recovered first.

"Nothing to worry about. A few minutes ago Sebastian startled Amanda when she was practising her chair climbing and nail hammering skills. Naturally, she fell into his arms. Nothing to worry about," he repeated as he withdrew a pristine handkerchief from his jacket pocket and pretended to remove something from his left eye. The handkerchief, manoeuvered with care, failed to obscure his enjoyment of Amanda's indignant response, but did cover his grin.

"Nonsense." She glared at Henry. "Not satisfied with roaring like a bull and causing me to lose my balance, your employer grabbed me about the middle. He claimed he was trying to save me from a bad fall. Which possibly may have been true." The last statement was uttered in a grudging manner.

Her expression showed extreme doubt of such a noble intention. She smoothed her skirt and checked her hair once again. "But if he had not interrupted me in that manner, or, in fact, in any manner at all, I would have been just fine."

Faith gazed at her sister's face, which became rosier and rosier as her explanation progressed.

"Well, I'm glad to see that you appear to be uninjured, but where is the supposed perpetrator of this near-accident? Were those his coattails I saw disappearing around the corner of the back room?"

She waited for a response, lips pursed. Pursing one's lips made it virtually impossible to smile. Amanda had exhibited increasing interest in her nemesis from the date of their arrival in Marcher Mills. She had no idea that her sister and mother followed the progress of the thorny relationship with avidity. Indeed, they frequently dissolved in laughter at the reaction they knew would be forthcoming, should they say so in her presence.

"It is most unlike our intrepid landlord to leave a skirmish before all is resolved," Faith observed. Amanda glowered. Henry appeared overcome by a fit of coughing.

Faith noticed that her companions were looking over her shoulder. She turned to see Sebastian, a glass of water clutched in his right hand. He checked his pace and nodded, greeting her in a perfunctory manner. "Miss Faith." His attention immediately focused on Amanda.

"Amanda, you should be sitting down after such a scare."

The other three occupants of the room observed his actions with interest. A suspicious tinge of pink dusted his cheekbones.

"Here." He drew forward a chair. "Sit and have some water. You'll feel better."

His embarrassment at being the focus of so many eyes showed in his rapid speech and rosy cheeks. Faith began to think the complexions of the two antagonists resembled peonies. Amanda was far from mollified.

"No, thank you. I'm quite recovered. Why don't *you* sit there and have some water and then *you'll* feel better. I still have to hang the picture and tidy up before Wentworth Optometry Services opens for business."

Faith knew that any reference to Wentworth Optometry Services affected Sebastian as a red flag to a bull. She also knew that her sister used it deliberately.

Then Amanda realized that hiking her skirt high enough to permit her to stand on the chair seat would result in an unseemly and immodest display of ankle and even calf. She handed him the hammer.

"On second thought, since you're such an expert, *you* hang the picture."

She turned her back, adjusted her cuffs, and smiled terribly at her audience. "I'm going to have a cup of tea. Faith, you're in charge of Wentworth Optometry Services until I return."

She turned her glance to Henry, inclined her body the least possible degree, and left.

"I've seldom seen such an effective exit," her irrepressible sister murmured, before volunteering to pass the picture to Sebastian.

CHAPTER 25

OCTOBER, 1885

Al heaved a sigh of relief. His busybody landlady who guarded the entrance to her home with the fierceness of a pit bull, stood in the backyard, chatting over the fence with her next-door neighbor. He knew that once those two started, especially on such a warm, sunny day, they would be at it for quite some time. What anyone could find to talk about when their lives were lived mostly on a small plot of land, was a mystery. He would be safe and undisturbed.

After a long and acrimonious battle, plus an extra payment, she had agreed he could supply the lock for his room.

"But if I see or smell anything at all out of the way from there, the lock will be removed. And so will you." She was loud and brash. Personally, Al thought her husband had reaped his reward by his early demise. Usually in his room only to sleep, since Bert had given him his latest assignment he had spent more and more time there. Al knew he wasn't the shiniest apple in the barrel, but Bert's constant derision and snide remarks pricked his pride. He was determined to show the bastard that Al Anderson was a force to be reckoned with.

Currently, his surroundings were unnaturally neat and tidy. He had learned, painfully, that when running experiments in order to acquire the necessary skills for his new task, it paid to make sure that nothing littered the floor, especially the bedclothes.

The first time he tried to improve his cork-removing technique, he stood between the table and the bed, stoppered bottle in one hand, cloth in the other. With a firm clamp of his teeth and dashing fling of his head, the cork flew across the room. Then he started to inhale in preparation for the next part—pouring the drug on the cloth.

He realized his mistake just in time to use his thumb as a plug. A whiff of the chloroform sent him staggering. He caught his foot in the sheets which trailed off the bed and across the linoleum. He fell half on and half off the mattress, and rolled onto the floor. His head collided with the handle of the chamber pot, almost empty, which caused him to see stars and take a bath. But he had kept his thumb on the mouth of the bottle, saving its precious liquid.

Subsequent trial and error led him to practice while sitting behind a table, the chair propped in a corner for additional support.

The second time he tried to refine his method, he maintained his seat. However, he forgot, again, to hold his breath. The resulting dizzy spell produced a small cut over his eye when his head and the fork on the table met with considerable force. Now the table stood in front of the chair—its top clear, if not clean. The problem of its customary clutter had an easy solution. The lamp occupied an unused corner of the room. A simple sweeping motion of his good right arm moved all other objects to the bed.

Multiple tests resulted in a marked reduction of the amount of chloroform. Asking for more was not an option. Much thought let him finally hit upon the idea, brilliant in his estimation, of obtaining another bottle and inserting a cork in its neck. This allowed him to practice his cork-pulling-and-flinging movements. The level of chloroform he felt would allow him to subdue his target was sealed in its original container. His handkerchief, indistinguishable from a well-used floor rag, stood in for the cloth he would use in the actual kidnapping.

After several hours of practice, he could inhale, remove and fling the cork, and make pouring motions towards the handkerchief, all without a second breath. Spitting out the cork had never posed a problem. He only broke three bottles before learning to put a pile of rags beside the chair to cushion their landing.

Bert insisted that once the chloroform saturated the cloth, the bottle was no longer important and could be dropped. But not flung. Only the cork could be flung.

His second incredibly clever idea involved shadowing Miss Faith on her way to and from work. Bert, as usual, was right. Nine times out of ten her route included a stop at the library, currently the only building in an entire city block. Both building and land had been donated by a caring citizen. Lilac bushes made a charming frame, lining the street and perfuming the air as a herald of summer. Grasses and weeds filled in any bare spaces. In the winter it became obvious that ample room existed for people to pass between many of the bushes. During the other seasons, they gave the appearance of a solid wall of green. Fortunately for his plans, early October left sufficient foliage remained to provide cover. Al also noticed that there were fewer people on the street at the end of the day.

Located two blocks behind the main thoroughfare, the library had an intermittent but steady stream of customers from the time it opened in the morning, at eight o'clock, to when it closed, at six. Saturday was the busiest day, as people came to town to do their weekly shopping. The librarians left about thirty minutes after the last customer, and Faith frequently waited for them. Between six fifteen and six-thirty, the usual time for Faith to meet her friend, the street was virtually deserted.

So, now he had the expertise with the chloroform, and enough remained for his purposes. He had chosen four possible places for the completion of his assignment; two on either side of the library. A seldom-used laneway ran behind the building, perfect for the wagon he needed to transport his victim to a pre-selected place a few miles from town. The nights were cool, but not cold. She might be uncomfortable, but she would not be in danger. He had no doubt that she would be found within a couple of days—more than enough time for the rest of Bert's plan to be completed, and for each of them to leave town without suspicion. Bert's insistence that he take the train out of town on different days of the week for the last few weeks ensured that no one would consider him to be leaving forever.

CHAPTER 26

Jenny continued to mull over her choices for killing Bert the Bastard. When she was worried or tried to solve a knotty problem, she knew that physical activity would help. There was nothing left to scour or polish in her house. Even the garden shed, ruthlessly turned out, featured shining windows, no spiders, and every tool cleaned and oiled. She and Stan had planned to paint the shed in the spring. But it took every cent they had just to pay the blackmail. Yet one more reason to hate Bert, blackmailer, bastard and destroyer of families.

The need for action, combined with anxiety about money, gave her courage to enquire if Zeke wished her to clean and organize the small, locked cupboard under the stairs leading to the Marshall's personal quarters. He agreed.

"I can't remember what all is in there, but I do know there are some animal traps. They were supposed to be sprung before storing, but sometimes one or two get missed—or reset as a very unfunny joke. They've been known to break bones or cause nasty injuries, so be especially careful. Keep the key until the job's done." He passed it to her, paused, scratched his chin, and invited her to enjoy the joke.

"Charity and I call that the one-of-these-days-cupboard, because we're always threatening to get to the very back of it one of these days."

Jenny laughed, assured him she would use the utmost caution with anything she found, and began to empty the space. Finally she achieved her goal. The traps, none reset as a bad joke, comprised the major part of the contents. She also discovered two buttons, half of a pair of scissors, spectacles with only one lens, a child's top, a knife, fork and spoon, and a bag containing white powder. Curious as to why it occupied the furthermost corner, she returned it to the cupboard, closed and locked the door, and went to check with Zeke.

Part of her mind kept whispering *poison, let it be poison*, but she refused to believe her luck had changed so much. Good things, and just now poison was a good thing, didn't happen to people like her and Stan. They were grateful if chances for a little extra work occurred even once a year.

"I found a bag of white powder in the cupboard, Zeke, but it isn't labelled. Because it was tied so tightly and placed at the very back, I just peeked in and then tied it up again. Should I throw it out?"

"My God, no! How could I have forgotten about that?" Zeke pulled a handkerchief from his pocket and wiped his perspiring face. "Are you sure you didn't breathe it in? It's strychnine. I got it to kill the mice and rats when we bought the store. Now that we have a couple of cats, rodents aren't a problem. I hid it in the back of that cupboard and locked the door so that no one would use it by mistake."

Jenny blinked, covering her mouth with her hand. *Or on purpose. I could use it on purpose. A good purpose. I'm only trying to protect my family, my children. That's not a bad thing. Surely God will understand.*

Zeke dabbed his face again. Jenny could see that he was quite upset as he plunked himself down on the third stair from the bottom.

"It's OK, Zeke," she hastened to reassure him. "I made sure to keep it as far away as I could. I know that strychnine is nothing to fool around with, and that breathing it can be as fatal as consuming it. I've even heard that if enough of it gets into a cut, it can be just as dangerous." *Thank you God, this is an answer to a prayer.*

"Perhaps it would be better in a tin, then there would be no concern that it might rip. Shall I get one from the store? And glue and paper to label it clearly and add a skull and crossbones?" Zeke still occupied his stair of choice, but the color was back in his face. He had stopped panting, and his breathing had returned to normal.

"Thanks, Jenny. You're a lifesaver—and I mean that literally. Take whichever tin you think is best. I'll get the glue and paper. And cover your mouth and nose when you transfer the poison. Let's not have any accidents."

"Right away. Thanks for the reminder about covering my face. And don't worry about the bag; I'll burn it." *After I remove what I leave in the bottom. Strychnine candy, or cake, or biscuits would do the trick.* She scurried to the shelf holding the tins, grabbed the one that was just that little bit too small, and hurried back to the cupboard. It was important to transfer the powder before Zeke returned with his supplies. She wanted the bag tucked into her apron pocket and safely out of sight as quickly as possible.

✿✿✿

Thoughts of ways and means to use the weapon she was sure that God had granted to stop a monster occupied her mind as her feet took the familiar route from work to home. More and more the idea of incorporating the poison in the coffee that Bert insisted be ground in the store and put in his special container attracted her. She remembered Stan complaining bitterly on more than one occasion that no one dared touch it. Bert marked the level each time he used it. Could she figure out a way to use this information?

Fortunately, in addition to store shelves and cupboards, cleaning the new coffee grinder was one of her duties. Every morning she removed the oily residue left after the coffee made the journey which turned it from hard beans to fragrant grounds. There must be a way to camouflage the poison to render it invisible. Since Bert permitted no one but himself to drink coffee made with his personal supply of grounds, there was no danger of hurting anyone else. But first she had to hide her weapon. Perhaps if she added fresh grounds to the residue she collected when cleaning the coffee mill, she could disguise the white color. The bitter taste of strychnine, further masked by the same flavor in the coffee and the three spoonsful of sugar Bert added would take care of her problem. At last freedom for her family seemed possible.

She decided to wrap the bag in a piece of oilcloth she had thriftily tucked away "just in case" and place it in the bottom of the trunk at the end of her bed. She would tuck the bundle under the quilts and blankets until all the parts of her plan were in place. For the first time in months, she felt able to breathe freely.

In the privacy of his room, Bert rubbed his hands together before pouring a generous measure of fine brandy into a crystal snifter. Earlier this afternoon he had made a quick trip to Hamilton to put the final touches on his plan. The two men hired to set the fires would appear in two days' time. Al was set to get Faith Wentworth tomorrow afternoon. In spite of himself, Bert had been impressed when Al revealed his plan.

He would "borrow" the two-wheeled cart from the Blenkins' farm. They had left for a week to visit their daughter and her new baby in Ottawa. Tucked away in a small barn at the back of their property, it proved easy of access via a track that joined one of the outlying sideroads. An old farm horse, put to pasture as a reward for many years of faithful service, dozed in a field that abutted the building. The harness hung on pegs beside the cart. Al had even found some discarded sacks to hide his passenger, in case someone should encounter him on his way from behind the library to the drop-off point.

After much thought, Bert agreed to leave their victim in the woods a mile past the old barn. Al could drop his passenger, return cart, horse and harness, and make his way back into town in time to be a prominent member of a bucket brigade.

They knew that, as a Londoner, Faith would have no idea of how to find her way in the bush. The hue and cry, which Bert saw as rapidly rising to panic, would keep the town focused on finding and rescuing the young woman. They would have little time to observe strangers alighting from the train. He still regretted that his scheme to loosen a wheel or two on the pumper truck, or even to damage the traces had failed to materialise. But kidnapping the younger Miss Wentworth would provide a fine diversion. Even better, common gossip insisted that, rumors about an engagement to his cousin notwithstanding, Sebastian was sweet on Miss Amanda. He would no doubt take his Montgomery's God-given place at the head of the rescue operation.

The bouquet of the brandy, released by a combination of a swirling motion and the warmth of his hand, caused a smug smile in appreciation of his good taste and anticipation of the Montgomery family finally getting its comeuppance.

In less than a week he would be out of Marcher Mills for good, secure in his alter ego of Bart Stone, up-and-coming businessman in the province's biggest and richest city. "Here's to you, you rotten bastards. May you rot in hell. And if the flames from your buildings get to you first, all the better."

CHAPTER 27

Stan was snoring with his usual enthusiasm, providing excellent cover for any noise Jenny might make. She marvelled once again that anyone could sleep through the ever-increasing volume. At its peak, Stan finished with a snort, smacked his lips, and started again. She made sure to leave the bed in her usual manner. Stan never heard the children call during the night. Trying to sneak out of bed would probably wake him up.

Donning her slippers and robe against autumn's chill, she crouched in front of the chest at the foot of the bed. She lifted the lid just high enough to permit her to slide her hand under the contents and grasp the cool smoothness of the oilcloth in which she had so carefully wrapped her weapon. She eased it across the bottom, up the side. Quickly sliding the bundle into her pocket, she inched the lid closed. A favourite saying of her father's came to mind. "The zookeeper never hears the lion's roar, but knows when a mouse skitters across the floor." Certainly that applied to her when it came to her children, and she had no reason to think that Stan wouldn't be the same with a noise that was out of the usual way of things.

Don't forget to skip the third step from the top. And tread as close to the wall as possible, she reminded herself. Her progress remained steady as she successfully negotiated the steps. The door between the kitchen and the hallway usually stood open, but tonight Jenny grasped the knob and softly pulled it shut. She had oiled the hinges on this and the outside door two days ago in preparation for her plan to save her family. Carefully slipping the latch into place, she took the lamp from the table and repeated the process with the back door.

Once outside, the night air soothed her flushed cheeks, and two deep breaths of its freshness helped to calm her nerves. There was no need to light the lamp until she was safely in the shed. The path from the house was well defined. The moon, in sharp contrast to its backdrop of infinite dark space and outshining the stars, provided more than enough illumination.

As she trod the familiar path, she remembered how hard it had been to get Stan's promise that from now on he would say good night to their daughter from the doorway of her room. He was hurt at what he saw as her lack of trust. She was hurt that she had to ask for it, but she wanted no grounds for anyone to accuse the Biltmore family of irregular behaviour.

Part of her wanted to ask for God's help to stop the monster who was threatening her family, but no amount of justification removed the fact that she planned to kill another human being.

Once inside the shed she crouched and carefully removed the potato sacks, freshly washed and ready for this year's crop, from under the work bench. Two sacks per window should dim the light sufficiently. Again her hand snaked under the bench to pull out a wooden tray filled with dirt. Only then did she grope behind some tins of paint for matches hidden earlier in the day. Striking one on the rough side of the tray, she lifted the glass and turned up the wick the smallest possible amount. The resultant glow satisfied her need to see without advertising her presence. As an added precaution, she kept the lamp on the floor. The many hours devising her strategy focused strongly on safety.

One of Stan's clean handkerchiefs, folded into a triangle and tied over her mouth and nose with a firm double knot at the back of her head, reduced significantly the possible danger of inhaling the strychnine. Carefully placing the package in the middle of the dirt tray, she gently helped the oilcloth, softened through much use, to fall away from the bag it had protected. She rose and grasped a tin from the shelf between the door and window. The delicious scent of freshly-ground coffee filled the air with its invigorating and inviting perfume. The soft light illumed a woman whose night braid fell fuzzily down her back creating a poignant vignette of domesticity—a sharp contrast to the hopes which governed her actions.

The rag covered with coffee oil and residue from the store's coffee mill was hidden inside. Using extreme caution, and slow, controlled movements, she poured the strychnine onto the rag. She returned the rag to the oilcloth, rewrapped it, and rubbed her hands vigorously over the outside. Then she repeated the process of pouring the poison onto the rag, this time adding coffee grounds. Long thought suggested that the grounds would assist in removing any errant bits of colour, oil and poison. She would return the bag to its hiding place until she was alone in the house and burn it in the stove. Better still, she would make a point of lighting a pile of garden waste, add some kerosene, and incinerate the bag in the open air. The ashes could be spread on the flower garden, well away from the vegetables. *No sense in taking chances.*

Returning to the task at hand, she added two more spoonsful of coffee grounds to the rag, folded it carefully, and placed it in a jar with a tight lid. *If some is good, more must be better.*

Placing the fruits of her nocturnal labour in the pockets of her robe, she dumped the dirt in the privy before returning the tray to its hiding place under the workbench. She would take care to burn the tray with the bag.

She opened the kitchen door, crept upstairs, and hid her booty in the bottom of the chest. After carefully folding her robe and hanging it over the footboard, she aligned her slippers carefully, and crept into bed. *A job well done* was her last conscious thought.

✿✿✿

"Good-bye, Mother. Don't forget I'm dining with Marianne tonight. She's promised to send me home in a carriage." No response.

"Mother, did you hear me?" Footsteps hurried along the upstairs hall.

"Yes, yes, dear. Sorry, I had my head in the closet looking for a scarf I'm sure I put there when we arrived. I'll expect you home by nine o'clock."

Faith, secure in the knowledge that her mother couldn't see her expression, rolled her eyes. She made sure that her exasperation at what she termed her mother's "cloying care" did not sound in her voice. "Just as we agreed, and you may set the clock by my prompt arrival. Good-bye," she called again and whisked out the door before any other admonitions or reminders should occur to her hovering parent.

Twenty minutes later, sandwich and apple safely stored in the cold room, she checked her appearance in front of the small mirror Amanda had insisted be installed in the back room. Her new suit, featuring a cuirass bodice, represented an appreciable amount of work and time. She admired her good taste once again, twitched her skirt to ensure that the folds fell exactly right, and entered Wentworth Optometry Services.

Her sister stood beside the display of colored eyeglasses, speaking quietly with a client. This particular customer took great offense at what she perceived as wandering attention on the part of those serving her always important and urgent needs. Faith lowered the hand she had raised to get Amanda's attention.

Avoiding the customer's line of sight, she went to the desk to check the appointment book, gratified to see three examinations scheduled; one this morning, and two for the afternoon. Her gratification increased when she realised that the second appointment finished before six o'clock.

Parental permission for tonight's meeting and dinner with Marianne marked a major improvement in her mother's returning health. Since the Wentworths had settled in their new home, Amanda and Faith had become increasingly aware of their mother as a wife grieving a beloved spouse. The sisters grew closer, shared their thoughts and tears, but resolutely presented a united, cheerful, and positive façade to their mother. Amanda began treating Faith as an adult, and not a younger sibling. Elizabeth's collapse, once settled in her new home, had frightened them badly.

Gladys was a godsend—a perfect antidote to melancholia. She came for tea, encouraged her new friend to go for quiet walks, and gradually included her in many social aspects of Marcher Mills. Her kindnesses freed them to establish themselves in the business community. They feared that after the first flurry of appointments and orders, the charm of their newness would wear off, increasing the difficulty of balancing both business and personal budgets on a sharply-reduced income.

Even as she mused and created busy work in order to avoid hovering, she kept one ear open to the murmur of voices in the background. Reiterated "good-byes" from both parties caused her to smile. Judging by the tones, the transaction had come to a satisfactory conclusion. She returned to her thoughts.

The inhabitants of Marcher Mills showed an agreeable willingness to take care of their visual health. Her suggestion that they add glasses in pink, blue, green, and amber as protection against the sun had turned out to be very profitable. The ladies purchased them for comfort and to avoid excessive wrinkling around their eyes. The gentlemen found that wearing them improved vision and added to their comfort. Many embraced the idea of fewer wrinkles, but none would admit it on pain of the rack.

Amanda returned from escorting their customer to the door. Faith forestalled her greeting with a happy reminder. "Did you remember that I have to leave a few minutes early today?"

She could hardly contain her glee. Marianne's suggestion that they hold a key strategy meeting on various ways and means of getting Amanda and Sebastian to admit their mutual attraction promised to be great fun.

When Marianne's real fiancé, Durwood Bosworth, had visited her in Marcher Mills, she and Sebastian relinquished their "protection through false fiancée" plan. Sebastian's rating as the community's most eligible bachelor soared to its previous peak. He frequently confided to his cousin that the vultures were circling. The two young ladies had some very innovative ideas about removing the harried look on Sebastian's face when confronted by a contender for his affections. Their scheme relied on the stubbornness of the parties involved.

"No, dear sister, I have *not* forgotten that you and Marianne have arranged for an evening together. Nor have I forgotten our agreement that you could leave ten minutes early, so I expect to see your back at ten to six exactly." She walked to the desk and removed a ledger from the top drawer. "Come and look at the figures for the past five months. In spite of our worries, and even though there is some fluctuation, we've been doing quite well."

"I know. Have you checked the other ledger—the one showing our personal funds? We've not only met all our expenses, but there is a small amount we could transfer to a savings account. What do you think?" Amanda drew out the second book and they perused the information together.

At precisely ten to six, Faith opened the door, turned, waved to Amanda, and scooted. Marianne had suggested the library as a meeting place, as she had to return some books. Faith agreed with alacrity. It was time to choose the name of another town for her collection of strange place names.

CHAPTER 28

The horse decided that a slow amble was his speed of choice, and no amount of coaxing, yelling, or swearing on the driver's part changed his mind. Resigned to his fate, Al used the trip to review his Great Plan. Over the past few weeks, he had added the capital letters to acknowledge the enormous amount of energy and thinking required. After all, if he could concoct one such Plan, who knew what the future might hold? He rarely felt proud of himself, but now realised that there was no limit to what he might do in the future. And to hell with Bert the Bastard and his nasty comments.

Brisk autumn air ensured that his walk to the farm had been pleasant. For the most part, he avoided roads and cut across country. There were so many rabbits that the urge to set snares was almost overwhelming. He knew several places in town where fresh rabbit delivered to a kitchen door meant sufficient funds for a beer or two. He sighed. Not today. Today he was determined to show that his ability to help create and follow through with a plan matched anyone's in the county. Excitement at projected success kept the spring in his step.

Dobbin, as he had temporarily named his plodding steed, proved amenable to wearing a harness and working again. An apple distracted him long enough to snap a line onto his halter and lead him to the building. The sacks in the bottom of the cart were unremarkable and found in virtually every barn. He made sure to bring twice as many as he thought he might need, acknowledging the necessity of covering her in the quickest possible manner.

Neatness didn't count. He patted his pocket. The bottle of chloroform was safe. A squeeze of the opposite pocket assured him that the rag to apply the drug rested in readiness. This mission would be an unqualified success.

Finding a spot to drop Miss Faith that was isolated, yet not too far from Dobbin's barn, posed no problem. Bert had explained at length the importance of being where people would expect to see him. Al's reputation guaranteed him a place at the top of the list of probable culprits, which meant he had to maintain his usual routine.

The problem was, of course, Bert, who seemed hell bent on finding something wrong with every suggestion, even though Al was the man who had visited each proposed site. But at last Bert was satisfied. They agreed that even if it took three or four days to rescue her—she would probably wander in circles—the temperature never got close to freezing at night. Besides, with those armored corsets and layers and layers of petticoats and whatever else they thought necessary, any woman would survive a chilly night or two. If she didn't know how to forage, then she could damn well go hungry.

Al's focus remained on the money promised for a successful completion of the job, an iron-clad alibi, and plans to leave town without stirring up a hornet's nest of gossip and speculation. It really didn't matter where he went. The large sum he would receive guaranteed lots of beer. The absence of Bert and his schemes in his future would be more than welcome.

He turned into the laneway behind the library, nodding with satisfaction at the barely-visible wheel ruts. *If anyone's been here in the last month, I'll eat my hat.*

He stopped with the cart in perfect alignment with the opening he reckoned as the best. He was sure it allowed room for a man with a body over his shoulder to slide through. The thin line of lilac bushes still sported most of their leaves. The fact that his Great Plan had failed to consider the bulk of skirts and petticoats, or the height and adornment of ladies' hats reflected his lack of social interaction with females.

To prevent any chance of his steed's going after a particularly juicy clump of grass, he gave Dobbin a nosebag containing a generous supply of oats. A lead fastened to a large brick and clipped onto the bridle made him confident that his transportation would be available. The horse's age and eager interest in the contents of the feedbag meant one less thing to worry about.

Checking the contents of his pockets yet again, he took a position behind the hedge, to one side of the gap. It gave a clear view from the corner to the library. He knew that he had to be able to see the woman coming down the street.

And sure enough, there she is. Move faster, bitch.

"Come on, come on, dammit woman. Get a move on." His patience, always in short supply, was waning quickly. Realising that he could hear himself, he clamped his lips shut. *What the hell is she doing, stopping so often, and looking around? There's nothing to see. If you can't kill it, eat it, or sell it, why bother?*

He held his tools at the ready: bottle in the right hand; cloth in the left. Finally she passed his hiding place. With practised ease and a gratifying sense of accomplishment, he inhaled, clamped his teeth on the cork, flung it wide, emptied the remaining chloroform onto the cloth, dropped the empty bottle, and eased between the bushes. Moving quietly, he gave himself a mental pat on the back for a job well done.

Yessir, Bert, it's shame you ain't here.

Faith remained oblivious to his presence. He rushed up behind her and flung one arm around her torso to keep her arms from flailing as he clapped the cloth over her mouth. Her body arched and she tried to kick. Best of all, she inhaled to scream, speeding her path to unconsciousness.

Her head fell forward, followed by her upper body, and she folded almost in half over his arm. He removed the cloth from her face and was about to sling her over his shoulder when he heard a shriek.

"Put her down, you monster. Help, help!"

Shit, it's that damned Montgomery woman. Now what will I do?

He dropped Faith. Tightened his grip on the cloth. And ran to meet Marianne.

"Here, bitch, you have some, too." With that, he grabbed her hair and forced the cloth against her face, ignoring thrashing arms and legs. No frail flower, Marianne used her parasol as a weapon, whacking him on the head before poking him in the belly. He ducked to throw off her aim, wrenched the thing from her hands, and threw it aside. He failed to see that it landed beside the walkway. Denied her substitute sword, she swung her reticule and connected with his left eye. With both hands full of fighting female, he closed the injured eye and felt the tears trickle down his cheek, over his chin, and onto his coat.

His prisoner was slowing down, but a glancing kick to his crotch almost brought him to his knees. Making a herculean effort to remain upright and not whimper, he responded with a well-placed punch to the side of her head. That, combined with the chloroform, finally rendered her unconscious.

Oh my God. Now I've two of the damned bitches to manage. And they're lying in the street for anyone to see.

Panic-stricken with fear, he tossed Marianne over his shoulder. Staggering the few steps to his other victim, he became aware of another problem.

Why the hell can't I have an extra arm? And goddam that Bert for insisting on no injuries. If I drag her by an arm, I might dislocate her shoulder. Shit. Shit. SHIT!

Okay, her leg. I can grab her ankle. He did so, only watch in horror as her skirt rose higher and higher. *Now God will punish me for being lewd.*

As a compromise, he obtained a vise-like grip on the neck of Faith's jacket and lurched toward his hole in the hedge.

Panting and listing to one side, he tried to drag his burdens through the bushes. Why was it so much smaller than when he charged through to attack his first victim?

Okay. Okay. I can do this if I angle my shoulder and go slowly. And lean forward so her damned hair doesn't catch on any twigs or branches.

One step forward and he was stuck. *Bend more.* This time he stepped on Marianne's skirt. Felt her body start to slide backwards.

No, no, don't fall. Fear threatened to overwhelm him.

Think, dammit, think. If you can make a Great Plan, you can do this.

Releasing his grip on Faith, he reversed direction and lowered Marianne to the ground. Panting and swearing, he grabbed her under the arms and tried pulling, instead of carrying. One step. Two steps. Damn—the woman refused to cooperate. Again.

Digging in his heels, he gave a mighty heave, lost his grip, and sat on a sharp stone. He ignored the pain, kicked the stone, and concentrated on the task in hand—one down and one to go.

Tempted as he was to get Marianne into the cart, he had to get Faith's body on this side of the barrier in order to escape detection. Rolling Marianne out of the way, he headed back for the second, only to notice that a sizable amount of her hair hung on a branch. No wonder she hadn't been cooperating with the Great Plan.

Hah! Gotcha! No flies on Mrs. Anderson's little boy.

He carefully removed the hair and put it in his pocket.

All right, bitch, your turn next.

Recalling once more Bert's instructions about not harming his victim, he lifted Faith in his arms. Stalemate.

Her length exceeded the width of the gap. Her shoulders and head hung over on one end; her lower legs and feet, on the other. Turning his body to permit either the top or bottom of her to go through was futile. Al plus Faith equalled one body too many.

Don't hurt her. Don't hurt her. Well, to hell with you, Bert. You're not here and trying to cope with two of them.

Swearing vehemently, he lowered her to the ground and reverted to the same method used with Marianne. He grabbed her under the arms, dug in his heels, grunted and heaved. The sweat ran down his face, tickled his cheeks, and interfered with his vision.

The combination of sweat and the poke in the eye he had received from the Montgomery bitch added to his rage and discomfort. He swiped a sleeve across his forehead to stop the drip and prepared to drag his trophy to the right side of the bushes. Once again his victim left a token of her passage—a glove had snagged on a protruding root.

Incipient hysteria added strength to muscles unaccustomed to such vigorous action. Her shoulders were through. Her torso was through. Success. Almost. As he prepared for the final pull, his foot slipped on the empty chloroform bottle. Losing temper, balance, and grip, he now sat in a patch of thistles. Consumed by the frustration of the moment, he released a string of world-class swear words, scrambled to his feet, kicked the bottle out of the way and yanked Faith the last two feet.

Good—now I'm on the home stretch.

Running to the cart, he dumped the sacks on the ground before dashing back to pick up one of the women. He was so rattled he had no idea which one he held. He dumped her into the wagon, then sprinted back for the other one. Taking time only to ensure that they were side by side and face up, he remembered to check that they each still wore a hat and carried a reticule. Frantically arranging the sacks to cover his cargo, he removed the nosebag, and leaped onto the driver's seat.

Good—not a clue to help those bastards figure out what I've done. You're a star, Al.

He slapped the reins on Dobbin's back. Obedient to the signal, the horse started forward.

Movement helped Al to settle down. Briefly. Suddenly Dobbin turned to the left.

"Whoa. Whoa, dammit. What the hell do you think you're doing?" Just before he used the ends of the reins as a whip, he realised that they would continue to circle until he detached the brick meant to keep Dobbin in place. Leaping to the ground, he unclipped the lead, ignored the brick, clambered back up to his perch, and got them on their way once more.

Beside himself at the near collapse of his Great Plan, terrified that someone might see or hear them, he flapped the reins with vigor and chirruped encouragement to the point of almost swallowing his tongue. Dobbin responded to the undeserved indignity by taking off with a jerk that practically toppled Al over the back of the seat and onto his cargo.

✿✿✿

Why can't I turn over? Cold. She was so cold. The draft whisked tendrils of her hair across her face, tickling her nose. A cool freshness to aid in getting a good night's sleep did not include a biting wind. She became aware of a faint rustling sound. Then a creaking noise. A squeak. *Squeak? Is there a mouse in my room?*

What was poking her in the back? It felt like a rock, but how could a rock get into her bed? She groped for her blanket. Her hand encountered wool, but something was wrong. She struggled to sit up and get a better grip.

She gave up pretending that cold and an uncooperative blanket accounted for the weight on her legs. Why was her upper body free to move, and her legs weighted down? Shivering, she struggled to pull the cover up to snuggle around her shoulders. Changing the angle of her grip, she felt something bumpy. Like beads. Beads? Beads on a blanket?

It was at that point she knew the irritating moaning sound was not the wind in the eaves, but a human voice. *A nightmare. I'm having a nightmare. I must wake up.* The moaning increased in volume, closely followed by the sound of retching.

Oh, God, now I need to be sick. Why can't I move? My eyes are open but I can't see anything, not even the thin bar of light under the door from the lamp at the top of the stairs. The wind tried to slide down her back. Frantic at the rising nausea, she grasped a handful of the non-blanket and pulled herself to a sitting position.

"Ouch," said the blanket.

"Marianne, is that you? Where are we? What happened? I'm going to be sick." She twisted to the side and suited action to words.

"Are you finished? I understand just how you feel. The answer is yes to your first question, and I don't know, to the second. If you release the death grip on my suit jacket, I can get up. I think." A soft grunt reflected considerable effort expended.

"We seem to be outside, but I have no idea where. The last thing I remember is coming to meet you at the library. It was to be a night of revelry and scheming."

"The last thing *I* remember is Al Anderson shoving a filthy rag in my face."

"Al Anderson? The creep who hangs around with Bert Stiles?" Faith's confusion increased. "How did Al Anderson get into this conversation?"

"He arrived via his successful attempt to subdue you. I guess

I was a bonus. But at least I whacked him with my parasol and hit him in the face with my reticule. I hope the bastard has a black eye."

Faith, concentrating on making some sense of the situation, ignored Marianne's retelling of the battle. Very carefully she rolled over and sat up. Standing up did not appear to be advisable just at the moment. Her mind was muzzy, her brain barely functioned, and the wind took fiendish delight in piercing her clothing and chilling more parts of her body.

"I thought I was in the middle of a horrible nightmare, but it would definitely be an improvement on our current situation. At least I could make a nice hot cup of tea." She wrapped her arms around her middle. " I'm freezing, Marianne. Are you?"

"Absolutely. I'd give anything for a shawl. I'm also totally confused as to why he would chloroform you—I recognized the smell. I know why he chloroformed me, but judging from the bump on the side of my head, he also punched me."

"Well, don't look at me for an answer. I have no idea why we're here. And speaking of that, where *is* here?"

"The leaves on the ground would indicate we're in the woods. Lost in the woods, I imagine."

"Yes, yes, I *know* we're in the woods, but *where* in the woods?" Discomfort and fear combined to make Faith cranky and impatient. Her friend obviously felt the same.

"How should I know? I'm chilled to the bone, tired, nauseous, and scared. My only comfort is that there are no poisonous snakes around here."

Faith decided to keep the information about rattlesnakes and their venom to herself. Besides, if they were still close to the town, the chances of encountering one, especially with the cool temperature, were remote. *Hear that, snakes?* But she could offer a little comfort to her friend.

"Well, even if there were, snakes like to be warm. I'm sure they're all tucked in for the winter." *I hope she doesn't realise that while the nights are cold, the temperature rises considerably during the day. Many a snake could take advantage of a comfortable rock and the sun.*

"What do you suggest we do? Apart from the bump on my head and a distressing wish to throw up again, all my body parts seem to be in working order."

Faith wondered how she had become the leader of the expedition. "Well, we can't do anything in the dark. My symptoms match yours, with the exception of the bump on the head. Let me think." *Think of what? My knowledge of the wilderness is precisely zero.* "Why don't we find a tree we can use for a back rest, and huddle for warmth. In the morning we can look for a stream and at least get a drink."

"Of course. Why didn't I think of that? And if we follow that stream we should come to a farm or town. Eventually." Marianne's voice, which began as robust and enthusiastic, dwindled sharply on the last word. Faith refused to give in to her own fears or those of her friend.

"Right. Now, a sturdy tree must be close. Take my hand so we don't bump into each other or get separated. We can do this, Marianne. Women can do anything." Hands clasped, the duo began their search.

A mournful hoot caused them to jump. "An owl, it's just an owl. They hunt at night."

"Right. I knew that. They do the same thing in Australia."

"Never mind a lecture on the birds of Australia. Find a tree." Faith reflected on her words and tone. "Sorry, I'm just a little overwhelmed."

"Wait. The ground seems different, here. Let me feel." Marianne crouched and ran her hand over the unknown object.

"It's cloth. I'm picking it up." Faith' dropped her friend's hand to help. Together they carefully explored the perimeter.

"Let's shake it out in case some insect finds it attractive. Whew, it smells like dust."

"Yes, and I know just what that dust is. This is a feed sack. A *warm* feed sack. I wonder if there are any more." Marianne folded and tucked it under her arm. The friends crouched and began patting the ground.

"Eau de grain dust—we'll be irresistible." Faith heard her friend giggle.

"To a horse."

"Damn."

"What's wrong? Are you hurt?

"No, but there is quite a sturdy thistle over here. However, since it's beside another sack, I'm inclined to be forgiving."

"And at the small cost of a stubbed toe, caused by a rock that leaped in front of my foot, I've found two more. Give me your hand, and we'll find a friendly tree."

"Right. Just lead me to it. We can use one sack to sit on, put one around our shoulders, and share one over our laps. It will be cosy, but at this point, warmth is our goal."

Hands clasped, the two young women shuffled in their search for a tree. Faith' foot caught in a bramble runner, causing her to drop the sacks. Marianne found a puddle or a small creek with her right foot. At last, shoulders touching, the two friends huddled against their chosen tree and waited for the dawn.

CHAPTER 29

Bert watched as Al rushed into the shack at the construction site only to pop out moments later. He looked around, a smirk on his face. In order to avoid the inevitable clarion call of "I done it" ringing over the site, Bert stepped out from behind the only remaining pile of building supplies.

"Over here, Al. Quietly, for God's sake." Al, jaw dropped and chest expanded in preparation for a shout, shut his mouth, exhaled, and hurried to tell his tale, panting with excitement. Bert just hoped to God that Al remembered he was to keep hidden from the busybodies. Someone would be sure to tell the world that Al Anderson had been seen creeping *back* into town.

"I done it, Bert. I done it. Just as smooth as cream. The two bitches are right where you said to put them."

"Bitches? More than one? Al, what have you done?" He was able to control the volume, but his expression caused Al to flinch and step back.

"Just what you said, Bert. I don't know why you're so angry. I remember that you said it might be necessary to grab both Miss Faith and her friend. You know you did." Al maintained a prudent distance, obviously mindful of the well-known axiom that the more space between you and an angry Bert, the better.

"All right, Al." Bert took a deep breath and lowered his fists. "Just tell me exactly what you did." Eager to receive praise, Al complied.

"I got the horse and cart, just like we planned. I cut through the woods so as no one could see me. It was a shame I couldn't take the time to set a few snares, though, because them rabbits just kept beggin' to be in somebody's dinner pot."

"Never mind the damned rabbits. Tell me what you did." Bert was now grinding his teeth. Al prepared to enjoy the telling of his tale.

"Well, like I said, I got the horse and cart and set them behind the library. I remembered the sacks, too." He stopped to give himself a mental pat on the back, then hurried on with his story.

"Like I said, it was goin' smooth as cream. I made sure the horse couldn't get away, checked that the stuff was in my pockets, and hid behind the lilac bushes."

Bert gave Al a moment to contemplate the glory of his magnificent performance.

"And then it happened. She came walkin' down the street, gawkin' at who knows what. Never could understand why wimmin can't just walk." A growl encouraged him to finish.

"Nobody else was in sight. As soon as she passed, I whipped up behind her and shoved the cloth in her face."

"I'm assuming that you're talking about the Wentworth woman. But what about the other woman? What. Other. Woman?" He shoved his hands in his pockets to keep them off Al's neck, even as his quarry backed up a couple of steps.

"Well, you see, Bert, I had no sooner got that Wentworth woman asleep, when I heard the other one whoopin' and hollerin'. And you should have seen me pull the cork, fling it out of the way, wet the cloth and drop the bottle. All without a breath." His chest swelled at the remembered glory, but Bert's red face and bulging eyes brought him back to the present. He increased his rate of speech and edged back another step.

"Sorry, Bert. Of course that was for the first one. The second one had come out of the library. I just ran up to her and shoved the cloth into her face." A small pause for breath, then he resumed.

"She was some fighter, but a clout on the side of her head shut her up."

Bert knew Al longed to boast of his solution to getting the women through the hedge and into the cart. He also knew that his life was in danger if he spun the story out.

"I dragged them through the hedge, dumped them into the cart, covered them with the sacks, and took them to that spot in the woods—just where we planned."

He stopped talking and grinned. Put his hands in his pockets and rocked back on his heels, obviously waiting for a word or two of praise. But Bert's focus was on other things.

"*Who* was the other woman?"

Al backed up another few paces and provided the answer.

"That Montgomery girl. The one you said hung around with the Wentworth bitch. You know, Bert. You told me about her." He backed up a little further.

"I don't know why you're so mad. I done just what you said. I made sure nobody saw me do it. The horse and cart are back in place with no one the wiser." His voice rose to match his sense of ill-usage.

"And not only that, I didn't stop for them rabbits that was just beggin' to be caught, but came straight back to report, *just like you said.*"

Through the red haze of his frustration at dealing with such a consummate ass, Bert realised that some praise of Al's accomplishment should be forthcoming. He still might be useful before everything was completed.

The plans were coming along nicely. The girls, tucked out of sight, formed an excellent diversion. The community would respond with its usual speed. The fires would start during the very early hours of tomorrow morning. Because the search parties would have expanded their areas to sites out of town, the volunteer fire brigade would take even longer than usual to form.

He contemplated returning to his scheme of cutting the reins and loosening a wheel on the pumper truck. But, knowing Phil Landers' legendary attention to detail, the rig would have someone watching it. Better to leave well enough alone.

He permitted himself a smile. If Al thought it related to his, admittedly, completed assignment, no harm done. Between the missing women and raging fires, a full crew of volunteer firefighters would be hard to assemble. The Montgomery house and pharmacy, located several blocks from each other, would divide the fire crew. Therefore, the total destruction of the two factories seemed inevitable.

Bert's mind sifted, readjusted and rearranged his plans, now that Idiot Al had been seen by Marianne Montgomery. Al would have to leave immediately, and on foot. Bert would guarantee Al's disappearance forever—his lack of brains and big mouth made him a considerable risk. But first he had to regain control of the situation. If Al thought something made sense, he would follow directions. Otherwise, he would argue and argue.

Months of meticulous planning jettisoned because of that idiot. Even through his rage, Bert remembered that the tentacles of his network reached far into the underbelly of Hamilton's criminal element.

To guarantee someone noted him as part of a search team or bucket brigade, he would make a point of talking to as many people as possible. Rumors of the ill will he had nursed for so long against the Montgomerys would surge, but his alibi would be rock solid.

Then he remembered Stan Biltmore and his wife strolling on the other side of the street just before he spoke with Al. Recreating the scene in his mind, he relaxed with the realization that they had no idea anyone else was on the job site.

Things were falling into place. But first there was more pressing business. He turned to address his biggest problem.

"Al, you need to leave Marcher Mills right now. Immediately. No questions asked. Here's fifty dollars to get you to Hamilton. Go to the Dog and Duck, you know where it is, and ask for the Jubal, the owner. He will give you a place to stay."

"But Bert, what about my stuff? I need to get my stuff."

Bert clamped down on the rage that threatened to overwhelm him. "Listen to me, Al. Marianne Montgomery *saw* you. Sometimes people don't remember things that happened just before a blow on the head. Sometimes they do. Sometimes they don't remember it right away, but later it all comes back to them." He raised his hand to forestall Al's objections.

"I'll have your things packed and sent to you. The money in your pocket, a bonus for a job well done, will get you all the clothes you need. It's only for two or three days until I can join you."

Al still showed signs of objecting to such an abrupt change of plans. Bert decided to let him have a sentence or two, just to calm him down. Push Al too hard and the stubbornness of stupidity settled in; then nothing would convince him to act against what he knew. When Al finished sputtering and expostulating, Bert continued.

"You know that there are a couple of men here to set the fires." Al nodded. Go through the woods until you are at least a mile out of town. I'll have them pick you up and give you a lift to the next railway stop.

"No one will recognize you in Hamilton, and it's big enough that strangers are of no particular interest." At last Al was nodding and smiling as he realised he would benefit from this financially. Bert knew that he thought in terms of pints of beer and good times, not next week or next month.

"Remember, *do not go home.* You must leave right now. No one has seen you since this afternoon." He watched Al check for observers as he headed across the road and into the bush away from Marcher Mills.

✿✿✿

Jenny and Stan strolled slowly along the main street. Their oldest daughter, Susie, had suggested, hinted, and almost badgered them about "the most beautiful hat in the whole wide world." Her birthday was next Wednesday, and they wanted to see if it would make an appropriate gift for a young lady of thirteen years.

Stan had promised to show Jenny the shack where he had spent so many Sundays. Little did he know that she was very familiar with it. And Bert's coffee tin. A few hours' of lost sleep were a small price to pay for the knowledge that the poison was finally in place. Soon Bert would be dead and her little family would be safe.

Bert, it appeared, did not have coffee there every day, but Jenny could wait. Justice would be sweeter for waiting. More time to anticipate and enjoy. Bert the Bastard would be no more. Marcher Mills and its inhabitants would benefit.

Jenny had spent a great many hours thinking about Bert. She had long since concluded that her family could not possibly be his only victims. Really, killing him provided a service to all and sundry—a boon to the community. Twinges of conscience died when she contemplated the damage caused by discovery of the Biltmore family's secrets.

CHAPTER 30

The fall and winter seasons got colder every year. And damp. *I'm getting too old for this out-of-town-and-in-the-country crap.* So far, so good. They had been the only ones in the passenger car. Cuddy almost fell into a seat as the train gave an unexpected lurch. Grasping the handrails beside the steps, he turned his head and addressed his companion. "Now for God's sake, Jude, be careful. You sure as hell don't want to break the bottles in your pockets. The rags around them make good wicks but are bloody useless as protection against cuts."

"Yeah, yeah. Christ A'mighty, you're like an old woman.

"Well then move, Jude, you stupid bastard, so we can get this over with."

Thoughts of the large amount of money waiting for him and Jude when they returned to the Dog and Duck acted as an incentive. He checked again to make sure the water tower was on the other side of the train. Bert had assured him that only a thin line of trees and small bushes screened the rail bed from the road leading to Marcher Mills. Keep the water tower behind him, and he'd head straight for the road. Starlight showed a slightly blacker line a few yards away.

"Those bushes Bert promised are real close, Jude. This is the first time I've hopped off a train when I had a ticket," He descended the steps, and jumped. Bending his knees to lessen the impact, he teetered once, then headed for cover.

He heard Jude grunt as he landed heavily. Caught the whisper of cloth and faint sound of steps. *Thank God we'll be done tonight and collect the rest of our pay from Jubal at the Dog and Duck. That stupid bastard didn't even ask if the remainder of our pay had arrived. Too bad Jubal will dole it out equally. But I should get more for being the brains of the outfit.*

"Where the hell did you go?"

Cuddy had suffered numerous repetitions of complaints about jumping off a train as it stopped for water and hiding in bushes. He knew Jude hated the country. It was full of things that bit, or howled, or made strange noises. Things hidden by a lot of bushes and leaves and other *green* things. *All this bloody fresh air, and not a pub in sight* had been another complaint. Jude just wanted to get the god-damned job done and return to civilisation. Cuddy couldn't argue with that.

"Keep your shirt on. You're almost here. Veer a little to the right."

Jude dutifully angled to his right.

"Not *your* right, asshole, *my* right."

"OK, OK, don't get your knickers in a knot. Can't see a bloody thing. Wish to God we had a light out here in the wilderness."

"Shut your cake hole. Two more steps and we can share the bush. We're damned lucky that the water tower is only half a mile from Marcher Mills. As soon as the train pulls out, we go a few more steps to the road, and turn right. In fifteen minutes we'll be getting our supplies." But Jude had more to say.

"Do you have the map? It's not hard to find the factories or the pharmacy on the main street, but getting to that house he wants fired would be impossible without it."

"Yes, yes, I told you I had the map. It's safe in my pocket." Jude still wasn't finished.

"And that's another thing, Cuddy. Why the hell do we have to cart the coal oil from the shed at the back of the general store all the way to the house?"

"Because, you dumb ass, that's the way Bert wants it. Just be glad he's made arrangements to conceal the fuel near the factories so we don't have to tote it there. Besides, a couple of gallons spread on the boardwalk and storefronts will do the job."

As soon as the last rail car passed, they began walking towards the town.

"Listen, is that a horse?"

They leaped for the bushes lining the road, and landed in a ditch containing just enough water to cover the tops of their boots. They crouched and watched a horse and buggy trot past. When the clop-clop of hooves had faded, they returned to the road.

"Jesus H. Christ. When will it stop? Now my god-damned feet are wet. I *hate* it when my feet slip in my boots."

"Shut up, Jude. Think of all that lovely money waiting for us. It's not often that we make this much on one job. Nifty Nancy will be more than happy to help me drink and carouse. Especially carouse. She has the biggest…."

"Yeah, yeah. You've told me a hundred times. I don't care how big her tits are. Saucy Sara gives a much better ride." The conversation continued with fond reminiscences and fewer recriminations until they reached the edge of town.

✿✿✿

Tick, tick, tick. No matter how many times Amanda checked, time ticked on at its irritatingly slow pace. She could understand that her sister might be a few minutes late, but she should have been charging in the front door at least thirty minutes ago, apologies spilling from her lips.

"Mother, I'm worried that Faith hasn't returned. I'm going to walk over to the Montgomery house to check." She hurried into the front hall to fetch her hat and cloak.

"Mother? Did you hear me?"

Elizabeth appeared in the kitchen door, a tea towel in her hand

and looking concerned. She wrung the towel tighter and tighter.

"Faith should have been home a long time ago. She's usually very prompt. Be sure to take a lantern." Having twisted the towel into a rope, she now began to wrap it around her hand, only to reverse the action, then start again on the other hand.

Amanda observed the telling sign of stress and hastened to provide what reassurance she could. The last thing she needed was her mother worried about her, too. "Probably the girls failed to realize how late it was. I'm sure she's fine. I wonder if I'll get to the end of our street before I hear their voices." The words did not reflect her thoughts.

Her sister had proven to be more adventurous than she would have wished. The lack of crime in their new community furnished some peace of mind. Also, Faith' explorations, usually incorporated into her walks to and from work, meant that there were always other people about. And she was a woman of her word. It was incomprehensible that she would be so late.

Thoughts tumbled quickly through Amanda's mind. Her feet kept pace. She raised her skirts almost to her knees to increase her speed. The lantern bobbed and swung in her other hand, flinging its light in erratic arcs. She shivered, but knew the cold came from within.

Just before she reached the end of her street, she heard a rumble of wheels, jingling harnesses and fast-moving hooves. Traditionally community members tucked themselves in at sundown. If there were an occasion to fetch something at night, vehicles proceeded at a moderate rate to avoid injury. Horses driven at speed meant an emergency. A chill ran down her spine until she recognized the Montgomery's buggy, its side lamps illuminating the driver and casting fantastical shadows to either side.

"Amanda. Miss Wentworth. Are Marianne and Faith at your house?" Sebastian's voice rose over the noise of the equipage. He pulled it to a stop. The steam rising from the horses attested to their efforts to respond to the driver's urging.

Why was Sebastian asking such a ridiculous question? Her heart pounded. "No. No, absolutely not." She took a deep breath in an effort to maintain her composure.

"We would have notified you immediately. As far as we knew, they were at your parents' home, and had forgotten the time. I just set out to fetch Faith." Fear surged into panic.

Sebastian quickly wrapped the reins around the brake and vaulted to the street. He extended his hand to assist her into the vehicle. She reached to accept his assistance, startled at the feeling of comfort at such a brief contact, then reconsidered. "Please. We're only a few steps from my home, and mother is waiting. We should tell her that the girls are missing." She failed to realize that she was asking for help from the man whom she regarded as her nemesis.

"Not just yet. I think we should look for them, first." He descended to the walkway and offered his hand again. "I'd promised to bring Faith home, but ran into a business problem. That's why I'm late. When I arrived, the house was in darkness, and my aunts and the housekeeper were in bed. The housekeeper explained that they thought they had mistaken the arrangements, and that the girls were at your house."

She accepted his assistance, and moved over to give him room on the seat. The very small, very crowded, very intimate seat. Those magnificent shoulders needed a great deal of room.

"In *bed*? Sorry, of course they'd be in bed at this hour. And if the girls hadn't arrived, they, too, would assume that plans had changed and they would be with us." She paused, then smiled wryly. "Marianne and Faith will both be in for an earful."

He expertly urged the team to reverse direction and set them to a brisk trot. "Let's do a quick tour of the streets between the two houses. If we don't find them, I'll get Henry to rouse Jeff Napier and Phil Landers. Our police and fire department heads can organize a search party.

Sebastian's fist pounded on the door. His fear that something had happened to the two girls increased by the minute. "Henry, open the… ." The door swung open, almost causing him to stagger inside.

"What's the matter? Is it at the factory?" Even as he spoke, Henry reached for his hat and coat. "I'm ready." He pulled on gloves and groped for his keys. "Or is it at the pharmacy?" Practically pushing Sebastian out the door, he fished his key ring from his coat pocket and locked the door.

"No. It's Marianne and Faith. They're missing."

"Missing? In Marcher Mills?" Henry stopped in the middle of turning the key.

"Yes. They were supposed to be with my aunts for dinner, but they never arrived. Faith planned to meet Marianne at the library." Henry finished locking the door and hurried to the carriage.

"Amanda, I am so sorry to hear this."

"Thank you. We need you to get the sheriff and fire chief and organise search parties. Sebastian and I will follow the route from our shop to the library. Hurry! Please." Her agitation caused her voice to quaver, but no tears fell.

✿✿✿

The carriage proceeded at a walking pace. Amanda and Sebastian each scanned a side of the street. Amanda broke the silence.

"I hope Henry will be back, soon. Phil and Jeff will round up a few dependable volunteers. I'm sure Phil will divide the group, assigning one to check buildings. He'll no doubt use the other to set up street patrols."

In spite of the fact that his head turned away from her as he checked his side of their route, his remarks were audible. She murmured assent, but maintained a close scrutiny of her part of the street.

"We're almost at the library, and there's no sign that anything happened." Just then she caught a flash of something. It disappeared. Winked again, then disappeared once more.

"Wait. Wait, Sebastian. There's something lying in the grass beside the boardwalk." Almost tripping in her frantic haste to alight, she jumped from the carriage before it came to a complete stop. Holding the lantern high, she willed the errant gleam to reappear.

Sebastian stopped the horses, wrapped the reins around the brake handle, and hurried to her side. "Look. Over there. It's a parasol. One of Marianne's. I gave it to her as a welcome-to-Canada gift." He scooped it up.

That fancy glass bauble in the handle is what I saw." She reached for the parasol.

Sebastian paused in the act of handing it to her. He pulled it back and scrutinised it again. "It's bent in the middle."

"Faith has been talking about an intrepid Englishwoman explorer who uses her parasol as a weapon. The girls are determined to have one just like it. They haven't been able to find one with a sufficiently thick steel shaft, but you can see that they've filed the end almost to a point."

"How the hell can you talk about fashion at a time like this?"

She clenched her jaw. *Right back to normal. So much for feeling like one of a team.* She faced him, hands on hips and the light of battle in her eye. "Not fashion, you idiot—defence. Has it escaped your notice that that bend in the shaft would fit nicely over the top of a head? I think someone attacked Marianne, and she tried to fight him off."

"That's quite a theory, given that the only proof is a warped parasol. But if you're right, there could be other signs." He raised his lantern to further increase the circle of light. "You walk toward the library and I'll start back the way we came."

Refusing to acknowledge his self-appointed position as leader of the expedition, she pushed past him and started back toward the pharmacy. "*You* walk toward the library. I want to check this side of the street more closely."

She realized that the tempo of her steps reflected her temper, not a deliberate pace which would permit her to check the perimeters of the path. She returned to her starting place and began again. At the end of the street, she retraced her steps, but this time on the narrow space between the boardwalk and the lilac hedge. Halfway back to her starting place her heart thundered in her chest. *Faith's glove.*

"Sebastian, I just found Faith's glove." He ran back to join her, sliding his arm around her shoulders as she seemed to wilt. She leaned into his strength, welcoming the support.

"My God, Amanda. Are you all right?" She nodded.

"Yes, yes. I'm not going to faint." Hastily she stood upright again. "Here. I found it in the grass, right where I'm standing."

"I found some broken glass and something caught on those bushes." They shone their lights on the spot, clearly illuminating trampled grass.

"Look—those are drag marks."

"Yes, and just the right distance apart if one person were pulling another." They followed the trail to a hole in the hedge. It was rimmed with bent and broken branches.

"Hair—and it has to be from Marianne."

"Let's tell the sheriff. Someone has definitely taken the girls." But he spoke to air. Amanda had almost reached the buggy. Under no illusion that she would wait or hesitate to drive the team, he rushed after her.

They retraced their route. When they had completed their investigation, they left one of the lanterns to mark the location of their clues.

✿✿✿

Cursing and stumbling, the men carried a two-gallon kerosene container in each hand. Bert's instructions, as usual, were right on the mark. The door to the storage shed behind the general store was open; the cans easily available.

Cuddy would fire the factories first, and then the Montgomery home. Jude was responsible for the pharmacy and one other building of his choice, but on the opposite side of the street.

Cuddy regretted that the equipment shed was gone. But liveries burned a treat, they did. Of course, it was hard on any horses that might be caught, but he always tried to get them into the corral beside the building. If some of the stupid bastards insisted on running back inside, well that wasn't his fault. He'd done all he could. People stupid enough to sleep in the stables deserved what they got. There were lots more people, and they were supposed to be smarter than horses—but he doubted that. And on cold and damp nights, like this one, the warmth was always welcome. He grinned as he thought of all the fires he'd set and then helped to extinguish. Or try to extinguish. Water in pails, or even jetting from a pumper truck availed little against a blazing building. Too bad it was so far from his assigned sites.

CHAPTER 31

Sebastian had agreed, reluctantly, to stay in town. If medicines were required quickly, he would be of little use in the bush. No one had passed the fire hall or required his services. The town was quiet.

"Mr. Montgomery, Mr. Montgomery, Doc Redding says it's a 'mergency!"

Sally Jessop pelted down the street, her right hand waving a piece of paper. Pride at performing such an important task shone in her face. A basket banged against her left leg with every step. The doctor, assisting at the birthing of her soon-to-be-born twin siblings, required several items. Sebastian held out his hand.

"Give me the list and we'll see what the doctor needs."

He took the paper from her hand and read it. Once again he was torn. He should be out looking for his cousin and Faith. Or at the very least, providing support for Amanda and her mother. Instead, his responsibilities were doling out medicine and ringing a bell.

The logic of his remaining in town paled in relation to his need to do something concrete. Well, providing urgently-needed medicines was concrete, but not particularly satisfying.

"Come with me, Sally." He grasped her hand, and started for the pharmacy at a pace that let her feet hit the boardwalk about one step in three. Focused on their destination, they failed to see the man who slid back into the alley, two bulky objects in his fists.

Sebastian dropped her hand to reach into his pocket for the key. He flicked the switch and blessed the electric lights for saving time. Then he consulted the list and forced himself to concentrate.

"You put these things in your basket as I give them to you." He placed it on a small stool his staff used for reaching the top shelves.

"Yes, sir, Mr. Montgomery." Sally seemed intrigued by the many things filling the shelves around her.

"Then wait until I fill the prescription. I will help you take them home."

Hard-won experience proved that children who felt important and were given specific tasks to complete spent less time exploring. He placed several items on the counter, then headed for the back room.

"I'll be right back as soon as I wash my hands. Don't touch anything while I'm gone."

"Yes, sir. I mean no, sir. I mean I won't touch anything." Sally nodded obediently. She watched intently as he made the pills.

"There, that's the lot. Let's see how fast we can get them to your house."

✿✿✿

Forty-five minutes later Sebastian stopped pacing in front of the fire station long enough to replenish his coffee. The warmth felt good on his hands, but turned into acid in his gut.

"Dammit, Phil, I agree with your theory that not all of the able-bodied men should be on the search teams. Ensuring that each farm has a minimum of three searchers makes sense. Family members can help with checking the outbuildings; the men will search the rest of the property as soon as it's light."

His comments were addressed to Phil Landers, currently patrolling the streets of town and well out of earshot. Sebastian stepped onto the road to look in vain for a rider bearing good news. Or any news. He continued his one-sided conversation.

"It's impossible to argue that keeping me on tap as a backup to

Doc when he's attending the Jessop birth ensures the town has a medical presence—even though your faith in my medical expertise is both touching and misplaced. But dammit to hell, it grates to be wearing out the sidewalk when I could be out there looking for those two girls and actually *doing* something."

He wheeled and strode back to the entrance of the fire hall. The fire horses waited patiently. They had hay, oats and water. *All's right in your world, even if mine is upside down. My God, not only am I talking to a man who isn't here, but now I'm talking to horses. What next?*

Twenty minutes later Phil returned from his circuit. He tightened his scarf, fastened the buttons on his heavy jacket, and patted his pocket to assure himself that his gloves were in place.

"Why the hell aren't you cold, Montgomery? You're only wearing a suit."

Sebastian ignored his comment. Phil tried again.

"This October certainly fulfilled its reputation for cold and damp."

"Sorry, Phil. I was a million miles away." He shivered. "You are right. It's damned cold and damp tonight. I just wish to hell we'd get some good news from the searchers."

"I know, I know. It's hard. Jeff feels the same. As sheriff he has to coordinate the search, but he'd rather be out and about, as well. It's just that with the recent vandalism and fires, we don't dare leave the women and children unprotected. I'd rather feel a little more useful, too."

Phil refilled his own cup and joined his friend in the doorway.

"Look, here comes my assistant fire chief, complete with hat."

Sebastian felt a smile tug at the corner of his mouth. It was a wonder that hat hadn't disintegrated from overuse.

"He must have finished rounding up all the ladies and taken them to the church."

Steve approached, his face sporting a big grin. “The Anglicans will be crowing for years that their church hall was the only one big enough to hold so many ladies and children.”

“You are absolutely right. With any luck they’ll be so busy making sandwiches and coffee and noting any mistakes made by the others that war won’t break out. Some of the women with little children stayed home, but most of them are at the church.”

The men shared a laugh and Steve outlined his next actions.

“I’ll do a quick check of the downtown and businesses, then get the reports from the men who are patrolling the town. I wish I could believe they’d tell me the ladies have been found in an outbuilding.”

✿✿✿

The raised boardwalks in Marcher Mills were definitely a bonus. Well maintained, they featured a small opening between each of the slats to allow dirt to fall onto the ground below, thus reducing the amount of dust kicked up by many passing feet. Those same openings also provided a lovely updraft for a well-set fire. Jude anticipated a lovely blaze.

Twenty minutes later from his hiding place behind the Montgomery house, Cuddy heard a runner approach, breathing heavily. Jude bent over and braced his arms on his thighs, winded by the eight-block run from the pharmacy. Cuddy decided to fill him in as he fought for breath.

“Of all the god-damned luck. The whole bloody staff was outside the factory when I arrived—something about one of the machines starting to smoke. The stupid knothead they call a manager ordered the building evacuated until they knew what was happening. Some idiot concern about the resins and glue they use.

“And before you ask about the second building, they had evacuated that, too, ‘just in case’. Looked like a bloody damned circus.”

He took a breath, spat, and continued.

"It will be a wonder if they don't find the kerosene Bert hid."

Jude looked at his partner and swore. "Well, couldn't you dump the kerosene around the trees and bushes and set them alight?"

"Jude, think. It's night. That means it's dark. That means there was *lots* of people seeking bushes and trees, either to take a leak or do a little grope and grab."

By now Jude had caught his breath and started to pull the bottles out of his pockets.

"Shit, shit, shit. Well, come on, nothing we can do about that. I was just about to start when the pharmacist and a little girl came down the street."

"How did you know it was the pharmacist?"

"Because he had a key to the place." Jude's tone indicated that Cuddy should have known this.

"I had to wait 'til they were finished inside, 'cause you know I don't do kids. I poured kerosene on the pharmacy, and one building across the street. Them sticks we got worked a treat. Just wound a bit of cloth around the end, dipped it in kerosene, and used it to start the blazes. Looked as if those pretty flames were taking a walk until they got to the mother lode."

"Well, just before you arrived, I filled a bottle, put in the wick, lighted it and heaved it through the front window. Figured with all the chemicals and stuff we should hear a boom and whoosh any minute now." Jude nodded.

"Thank Christ something went right. Bert promised to have every able-bodied man out of town looking for two stupid women who got lost, but I've seen a couple of men in the street. And there's someone at the fire station, too." Jude checked for foot traffic.

"Let's get this damned house fired. The next train goes

through at five o'clock. That means it's still dark, but we have to get through town without being seen and be at the water tower to pick it up."

"Oh, yeah? And what if we meet some of those searchers?"

"You know Bert; he always has an answer. We just tell anyone we meet that the girls are home, and everyone is to go back to town. If we shout, no one will recognize our voices. And we sure as hell don't hang around for a chat!"

CHAPTER 32

Branches rubbed together, creaking and groaning. Their movement caused bushes to stir, adding rustling to the ominous chorus. Leaves, some old and dry, others freshly fallen, created a thick mat, the better to muffle nocturnal prowling.

"I'm sure they're looking for us by now. How long do you think it will take?" Iron control almost eliminated the quaver from Marianne's voice.

"Well, I have no idea how long, but I'm sure they'll find us by tomorrow." Faith struggled to make her tone matter of fact.

"I wonder why he did this to us."

"Didn't you say that Al person often worked for another man?" Marianne really had no idea why they had been chloroformed and abducted.

"I just wonder if it has anything to do with the fact that Amanda and I are running a business, and not a traditional one for women. Some men are really weird, not to say stupid, about things like that."

"You might have something there. Just look at all the nonsense about women wanting to ride bicycles. It's ridiculous."

"True, but I really want to find the answer." Faith shook her sacks vigorously in a vain attempt to eliminate the dust.

"In Australia we have poisonous snakes and spiders. Fortunately it's too cold here for crocodiles."

Masked by darkness, Faith smiled. "Well, none of them live here, Marianne, so not to worry." She hoped. Crocodiles were definitely off the list, but rumors of rattlers still circulated. And, in the case of spiders, just being a spider was cause enough for panic.

The two young women propped themselves against a convenient tree and pretended to sleep, their bodies rigid with fear. Logic held no power over the universal dread of the unknown. And when darkness joined with fear, their apparent courage masked a mounting terror. Courage, in this case, contained mostly pride and a determination to hide perceived cowardice

"What's that? Did you hear it? What do you think it is?"

"Whatever it is, Faith, it's been going on for some time."

"Really? Are you sure? I only heard it now."

Marianne grunted and turned her back to her friend. Pretending nonchalance, she smoothed the rough burlap which comprised their only defense against the chilly October night. "Go to sleep," she said firmly.

Suddenly, her scream shattered the darkness.

"What, what? What is it? Are you all right?" Faith grabbed her friend in a death grip, then released her and began to check for injuries, starting with her head. "Ouch. That hat pin is lethal. I had no idea we each had a weapon."

Completing her inspection, she enveloped her fellow abductee in an enthusiastic hug. Loving concern met resistance and an appreciative shoulder pat.

"For heaven's sake, stop. I'm fine. Oh!" Faith felt her jerk in surprise. "Something just dropped on my face."

"Are there birds above us? Was that it?"

"I really don't think so. It landed on my forehead, bounced off my elbow, and disappeared. I think it was a tree fruit."

"Tree fruit?" Faith wondered what her friend could mean. Sometimes Marianne spoke Australian.

"Oh, now I understand. This is a pine tree, so it was probably a pine cone."

"Well, it was hard. And rough. But it's gone. Let's go back to sleep."

The two friends pretended to settle down once again, their shoulders touching for comfort, covers meticulously rearranged. Dusty, smelly, and much used, their benefit was two-fold: warmth and a solid reminder that others would be looking for them.

A loud crash brought them to their feet, hearts pounding and eyes straining to penetrate the heavy darkness. A stag and two does, disturbed by a sound they failed to identify, crashed through bushes, sounding like a herd of thousands.

"A herd, it was a herd."

"A big herd. And close. Very close. I could feel something rushing right past me."

"Could it be bears? Or wolves? Horses? Or cows? Cows have horns and big, big heads. Cows chase things that come close to them. Horses would be better."

"Did you have to mention cows? I could handle the bears, but cows are much, much scarier. I've never seen a bear, but I know those great big cows with their great big horns are very dangerous."

They clutched each other, panting. But even heart-pounding terror dissipates unless fed, and gradually their fear subsided as their breathing returned to normal.

By mutual consent they sat again, shoulders no longer touching gently, but pressed together, bodies braced against the tree. Their very own tree. Their very own, safe- except-for-pine-cones tree.

"I know it's ridiculous, but I could almost hug this tree," Marianne whispered, her voice barely trembling.

"Why?"

"Because it's big, it's solid, and it's ours."

"How do you know it's ours?"

"Because it's holding on to me. The sap is very sticky."

She pulled gently at the hairs trapped by their very own tree.

"There, I'm free." She settled back into her original posture.

The woods repeated noises that had become familiar. The women began to relax, eyes drifting closed in spite of their best efforts. Exhaustion conquered terror.

Suddenly they were sitting bolt upright. An eerie sound floated in the air, neither advancing nor retreating. It came from the left. There it was again. Closer. Then silence.

"Did you hear that? What kind of animal makes such an awful sound? Like a soul in torment." Marianne clutched Faith, clamping her arms to her sides. Faith, unable to move, tried logic.

"Well, that one I know. It's just an owl. They hunt at night. Don't you have owls in Australia?"

"Yes, but they are much kinder to people stuck in the woods. They certainly don't make noises like that. Australian owls are quiet. Polite. Refined, even. Considerate."

"Well, this isn't Australia, or even England. But English owls hoot, too."

"Are they dangerous?"

"I wouldn't want to get in the way of their beaks or feet. They are silent when they fly. The farmers like them in the barn because they feed on mice and rats. Probably other things, too, but I only know about mice and rats."

"Even if they aren't dangerous, they're scary. I'm going to try to rest and store energy for our escape tomorrow. Surely this night must be coming to an end."

Faith gave up and addressed her friend.

"Marianne, are you awake?"

"Why would I be awake? I'm so cosy under these soft, burlap blankets. No lights shining in my eyes."

Faith snorted. "And quiet—have you noticed how silent it is? No wonder you are so comfortable." Her companion propped herself on one elbow and prepared to respond. But Faith had more to say.

"The main reason that you are so comfortable is that you like to share. You put every knobby stick and large rock on my side."

"Of course, but I missed a very large one. It's under my left hip and working hard to reach the mate. I think it's trying to burrow through my entire body." She threw aside the sacks, sneezed at the dust, and stood.

Faith followed suit. "I think those cows we heard were really deer. I am convinced that no self-respecting bear would make that much noise. Besides, the bears are tucked up in their warm dens."

"There are no wolves. I know there are no wolves. Tell me I'm right. *There are no wolves.*"

Faith, hearing the real fear under the pretended humor, relented. "No wolves, Marianne, but I agree with you about that enormous herd of deer." Bedding folded, both girls brushed their skirts and adjusted their hats.

"You know, it always amazes me that hunters tell you how sneaky and quiet they have to be to get a deer. The deer, they assure you, can hear you if you breathe deeply. But they won't fool me again—now that I've heard them. I know the hunters are just flapping their jaws. The deer wouldn't be able to hear them over their pounding hooves and crashing advances."

Faith giggled weakly. She knew that her friend was trying to buoy their spirits. "You know, I just realized that I have not one bit of pioneer spirit. No desire to explore the wilderness. And I *hate* sleeping out of doors."

"You're right. There is a great deal to be said for four solid walls, a soft mattress with linen sheets and quilts, and hot cocoa." Marianne inhaled deeply. "I would give anything for a cup of hot cocoa. Hot anything, really, but hot, sweet cocoa sounds just about perfect."

"No talking about food or hot drinks. I'm really thirsty. Do you think you could step in that small creek again so we could get a drink?"

"Not the least bit funny, Faith." She sniffed. "But I think if we go a few steps to the left of our tree, I could probably manage to bathe my toes. And you're right, a drink is a wonderful idea."

"Have you noticed that the stars are extremely bright? I can't claim to see, but I most certainly can make out degrees of darkness. Take my hand, and we'll march ourselves to water."

"Very well, but let's put the bedding at the base of the tree. Gifted as I am in tripping over branches, I have no desire to add sacks to my list."

The two young ladies joined hands for support and comfort. With one arm sweeping in front and beside them, taking care to test each step for stability, they headed for the creek. They hoped.

CHAPTER 33

"Papa, what's that in your hand?" Since Jenny had started working at Marshall's Emporium, certain kitchen duties and housekeeping were now part of Stan's world. He had mastered bacon and eggs, but toast defeated him most of the time. It seemed to go from white to black in the blink of an eye. That lovely golden color that Jenny achieved had escaped him so far. But conquering bacon and eggs and striving for golden toast paled when compared to scrubbing the floor. He had a whole new understanding of just how hard, especially on the knees, housework could be. He embraced any excuse to have the children eat outside, encouraging picnics under the tree as the ultimate treat.

"Mr. Stiles thanked me for doing such a good job watching over the building supplies. They have all been moved inside, so now I will be home on Sundays."

"What's in the tin?" When Adam started on a quest, he stuck with it until he received a satisfactory answer.

"Mr. Stiles gave me the rest of his special brand of coffee as a thank you. I'm going to make a pot as a surprise for Mommy, and you may all have some, too. It will be a celebration."

The children's excitement was wonderful to behold. Treats did not often come their way. Their parents never let them have tea or coffee, claiming it would stunt their growth. The boys ran outside to give their friends the news. Susie entered the room and started to set the table.

Stan muttered to himself. *Why the hell am I making coffee? Susie is old enough.* Then he remembered he was the reason for learning how to make coffee, cook, wash floors, and mind the children.

He emptied the old grounds and rinsed the coffee pot before adding fresh water. He opened the tin, took his time selecting a spoon from the caddy on the table, then stopped. Jenny made the breakfast coffee. He had absolutely no idea of how much he should add. Since this was Bert's special coffee, it would be good. Did that mean that it required fewer spoonsful of grounds? Or was it the same and the results just tasted better? Or, in case it was delicate, would more grounds be better?

In order to mull over these monumental choices, he made a production of lining up cups without saucers since Jenny wasn't here. Hers he put at her place at the table, with a saucer. He checked to be sure the sugar bowl held enough for a heaping teaspoonful per person.

Putting the three kitchen cups on a tray, he carefully aligned the handles to the right. His own cup rested on the counter. He moved Jenny's cup and saucer to her place at the table.

He eyed the tray again. Treat or no treat, especially when the children would be taking them outside, the usual mugs would serve the purpose much better. He removed three cups and replaced them with mugs. Aligned the handles again. Adjusted the spacing between them. Put his cup and saucer back in the cupboard and retrieved one more mug.

Then, unable to think of a way to stall any longer, he added one heaping spoonful of coffee per person, clapped on the lid, and placed the pot on the hottest part of the stove.

That bastard should mind his own business. What happens in my house is my business, not his. How could he possibly know what happens here? And he's got Jenny so upset that I have to say goodnight to my daughter from her bedroom door!

Potatoes and carrots, peeled and chopped by his wife before

she left for work, sat in a bowl of water. He remembered to use fresh water for cooking. As he threw the old water off the porch, he realised that since the arrival of that damned letter, his wife made a point of rising earlier than ever to prepare some of the supper. Just one more way the bastard was affecting their lives. He suppressed the useless rage, unsurprised to see his hands trembling.

Just concentrate on the job. There's nothing you can do about the other. And where will I find another Sunday job? That smarmy bastard blackmailer. I bet he's been laughing up his sleeve the whole time we've struggled to meet his demands.

Adding a small amount of salt, he placed the vegetable pot beside the coffee. Later, Susie would slice the bread. Adam and Roger would clear the dishes at the end of the meal. Family life would continue.

Soon the delicious aroma of freshly-brewed coffee filled the room. He added milk to the four mugs—a little for him, and a great deal for the children—then poured the fragrant beverage before shouting through the screen door that the treat was ready. "Roger, hold the door open for Susie."

"Why do we have to drink it outside?"

"Because I don't want to scrub this floor again." Solemn looks from his sons greeted the explanation. Papa hated scrubbing the floor. He used many, many words that would have got them a whipping if they repeated them in their mother's hearing.

"Now scoot—you can have a coffee picnic under the big tree. It will be a celebration that I no longer have to work on Sundays.

"Don't slam the door." Right on cue, before the last word was uttered, the screen door gave a mighty bang. He now understood why his parents had said those same words to him and his brothers. The two boys pelted down the stairs and raced for the tree, all thought of holding the door for their sister forgotten. Two of the roots had formed a kind of seat—the place of choice for their picnics.Suddenly the banishment turned into fun.

Susie picked up the tray and smiled at her father. "I'll keep everything safe, Papa."

Stan watched his daughter push the door with her hip, the tray rock steady in her hands. She was taller than her mother, and would be a beautiful woman, slender and graceful. He reflected, once again, that his father had always visited his sisters at bedtime, and they had made happy marriages. And he was always, always gentle. Susie had never cried after the first time, which was unavoidable. How could there be any harm in showing affection?

"Ouch!" A shriek of pain rent the air. A crash followed on its heels. Stan charged through the door, oblivious to the loud bang that followed him as he took the stairs two at a time.

"What happened?"

The tray lay on the grass. The three containers rested on their sides, their contents rapidly soaking into the ground.

"I'm sorry, Papa. A bee stung my cheek."

She turned a woeful face toward him, an angry lump already visible, as she hurried to the pump to apply cooling mud. When she returned, a trail of discolored water seeped under the hand covering the sting, trickling down her cheek and onto her neck. Stan gave her a hug. The boys put the mugs back on the tray, hopeful that the treat was still forthcoming.

As the drama unfolded in the backyard, Jenny placed her reticule on the small table in the front hall before hanging her shawl on one of the hooks. Her hat always rested on the shelf in her closet, safe from curious hands.

Barely-heard childish trebles mixed with the richer tones of Susie's developing contralto and Stan's light tenor. With a smile on her face, she hurried to see what it was all about. Tiptoeing down the hall, she stood in the doorway and viewed her family.

Stan was holding a coffee pot in his right hand, one of her good tea towels padding the handle. She shook her head in resignation. Some of her linens suffered almost as much as their bank account with Stan in the kitchen.

The children's mugs sat in a soldierly row on the counter beside the back door. Another mug was set to one side. She noted that her own place at the table had both cup and saucer.

"Hello, everyone. Why are the mugs marching in a line?"

Susie turned and greeted her with a smile. She opened her mouth to add words, only to be interrupted by Roger and Adam.

"Mommy, Mommy, we're having a celebrater."

"Celebrater?"

"He means a celebration. Papa wants to tell you all about it."

"Is the celebration because I smell something good cooking?" She looked at her sons, who continued to bounce with excitement.

"We can't tell you," they chorused. Adam ran to the back door. "Hurry up, Papa. Mommy's home."

Jenny heard Stan's voice coming through the screen door. "Did you tell her?" He directed his remarks to the boys.

They grinned. "Nope, 'cause you said it was your turn. But we really wanted to."

"Good." His eyes twinkled as he viewed his wife. Large grins and breathless anticipation ensued.

Jenny inhaled and put her hands on her hips in pretended indignation. Happy family times occurred with diminishing frequency as the parents struggled with their burden. "Well, I like that—my family plotting against me."

"Guess, guess."

"Did you bake a cake? Oh, dear, I can just see your father baking a cake." The children recognized the joke for what it was. They had endured far too many of Stan's culinary attempts. They shook their heads, hands over mouths to muffle the giggles.

"Did Papa do the laundry?" This was so far beyond the realm of possibility that they just stared.

"Very well, I give up. So what's the big surprise?" He crossed the kitchen and kissed her on the cheek, then continued on the stove and pointed to the coffee pot.

"We have a very, very special drink for supper." He flourished the pot. "Bert Stiles broke down and gave something away."

A terrible foreboding caused Jenny to grasp the back of a chair with one hand, the other pressed to her chest. She swallowed. "Susie, I want you to take three pennies from my reticule. You, Adam and Roger may go to Mr. Marshall's store, *right now*, and buy a penny's worth of candy each. When you return, sit on the front step if the door is closed and wait until you are called. Be sure to close the door on the way out. I have something to tell your father. Don't come back inside until I call you."

The happy faces fell. The boys looked scared, grins fading. Susie, forgetting all about the mud on her face, grabbed them and headed for the front hall. "Come on, come on," she hissed. "Let's go and get some candy." The grimace on her face was frightening. She appeared oblivious to the tears coursing down her cheeks, causing the mud to trickle onto her dress.

Jenny and Stan stood as if frozen in place. The echo of the front door closing released them. Stan inhaled, expanding his chest to a degree which threatened the buttons, prepared to roar. Why had his wife spoiled his surprise and a happy family time? As he opened his mouth, ready to roar, he took a good look at her. She now had both hands on the chair and was shaking so hard it rocked.

"Please listen, Stan. I poisoned that coffee. You mustn't drink it." She sank onto the seat, hand pressed to her chest as she fought for breath. The part she dreaded, and prayed she would never have to confess, was over.

Stan banged the pot on the stove. Instead of his usual bellow, his voice was low, frighteningly controlled, and full of rage.

"What the god-damned hell are you talking about, Jenny. Poison? Have you lost your mind?"

She struggled to control her tears. "You know the blackmail would never stop, Stan. We would pay and pay and pay. That would ruin us financially. But if people discovered…." A sob escaped. "If people knew…." She used her skirt to mop her tears. "It would be so much worse if anyone found out. We could never recover from that. They could hang you.

"I discovered that Stiles was the blackmailer, but never told you. If something went wrong, and I got caught, you could still care for the children."

Stan staggered to the table and dropped onto a chair, reaching for her hand.

"Stiles? How in the hell could you possibly know it was Stiles?" He was terrified.

"And poison? Where did you get poison? What kind of poison?" Overwhelmed with his wife's actions and revelations, he panted.

She answered his last question first. "Strychnine. I found some in a cupboard in Zeke's store. He said to destroy it. I did. Well, most of it, but I kept some."

"Jenny! Didn't you care or worry about the children?" Stan eyed her with disbelief.

"Of course. I collected the scrapings from the coffee grinder at the store and combined them with the strychnine. Then I put them in another tin of that coffee, making sure that there was good coffee on top. I think the poison was about half-way down the tin. Anything that I didn't use went straight down the privy. That way we didn't have to worry about a dog or cat or something digging it up.

"I knew that he had bought some just a short while ago, so he wouldn't have used a lot. I just guessed at how much would be there, and exchanged the tins."

"But how did you get into the shack?"

"I waited for a chance to duck in on one of the times I visited you, and you thought you heard something. I told you I thought I heard something too, and while you investigated, I switched the tins."

Stan wiped his brow. His Jenny. His sweet, adoring wife was a would-be murderer. Murderess. The mother of his children. He swallowed twice, then spoke.

"What are we going to do? We can't keep paying that bastard. Frankly, I don't trust myself near him. I will choke the life from him, right after I beat him bloody."

"No more than I want to do myself. But we have to think. Perhaps the solution is to move to another town where no one knows us. We could say we were going to Toronto because my sister's husband has found a place for you."

"But she hasn't, and I'm not sure we should move without me having a job to go to."

"You could go to Toronto. Miss Mavis at the library has newspapers from all over Ontario, and some from other parts of Canada, too. You can't check the ones here, but if you did it in Toronto, no one would know. And even if you didn't find a job for sure, you could at least find a place where they are looking for good, strong workers."

"I don't know. It's a terrible risk." But hope, which he thought was dead, raised its head.

"Not as much as staying here. You have experience working in a mill. And you are good with horses. And you can be handy with simple carpentry. Just not cabinetmaking." She warmed to her theme. "And maybe I could find work, too. It seems that Susie is able to mind the children before and after school. We can do it, Stan. I know we can."

He reached for her hands, pressing them against his lips. "Jenny, Jenny, whatever would I do without you. I'm sure Barry Masters will give me tomorrow off for urgent personal business. If I catch the first train, I can go and return the same day."

Soberly they looked at each other, hands clasped. Jenny shuddered, then straightened her shoulders.

"I'm sure the children are back and probably full of candy. You fix the vegetables and bacon. I will dump the rest of the coffee down the privy and then let them in."

CHAPTER 34

"FIRE! FIRE!"

Barry Masters, head of the crew patrolling the eastern part of the town, sprinted down the street as fast as he could. The dreaded word caused Sebastian's heart to leap to his throat. He ran to the fire bell and began ringing it in the agreed-upon sequence. Three rings. Pause. Three rings. Pause.

As the clapper tolled its frightening message, he waited impatiently as Barry braced one arm on the doorframe, his chest heaving as he fought to regain his breath.

"Where, Masters? Where is the fire?" Then words he had hoped never to hear assaulted his ears.

"The pharmacy—and it's spreading to either side. The sidewalk is in flames, too, which will make it difficult to gain entrance from the front."

Catching sight of other figures running towards him, he stopped ringing, only to hear Barry continue.

"There's another fire, too, right across the street." Sebastian resumed pulling the bell rope with renewed vigor.

"Miller's Saddlery? The bank?" Barry nodded, then shook his head.

"It's the Saddlery just now, and doesn't appear to be nearly as bad as your store. That's burning like a son of a bitch."

The two men ran into the stable attached to the fire station to lead the horses to the pumper. Phil, who had been checking and rechecking the equipment, met them, the horses almost pushing him along as they placed themselves under the harness suspended from the ceiling. Several men came panting into the station, many bracing hands on thighs as they battled for breath. Jeff, back from a tour of the partially-rebuilt machie shed, shouted that he would notify the crew on the other side of town.

"Sebastian, Barry, thanks for taking over." As Fire Chief, Phil was now in charge. "Sheriff, you wait for the rest of the crew and tell them to go to the pharmacy. Phil did a final check of the harnesses, clambered onto the wagon seat, and picked up the reins. Just then his second in command, Steve, tore into view.

"Fire! Fire!"

"We know, Steve. It's at the pharmacy. And at Miller's."

"Oh, yeah? Well it's also at your house, Sebastian. Where are your aunts?"

"My God." Sebastian froze, shocked. Then the shock holding him immobile lessened. "They're at the church. One of the ladies told me when she brought coffee and sandwiches."

He started toward the downtown, then stopped and returned as he registered what Steve had said.

"On fire? My parents' house is on fire?"

"It's almost fully engulfed. There's no way we can save it; we have to contain it and keep it from spreading. Good thing those places have some space between them."

Sebastian nodded, torn between his business and his home. As his home was beyond saving, that left the pharmacy. Phil took command.

"Steve, you take the men patrolling your side of town and work on the Montgomery place. Sebastian, you decide which crew you want to join. The rest of you men, head for the pharmacy and Miller's.

"All of you listen to me. Don't forget your fire helmets. Don't forget the pole hooks. Each of you, grab a bucket.

"The crew going to the Montgomery house—two of you take

the ladder in case anyone is trapped upstairs in a neighbouring house."

"There's a twenty-five foot ladder in the garden shed, if it's not on fire."

Sebastian's voice was almost lost as the team thundered out of the station and headed downtown. He held Steve by the arm until the noise subsided somewhat, then repeated his comment. Steve nodded. "The shed is fine; we'll use your ladder.

Sebastian grabbed his own pail and turned to leave. He started to leave, and then turned back. Young Caleb Stanhope, trying to look considerably older than his fourteen years, hovered near the door.

"Why are you here? You live in the country. Did they find the women?" His body tensed, braced for news which could be good or bad.

"Some men came by and told us about the missing ladies. They will stay all night. Right now they're helping Dad search our farm buildings. Tomorrow they'll do the property.

"I drove Mom here to see if we could help. She's at the church. Emily is watching the little ones."

Caleb had dreams of driving the water wagon, standing and flourishing a whip as they exploded from the station and galloped headlong to rescue people caught in a burning building. Of course, those caught were pretty young girls, perhaps caring for younger siblings. And they always rewarded him with a kiss.

"Caleb, you stay here and direct the men downtown or to the Montgomery house, depending which side of the town they were patrolling. Tell them that if they aren't needed elsewhere, to report downtown."

"Yes, sir, Mr. Montgomery. I will stay until you return."

Straightening his shoulders and hooking his thumbs in the waistband of his trousers, Caleb strutted into the building. He could hardly wait to tell his family of the great and grave responsibility granted to him.

✿✿✿

Amanda tilted her head. The stone walls of the church's basement kitchen tended to muffle outside noises. She placed the hard-boiled egg she had just finished peeling on the table. *Surely that was the fire bell? Had they found Faith and Marianne?* Cold air rushed past her as she opened the door, the sound of the fire bell now clearly audible.

"Quiet, everyone. Listen! Something has happened." As one, the women rushed to join her, their voices muted into fierce whispers.

"What's happened?"

"Have they found the girls?"

Questions peppered her from all sides.

"I don't know, but I am surely going to find out." With that, Amanda picked up her skirts and ran toward the sound. Many followed her. The remainder, including Gladys and Elizabeth, too old to dash about, stayed and continued their work. Those men would need a great deal of food. Gladys put down her knife and went to the door of the Sunday School room.

"You children must be especially good. All girls and boys who are nine or older come to the kitchen immediately. Be sure to wash your hands. We need your help. Portia, we need Emily in with us, so you supervise the little ones. The older children will help the younger."

Amanda had chafed at her confinement in the church. She wanted to be out with the men, searching for her sister. She knew that Gladys would take good care of her mother. She also knew that any real searching beyond outbuildings was impossible until daylight. But still she chafed.

The fire bell stopped its dreadful message, then resumed.

She turned onto Main Street, toward the station, only to meet the pumper truck headed for downtown. A sinking feeling, an ominous *knowing* stole her breath. *The pharmacy. Wentworth Optometry Services. All our equipment and supplies. Our only means of support.*

Quickly reversing direction, she hiked her skirts above her knees and flew down the street in pursuit. Flames leapt into the air, clearly visible over rooftops. Smoke filled the horizon. It *was* the pharmacy.

Gasping and lightheaded, she saw two pillars of flame bracketing the road. That meant that Miller's Saddlery or the bank was also alight. Sebastian. Dear God, *Sebastian* was on duty in case of medical emergencies. What if he were trapped inside?

Then she saw him, his chest heaving as he fought for breath. Those members of the Marcher Mills Volunteer Fire Brigade already at the scene were busy dragging hoses and manning the handles of the water truck, building pressure to throw water onto the flames. Knowing this irritating and strangely important man was safe, she put her hand over her mouth in an attempt to stifle sobs of relief.

Suddenly, she wondered if Faith had made her promised trip to the bank.

Zeke and his oldest son arrived, arms full of shovels, axes and sledgehammers. Amanda grabbed an axe and started to chop the boardwalk. The axe refused to cooperate; it either bounced sideways or stuck in the planks. The flames chewed hungrily at the dry wood. She began her work at the edge of the alleyway. Swinging the axe with more enthusiasm than skill, she gauged her chance of slipping between the buildings and into the rear entrance of her workplace.

As she swung and muttered at her ineptitude, her thoughts returned to her own plight. *Had Faith taken the week's receipts with her to deposit in the bank? Or was the money still in the tin they used in lieu of a cash register?* The question refused to go away. She could see that tin so clearly in her mind, tucked into the drawer of their large desk.

Those precious funds represented the income for a week's work, and almost the only reserve, no matter how inadequate, she and her family would have for the foreseeable future. What little money rested in the bank would have to be used to re-establish the business.

As far as she could see, the fire was only on the boardwalk and the front of the building. The key rested in her pocket, heavy with possibilities. The axe was jerked from her hand.

"Ma'am, give me that. You get with the other ladies." She felt the axe ripped from her grasp and almost fell from being roughly shouldered aside. "What do you think…oh, of course." A man she didn't recognize ignored her and began to wield the axe in a vigorous and effective manner. Left with no choice, she stepped in the direction of the crowd, noticing some of them running in various directions.

Women streamed down the street, some with their skirts kited to their knees, others trotting or walking as quickly as they could. Exclamations of shock, unanswered questions and cries of anguish permeated the air. One of the older firefighters, gasping from his run to help, insisted they stand well away from the inferno.

Checking that the order giver's attention remained on his task, she edged toward the side of the crowd, craning to see if there was even the slightest chance to enter the building. Determined to take advantage of the confusion and lack of light at the side and rear of the crowd, Amanda melted further and further into the shadows, well beyond the flickering light thrown by the fire. Once hidden from view, she sped toward her goal. *Thank God the fire hasn't reached the back of the building.*

She pulled the key from her pocket and started to open the door. At the last moment she remembered to step aside in case the flames *whooshed* out. It swung open. Neither smoke nor flames erupted. She peered around its bulk. No sign of fire anywhere in the back room or as far as she could see into the next room. An eerie, flickering light revealed a clear path to her objective.

She flew across the room and along the aisle to the entrance to her premises. An ominous crackling, accompanied by an abrupt increase in temperature failed to slow her progress. The brightness of the fire lighted her path. Reaching the desk at the back of their area, she opened the bottom drawer, snatched the precious tin, rose, and began to retrace her steps.

The fire was gaining ground. The heat approached unbearable. A quick glance into the pharmacy encouraged her to risk a few more seconds. She convinced herself there was a tiny margin of safety.

The display case just inside the door held several pairs of spectacles. The cupboard upon which it rested contained some of their most commonly-used instruments. The money tin dropped into the pouch she had made with her skirt. Flinging open the cupboard door, two frantic sweeps of her arm tumbled the contents of the top shelves into her improvised reticule. They fell, higgledy-piggledy, onto the money tin. Finally she carefully placed the ophthalmoscope, an expensive tool critical to their work, on top. The fire crackled and roared—a monster chewing and gulping its way through wooden beams and shingles, sending tongues of destruction in advance of the juggernaut of its wrath. Sweat ran off her forehead, blurring her vision. The intense heat made her feel faint.

Not now, I can't faint now. Just another minute, and I will be out the back door.

Acutely aware of the danger and foolhardiness of her actions, she felt the fire creeping closer—a malevolent beast determined to engulf its prey. Its flickering illumination impelled her to leave. Smoke obscured all but the largest objects, Thickening, coiling, its noxious vapors increasing the chances of suffocation.

As she prepared to retrace her steps, she stopped for one foolhardy second. The spectacle display held the results of many hours' work. She made two lightning grabs to reap as many as possible, tumbling them into her skirt pouch with rest of her loot. But had she left it too late? Would the weight of her skirt and its contents make escape impossible?

She shoved her eyeglasses back in place. Perspiration encouraged them to slide down her nose. *Why didn't I tie my handkerchief over my mouth and nose?* She raised her shoulder and tried to cover part of her face as she coughed. *How much more of this heat and smoke can I stand?* She wiped her brow on her arm, her hands maintaining their death grip on her skirt and petticoats. Leaping through the door to the back room, she rocked to a stop.

The fire had worked its way down the outside of the building, devouring everything in its path. Smoke curled and writhed in menacing patterns, subservient to drafts. It seeped around the window frame, coalescing, then parting, granting tantalizing glimpses of her goal. Terrifying creaks and groans indicated well-weathered shingles had joined the inferno. Still coughing and sputtering, she stumbled across the room, racing to reach the back door before she collapsed.

Her right hand reached for the door handle. She started to grab the knob, then jerked her hand back. It was much hotter than before. She snatched a handful of petticoats as a barrier between hand and heat. It worked!

Panting with fear and relief, she clutched her precious bundle with renewed strength and both hands. She pushed at the door, then found herself flying through the air.

CHAPTER 35

Sebastian relinquished his place on the pump handle. Sweat pouring down his face mixed with soot to form a grotesque mask. He felt he needed a gallon of water, and looked for someone with a pail and dipper. Replenishment of body fluid was crucial to fire crews. Phil designated the responsibility for monitoring the others to keep them supplied with liquid on a rotating basis.

He became aware of a number of women rushing toward the crowd. They came from the direction of the church and carried heavy baskets of food. More followed, hard on their heels. Two carried a trestle table top, the next two each had a saw horse to support the table. Even in his panic and despair, he noticed that one more trailed the group, linens over her arms. A tablecloth for feeding a work gang of grubby, sooty firefighters—he saw the hands of his extremely prim and proper aunts. *I wonder if they brought napkins?*

Grabbing the tin mug of water, he looked over the group of concerned citizens, mainly women with children. He understood their fear that the fire might sweep through the town's many wooden buildings. They had one thing in their favor; there was no breeze to carry the sparks. He bent to fill the cup again, and noticed two small bucket brigades. Somehow these enterprising women had carted ladders to the buildings on either side of the pharmacy, and of Miller's Saddlery. They were wetting down the roofs of adjacent businesses.

Suddenly, he realised that Amanda neither pumped nor passed, climbed nor threw water. His heart rate doubled as he realized where That Woman had gone. That *damned* woman, regardless of the danger, had gone to save what she could of her precious business. While part of him applauded her courage and resolve, his first thought was to shake her. Or kiss her. He needed to feel her against him. Know she was safe.

He finally capitulated to what he had fought so valiantly: he loved her and all her quirky, unfeminine, irritating ideas. Dropping the cup, he ran down the alleyway, cursing with every step. Her only chance to enter the building was through the back door.

Even as he ran, he could smell the smoke escaping between the slats of the siding. Tendrils hung in the air, then swirled as directed by the flaming monster inside.

Rounding the corner to the stone-paved area at the rear, he took the four steps to the door in one giant leap, a feat he would have claimed impossible until that minute. Even as he leapt, he heard the heart-stopping crash of the first of the roof timbers collapsing. He grabbed the doorknob, only to release it with a curse. Pulling the tail of his shirt free from his trousers, he formed it into an inadequate pad. It burned painfully, but he no longer felt he was leaving several layers of skin behind.

Bracing himself in case the door stuck, he yanked as hard as he could. A small, feminine bundle landed on his chest, causing him to stagger and fall down the steps. He almost regained his balance, but the armful of woman did him in. At least he took the brunt of the fall, he mused.

Hugging her as hard as he could, he realized that her right arm circled his neck in a most satisfactory manner. Her left arm and hand, however, pressed against that part of his body enthusiastically exhibiting the powerful effects of adrenaline plus propinquity. Ignoring propriety, he pulled her head down and kissed her roughly, relief and rage warring for supremacy.

The far-from-fragrant bundle in his arms caressed his face.

Her reddened eyes wept copious tears as she gazed at him. Most of the pins had fallen from her hair, causing hanks to hang in disarray.

"Sebastian," she murmured.

"Yes, Amanda." For the life of him he couldn't think of anything else to say. Relief made him weak in both mind and body. The beauty of her loving smile momentarily blocked the terror engendered by her next statement.

"I think my skirt is burning."

He threw her to the ground, tore off his jacket, and covered the smoldering cloth. Satisfied that she was in no danger of resembling a torch, he swept her into his arms and ran for the street.

CHAPTER 36

"Listen. Did you hear that?"

"Yes. Am I losing my mind, or was that a shout?"

"It's a shout. Let's answer it." The two young ladies cupped their hands around their mouths and shouted in unison.

"HERE. WE'RE HERE." Faith tightened her grip on Marianne's hand, lifted her skirts with the other, and headed toward the sound.

"Stop, Faith. Where do you think you're going?"

"What any sane person would do, after having spent a night in the woods with every living creature in two counties trying to share the same space. I'm off to be rescued."

"Well, I'm all for being rescued, but you're going the wrong way."

Another "Helloooo" shattered the air.

"That way; it's that way."

"Absolutely not, Marianne. It's definitely the way we're going."

"No, it's not."

Faith heaved a sigh of exasperation.

"Very well, then. Let's answer it again and we'll both listen carefully."

Once more their shrill "Here, we're here" rent the air.

The direction of the response was unequivocal. They looked at each other and giggled with relief.

"We're both wrong."

"Yes, we are."

They reversed their direction. With one hand maintaining a death grip on their skirts, raised almost to their knees to increase their speed and avoid tripping, they raised the other to protect their faces.

"Hello, ladies. Keep calling."

Obediently, they took turns, shouting every few steps.

Dawn's light burgeoned, first making silhouettes visible, and possible obstacles easier to identify, then adding color. The shouts of their rescuers came closer and closer. Someone rang a cowbell with great vigor.

In less than ten minutes the two parties could see each other. Throwing propriety to the winds, the girls embraced the two men who had searched so diligently.

"How did you find us?"

"What are you doing in the woods?"

"Who put you here?"

"That Al person."

Finally the questions died down, and responses heard.

"We found you because you responded to our call, of course. I'm Jackson Stanhope. You're in the part of my farm that is still the original bush."

"Thank you, Mr. Stanhope. We've met your family at the library." Marianne paused for breath, and Faith chimed in.

"How did you know we were missing? Are my mother and sister all right?" She fought to control tears of relief and apprehension.

✿✿✿

Amanda paused at the parlour door, a tray with a teapot and two plates of cookies clutched in her hands. She felt her eyes fill as she gazed at Faith and Marianne, miraculously rescued from the bush. The loss of their workplace had been a blow, but seeing her sister home and safe went a long way to assuaging her grief.

Sebastian's presence was oddly reassuring. She sent him a small smile and received one in return. The heat in his glance made her uncomfortable in a very satisfying way.

"Tea and cookies, everyone. Mother, will you pour?" Sebastian and his two aunts had joined them.

"Faith, could you and Marianne tell us what happened?"

Faith blushed, carefully returned her cup in its saucer, and began.

"I left the shop shortly before six o'clock. Marianne and I had agreed to meet at six, when the library closed. We planned to spend the evening together. I was about half a block from my destination and could see the building just ahead. Then I woke up in the woods with a sore head and a feeling of extreme nausea."

She looked at her friend to continue the tale. Marianne gave a small shudder and straightened her shoulders.

"I had just left the library and started towards downtown. I thought I could meet Faith on the way. Then I saw them."

"Whom did you see?" Elizabeth chimed in, then waved her hand in the air as if to wipe out the interruption.

"Al Anderson. He had knocked Faith' hat askew, and was embracing her."

"Embracing her?"

Elizabeth echoed, leaning forward with a look of amazement on her face. *"Embracing* her?" She slumped and leaned back in her chair, stunned at the revelation and close to fainting.

"Yes, embracing her. He was behind Faith, with one arm around her waist. The other hand held a cloth over her face."

Amanda left her seat to stand beside her mother for both moral and, if necessary, physical support.

"That was when I realised that he was up to no good. I ran as fast as I could and started to beat him. First I hit him in the face with my reticule." Her audience had no trouble believing her. She looked fierce.

"I trust he has a very big black eye. Then I whacked him with my parasol. I struck him on his head hard enough to bend my weapon. I think I hit him a couple of other times, but by now he had dropped my friend on the sidewalk and shoved that cloth in my face."

She paused to swallow some tea.

"When I opened my eyes, I was laying on every sharp rock in the vicinity. I was cold and felt ill. Faith was beside me, and we seemed to be in a wilderness."

"Then what did you do?" One of the aunts stopped fanning herself long enough to inquire.

Faith took up the tale. "We tried to determine where we were. We shuffled around and found a pile of sacks. They were dusty and musty, but at least they provided some warmth."

Marianne added. "I will never view feed sacks in quite the same manner again.

"We attempted to sleep, but a tree makes a hard back rest, so we decided to explore. I found the creek with my left shoe. It's not deep—barely above the boot top." Smiles flickered over the faces of her audience. Faith continued the narrative.

"We also discovered that our choice of resting place was in the centre of all nighttime activities. An entire herd of deer—we think they were deer—thundered through our clearing. Owls hooted. Things rustled in the bushes. But at least we were spared a visit by a skunk." She shuddered in memory.

"Because we couldn't sleep, we thought we would see if we culd find the creek and follow it to a farm or community."

"Yes, that's right, Marianne. And I didn't mention the rattlesnakes, though we did think about wolves and bears."

Marianne shot to her feet. "Snakes? There were snakes? *Poisonous* snakes? And you didn't think it worth mentioning?"

"Now, girls, let's not lose track of what we're trying to do, here. You can discuss snakes when we've finished." Elizabeth attempted to smooth the waters and bring the discussion back to the point. Marianne sat down.

"Well, then, we did find the creek. Or at least Faith did."

"Yes. And I surpassed Marianne's efforts by using both of my feet to do so. She's right, by the way, it just covered the tops of my shoes." Tension lessened as hands or teacups hid smiles.

"Well, that's about it. We heard Mr. Stanhope's shouts, responded, and met with him and two others."

"Those sandwiches and the water they carried were very welcome, we can assure you."

"Thanks for telling us what happened." Amanda smiled at the two girls, then turned to Sebastian. "Do you and your aunts have a place to sleep?"

"We'll stay at the house I've been renting. It's a little spartan, but tomorrow we can begin to put things in order. Jeff has called a meeting for ten tomorrow morning for all those affected by the fire."

Soon only Amanda, Elizabeth and Faith remained. The girls began to tidy and return the chairs to their proper places when a brisk rat-a-tat-tat sounded at the front door. They looked at each other and said "Gladys". They were right.

As her foot crossed the threshold, she started speaking. "I just saw the Montgomerys leaving. Now don't you ladies worry about a thing. I brought you some baking to tuck in your larder, and I'll be back at eight tomorrow to make breakfast for you." She beamed, exuding good will and rampant curiosity in equal measure.

Elizabeth, by virtue of age, acted as spokeswoman. "Thank you, Gladys. We certainly appreciate your kindness. Instead of breakfast, please come for lunch when we can have a comfortable chat. We'll look forward to seeing you then."

The two girls found things to do to hide their smiles. Elizabeth was a match for Gladys any day. She shepherded their unwanted visitor out the door with exquisite manners and great dispatch.

"Luncheon will be served at noon. See you then." With a final wave and a firm and gentle thud, the door closed and all three occupants heaved sighs of relief.

CHAPTER 37

Sebastian stopped the buggy in front of the Wentworth residence. As he prepared to descend, Amanda rushed down the path, a harried expression on her face.

"What's wrong, Amanda? Has something happened to your mother or sister?"

"No, no. They're all fine. I could not bear one more minute of 'are you sure you're feeling well enough to go out today? Be sure to wear your scarf. Where are your gloves?'." She expelled a long breath. "It's enough to drive a person mad."

Sebastian smiled. That was his Amanda, ready to take on all comers, but unwilling to cause any hurt to her mother or sister. *Wait a minute. Where did "his Amanda" come from?*

He was more than willing to admit that their relationship had warmed and softened since the fire and subsequent discovery that Faith and Marianne were safe. But "his Amanda?" That was just a little too fast.

He helped her into the vehicle, silently enjoying a glimpse of ankle, and tucked the lap robe around her. "Are you sure you'll be warm enough?"

She started to bristle, then caught the twinkle in his eye. Ostentatiously adjusting the robe, she changed the subject.

"So, what building have you found for us? I thought there were no more spaces. Miller's Saddlery has rented temporary quarters with the blacksmith, but nothing else is available."

He gave his companion a sidelong glance, and pretended to concentrate on merging with the two vehicles on Main Street.

"Little do you know, Miss Wentworth. I have a clever mind and am a shrewd negotiator."

"Shrewd, indeed, if you have managed to winkle out even six square feet of commercial space."

"Ah, but you close your mind when you specify our requirements as 'commercial space'. Reduced to its lowest common denominator, we require two things: enough space to conduct our separate businesses, and a presence on, or very near, the main street.

"Yes? I'm still waiting for the big announcement." She smoothed her gloves and checked her hat pin, fighting to conceal her smile.

"And here it is: Betty Keppel has graciously agreed to move her business to the former storeroom in Zeke's store. He'll put the goods in the shed, or cram them onto the shelves. Betty is renting her store to Wentworth Optometry Services and Montgomery's Pharmacy for the next six months."

"Sebastian, that's wonderful! You are absolutely amazing. It must have taken a great deal of negotiation to achieve that." She realized that her hands rested on his arm. Blushing, she returned them to her lap.

"Well, yes, but it was worth it. The part of our building that as stone survived quite nicely. Six months will give us ample time to rebuild the front and replace the roof. But before we touch the interior, we need to think about any changes we might need."

He waited in vain for more praise for his acumen and skill as a negotiator *par excellence.* Amanda's attention obviously focused on plans for the future. He wondered if she realised, yet, that their futures were together.

He tied the horses to the hitching rail in front of their new premises, and helped his partner to alight. She stood, entranced, a burgeoning hope that Wentworth Optometry Services would continue and thrive. The fact that within six months they could move into a renovated and updated structure designed specifically for them still seemed the stuff of dreams. Only when she felt Sebastian's hand on her elbow, urging her forward, did she leave the Elysian fields of what-could-be.

Later that evening she told her family of Sebastian's cleverness at finding a temporary setting for their businesses. And of Sebastian's incredible ideas for redesigning the old workplace. And of Sebastian's amazing ability to think ahead and place an order for the building supplies they would need. As she waited for agreement of his wonderfulness, it occurred to her that *Sebastian* was a word which cropped up with ever-increasing frequency. *Don't be ridiculous. Of* course *his name would occur frequently. After all, we're practically business partners, aren't we?*

Then she became very quiet. The word *partners,* which had slipped out so naturally, seemed impossible when reviewing their past history.

✿✿✿

Gladys rapped loudly on the front door, opened it before the echo of the last knock had faded, almost ran the short distance to the parlour entrance, and paused for effect in the doorway. The Wentworth ladies clustered around the table.

Elizabeth frowned over instructions for a pattern, her crochet hook and work suspended in mid-air. Amanda held her place in the optometry catalogue with a finger as she dictated to Faith, who was making a list of supplies.

Based on the delicious aromas emanating from the kitchen, cookies were cooling on the table, thus forcing the group to foregather here. She remembered Elizabeth's frequents laments that the size of the house precluded a separate dining room.

Big with news, Gladys braced one hand on either side of the door jamb, inhaled, and announced:

"They found Al Anderson!"

Gratifying looks of astonishment met her gaze. Elizabeth's finger stopped abruptly. Amanda's hand jerked and she lost her place on the page. Ink dripped unnoticed from Faith's pen. Eschewing such niceties as an invitation to enter, and still wearing her coat and hat, she advanced, pulled out a chair, and joined the group.

"They found Al… ?" Elizabeth phrased her query in such a way that her voice died away in the manner indicating affirmation would be appreciated.

"Yes, yes, they found him."

"Where? What was he doing? I have a few hard words to say to that miserable excuse for a human." The blood in Elizabeth's eye promised harsh verbal retribution for the man who had injured, then kidnapped her precious baby.

Gladys, pleased with the receipt of her bombshell, settled back in her seat and continued.

"I should say one of the search teams found him. It was terrible. Apparently he had been strangled, dragged a short way off the road, and partially covered with leaves and branches."

Exclamations of horror and satisfaction circled the room. Without missing a beat, she removed her gloves and unbuttoned her coat.

"They've put his body in the livery. Jeff Napier has ordered a coffin, but they have to wait for a Toronto detective to see if he can find any clues as to the murderer. Or murderers."

Superb breath control notwithstanding, even she found it necessary to pause for air. Her hostesses, adept at taking advantage of any pause in their conversations, leapt at the chance to express their unchristian gratification.

Gladys handed her coat, scarf, and gloves to Amanda. Once again, she savored the rapt attention of her audience. Italics now peppered her discourse.

"I'm *convinced* that terrible Bert Stiles must have been involved. Do you know that they still can't find him? Someone saw him get on the train yesterday *with a suitcase.* The fool *can't recall what time.* So they have *absolutely no idea* if he headed for Hamilton or Toronto. *A suitcase, mark you.* He *never* takes a suitcase on his weekly trips." When she finally paused for a sip and the vital task of selecting another cookie or two, her hostess was able to demand answers to clear some of her confusion.

"What makes you think Bert Stiles had anything to do with it?" Elizabeth had apparently decided to take the information in reverse order of the telling. Having obtained the floor, she took full advantage of the phenomenon. "And exactly where did they find Al? Do they think he had anything to do with the fires, too?"

Swallowing the final bite of her first cookie, Gladys smiled at the treat to come, safely perched on her saucer, and prepared to respond to any and all questions. *Even if she didn't* know *the answers, she was pretty smart at figuring them out. After all, hadn't she been the best speller all through school?*

"They found him on the Douglas farm, heading for the next railway stop, no doubt. Since he was such a close companion of that unprincipled scalawag Stiles, why wouldn't he have been involved in the fires? And not just the latest ones. You can just bet your boots that he had something to do with all those other fires." She paused to replenish her lungs—even Gladys needed to inhale occasionally.

"And, if he was the person behind all those other fires, then you can be very sure that he and some of those reprobates from the hotel were the ones who put the stones on the hotel kitchen steps. And moved the outhouses."

She leaned back in her chair and prepared to savor the questions and exclamations which had already started. The ire of the

Wentworth ladies promised painful experiences to those they identified as connected to such heinous acts. But since their biggest guns had been aimed at Al, they were now bereft of their main prey.

CHAPTER 38

Faith had used the current issue of the *Marcher Mills Clarion* to cover a good portion of the Wentworth's kitchen table. Because of all the exciting and terrible events during the past week, they had not read the current issue, other than to glance at the headlines.

Today the paper's job was to protect the table from flying fish scales. Amanda and her mother had always scaled them in the past, and insisted that the woodshed or outdoors was the only place to do so. They claimed the scales flew everywhere, even as high as the ceiling. Fifteen minutes of scaling indoors would be followed by hours of washing walls, furniture and themselves.

Faith felt confident that less vigor in applying the butter knife against the grain of the scales would result in a clean fish and clean room. She centered her prey, tail anchored with her left hand, butter knife gripped in her right, glanced down to ensure that everything was in place, and shrieked.

"Mother! Amanda! Come and see the terrible note in the Social Column." Gripped by the horror of the situation, she read aloud the few lines that promised to unleash a firestorm. The forthcoming crisis took precedence over a fish.

This reporter understands that some very interesting news will be forthcoming in the near future. A certain pharmacist is rumored to have a keen interest in a lady who knows all about eyes. Watch this space for further developments.

Faith heard the rustle of her mother's dress as she moved swiftly from parlor to kitchen. Amanda's feet pounded down the stairs, wrath evident in her every step.

"What are you talking about?" Elizabeth and Amanda asked simultaneously.

"Here. It's right here. Page eight." All three women bent over the table, gazes locked on the pertinent paragraph.

"I am marching straight down to that newspaper office. When I get my hands on the unprincipled wretch who *dared* to write such trash, he or she will crave death."

Amanda's words floated behind her as she hurried to the front door. Jammed her hat on her head with little attention to effect. Flung a scarf around her neck. Fighting to get her arms into her coat sleeves, she yanked the door open with her right hand while attempting to fasten buttons with her left. The door yielded to force. Her nose collided with Sebastian's chest. His arms clasping her tightly, he asked if she were hurt.

✿✿✿

Ever since the fire Sebastian had made a point of going home for lunch. Marianne now lived with her friend Betty Keppel, as his house had only three bedrooms. His elderly aunts, still quite shaken at their near escape from the fire, appreciated the effort required to restructure his day to accommodate them.

Two months' time had failed to alleviate all their fears. They still rose several times during the night to check for fire and intruders. But at least they had stopped getting dressed and inspecting the outside of the building. Sebastian's lack of undisturbed rest, combined with overseeing the renovations and rebuilding of the pharmacy, plus working in a space proving to be very makeshift, indeed, combined to shorten his temper.

He unlocked the front door and called, "it's Sebastian." Loud exclamations of surprise, accompanied by expressions of hurt and anger greeted him.

"Sebastian, what is the meaning of this social note? We thought you would tell us, first." Aunt Maria, always the most vocal, beat her sister Beatrice to the gate by a short length. "We definitely require an explanation."

Maria grabbed the spotlight again, still robbing her nephew of a chance to respond. She ignored, for the moment, his failure to remove his coat and hat.

"And another thing, how could you do something like this when your parents are in the middle of the Atlantic and not due home for another ten days?"

Sebastian, raising his voice in order to be heard, demanded to know what they were talking about. Each sister waved her paper in front of him.

"It all but announces your engagement to that young Wentworth woman."

"Yes, the older one. The one who should stay on the shelf where she belongs."

He snatched the closest copy of the *Clarion* and rapidly scanned the social column. Clutching the paper in one hand, he charged out the door and headed for the Wentworth home at a dead run.

He knew that Amanda returned home each day to eat with her family. Sometimes Faith spelled her at the store, but usually they both spent a couple of hours with their mother. He could be sure of finding her there.

Turning the final corner, the mangled paper in his right hand, he leaped up the porch steps two at a time and raised his fist to demand entrance. His hand was descending for a hearty knock when the door flew open and he barely escaped hitting Amanda.

Her hat bounced. Her scarf trailed over one shoulder. Head down to align a recalcitrant button and buttonhole, she ran straight into his chest. Even in a state of flaming temper, he noticed again how nicely she fit into his arms, as he grasped her in a reflexive manner.

The two swayed, then recovered their balance. And their sanity. Voices in the kitchen reminded them they were not alone. Sebastian reluctantly released the fragrant bundle. Amanda took a very small step backwards. Besides, with the exception of that one kiss, easily excused in the heat of the moment, and the fact that they now addressed each other by their first names, their relationship had not changed. Each, in turn, strove to quiet that inner voice. The one that told the truth, no matter how unpalatable. Or exciting.

"Oh, Sebastian, the most terrible thing. Have you seen the paper?"

He waved his copy in her face.

"I have, indeed. As soon as our meeting is over, I'm marching right over to that benighted establishment, place my hands around the neck of the unprincipled scoundrel who wrote such tripe, and squeeze. Hard. I doubt he will survive the experience."

In spite of the gravity of the situation, Amanda laughed. "Sebastian, Sebastian, your instincts do you proud, but it's a woman who writes the column, not a man. I could see you trying intimidation, but you wouldn't get very far. Just the sign of a tear and you collapse." He eyed her gravely.

"Do you mean to tell me that *you* have been so unprincipled as to use that technique on me?" Instead of shame at her behaviour, she grinned.

"It worked, didn't it? And besides, as a woman I have different, but equally effective, ways of defending myself." Reluctantly she considered the wisdom of taking another tiny step back. Her feet seemed to be locked in place.

"Just think—men have the power, the money and the backing of the law. Women have very, very little to combat that." He growled, but let it go. Now was not the time to enter one of their heated discussions on the downtrodden and discounted state of women.

Changing the subject seemed the safest way out of the quagmire awaiting him if he started to discuss the rights of women. "We need to talk about that note in the social column. Do you have any ideas about it?"

He raised his head and noticed Elizabeth and Faith hovering in the kitchen doorway. "Would you care for a walk?"

"Yes, please. I'll just tell mother where I'm going." She turned to see her mother and sister in the doorway at the end of the hall.

"Oh, I guess you heard that. I'm going for a walk with Sebastian so we can discuss the article in the paper. Purely business."

Turning to her former nemesis, she adjusted her hat and scarf, buttoned her coat, removed her gloves from a pocket, and waved goodbye to her family.

They paced in silence to the end of the walkway and through the gate. With one accord they turned to the left, a route which would eventually lead them out of town. Away from prying eyes. Amanda noticed with amazement that her hand was nestled in the crook of Sebastian's elbow. And his hand rested on top of hers. She had no recollection of how that happened.

An hour later, they approached the Wentworth's front porch. Without breaking stride, they passed through the gate—which they had left unlatched—up the walk and thus onto the porch.

"Well, I guess we are agreed on our actions. Right?"

"Right, Amanda. We admit nothing, say nothing, and carry on as usual. In no time at all this will all blow over and another nine days wonder will take its place."

While admiring the firmness of his tone, she had many serious doubts that their plan would work. Especially when, as they left town and its accompanying prying eyes, she found herself leaning into his shoulder. Instead of apologizing and moving away, he compounded the problem by remaining silent. And putting an arm around her shoulders.

In one of their many, many pauses to work out a knotty aspect of the dilemma, he had stopped talking all together, leaned over, and kissed her. On the lips. And no chaste salute, either.

She blushed and smiled when recalling her enthusiastic response. The response which included stroking his cheek as his lips met hers. The response which seemed to demand her arms circle his neck. The response which led to an abrupt—and delicious—vertigo when the kiss ended. She felt like a heroine in a gothic novel when her knees threatened to give out.

Of course, she was not totally without blame when he repeated the offence. As a well brought up young lady, one, moreover whose innate honesty demanded she admit her own culpability, she could hardly rail at the man. Best to say nothing.

She realized she had no recollection of much at all after the kiss. Kisses. *Honesty, Amanda, honesty.* The next thing she knew, they were at the front door.

Elizabeth and Faith seemed to have left. Amanda knew better. As they began to ascend the porch steps, she caught the tiniest twitch in the parlour curtains. Wherever they had secreted themselves, they were very quiet.

Sebastian, man-like, seemed to take everything at face value. He bid her a very proper verbal farewell, but his eyes told an entirely different story. She, too, said all that was proper. But even the most casual of observers would have noticed the two bodies leaning toward each other.

✿✿✿

Renovating a seamstress' shop into suitable quarters for a combined pharmacy/optometry business meant many, many hours of collaboration—some of it spent actually achieving the goals Amanda and Sebastian had created. It also permitted "a great deal of unnecessary canoodling," according to Gladys. Elizabeth found it difficult to disagree with her friend's statement. The canoodlers, on the other hand, found nothing about which to complain.

Sebastian used the opportunity to let Amanda know that she had been his blind spot from the very beginning. She felt obliged to agree. And every time she did so, Sebastian complained that he was not alone in his singular lack of vision. He insisted that, spectacles notwithstanding, he had been her blind spot, too. She never admitted it to him, but in her heart, she knew he was right.

Soft, loving glances silently exchanged stoked the fires of attraction and desire. Fierce, hot stares caused two hearts to beat harder and harder. Breathing required a conscious effort. Hands were thrust into pockets or busied with unnecessary tasks.

The participants savored both frustration and joy. They tempered their emotions with the realization that some months must pass before they could tell the world of their commitment to each other. Neither recognized that the community was fully cognizant of the situation.

Finally, six months later, they read the following tidbit in the Marcher Mills Clarion social column.

This reporter is pleased to direct the attention of the Clarion's readers to the announcement of the upcoming wedding of a local well-known pharmacist and a certain newcomer who is an expert on eye care. The nuptials will take place on June 12, 1886, at St. Luke's in the Meadow. You may be sure this reporter will provide a complete report of the joyous event.

ABOUT THE AUTHOR

Words have always fascinated Marilyn—their taste, sound, and ability to precisely capture a word or emotion, and, of course, their connotations. But it was not until her third decade that she thought of putting all this experience and knowledge into writing a book. Letter writing (before computers made everything easier) had always been a genuine pleasure. She loved telling stories of daily life, and friends and family enjoyed reading them.

When she finally decided to sit down to write a book, a friend, Maggie Petru, by asking very pertinent questions, gave her guidance with the plot and helped flesh out the characters. Marilyn then set out to develop the words, sentences and paragraphs of her book.

Blind Spot, her second novel, is also set in Marcher Mills, but ten years later. It will be avalable on Amazon and Kindle. The characters in her third book are demanding attention

OTHER BOOKS BY MARILYN TEMMER

Wife Seller!

In 19th Century England, it was legal to sell your wife! Susannah Ashton, the victim of a brutal and cheating husband is desperate to escape the threat of death at his hands. She and her friends arrange to have her sold and then escape from Yorkshire to Dorset to manage a dairy. Like so many hastily thought-out plans, she is sold to the wrong man, married by proxy, and sent to Canada. Fortunately, even the darkest clouds are lined with light, because an ocean and a new identity might save her from charges of bigamy. Can her conscience allow her to be wife to a stranger and to mother his two small wards?

Available on Amazon and Kindle

What others are saying about Wife Seller!:

Little House in Canada. By Catharine Bramkamp "Writing Coach" (Santa Rosa, CA USA)

This was like reading a Little House book based in Canada. I loved the detail and regional flavor of Wife Seller. The plot was original and engaging and I loved the hero! Romantic and redemptive, I'm obviously not the only person to curl up and while away my winter afternoon with a good book!

Wife Seller! By Margie

I couldn't put Wife Seller! down. The author, Marilyn Temmer, is a wonderful story teller. She weaves stories of the characters against a background of very descriptive farming details from both England and Canada. Her dry sense of humour permeates the novel. A perfect book to curl up with on a cold winter's day.